CHEVY

IN THE

HOLE

CHEVY
IN THE
HOLE

A NOVEL

KELSEY
RONAN

Ⓗ

HENRY HOLT AND COMPANY NEW YORK

Henry Holt and Company
Publishers since 1866
120 Broadway
New York, New York 10271
www.henryholt.com

Distributed in Canada by Raincoast Book Distribution Limited

Library of Congress Cataloging-in-Publication Data

Names: Ronan, Kelsey, author.
Title: Chevy in the hole : a novel / Kelsey Ronan.
Description: First edition. | New York : Henry Holt and Company, 2022.
Identifiers: LCCN 2021047490 (print) | LCCN 2021047491 (ebook) |
    ISBN 9781250803900 (hardcover) | ISBN 9781250803917 (ebook)
Subjects: LCSH: Flint (Mich.)—Fiction. | LCGFT: Novels.
Classification: LCC PS3618.O65626 C47 2022 (print) | LCC PS3618.
    O65626 (ebook) | DDC 813/.6—dc23
LC record available at https://lccn.loc.gov/2021047490
LC ebook record available at https://lccn.loc.gov/2021047491

Our books may be purchased in bulk for promotional, educational, or business use. Please contact your local bookseller or the Macmillan Corporate and Premium Sales Department at (800) 221-7945, extension 5442, or by e-mail at MacmillanSpecialMarkets@macmillan.com.

First Edition 2022

Designed by Meryl Sussman Levavi

Printed in the United States of America

10 9 8 7 6 5 4 3 2 1

For my mom.

I could scarcely wait to tell my father the great news: "*Pops, I've ridden in a horseless carriage!*"

He made me say it twice. He, William C. Durant, the man who was presently to do more than any other living man to sell the United States on the idea of the automobile as a means of transportation; he who was to make his creed "a motor for every family," said:

"Margery, how could you—*how could you* be so foolish as to risk your life in one of those things!"

Margery Durant, My Father

CHEVY
IN THE
HOLE

PART 1

CHAPTER 1

2014

Had August Molloy not returned from the dead that morning in Detroit, the Molloy family line would've ended in the bathroom of a farm-to-table restaurant midway through lunch service. After the Narcan and the ambulance, he would pass this sanity check: yes, August was his real, stupid name and not the month, which was May. He was twenty-six years old. Barack Obama was the president. No, he wasn't trying to die; he'd just misjudged his tolerance. He'd been clean nearly two years if you didn't count—and he had decided not to—the shift drinks and occasional Xanax he bought off the sous-chef. But his car wouldn't start that morning, and when the man on the crosstown bus asked if he was looking for something, he considered the day stretching in front of him and decided he was.

He'd died this time, he'd later grow sure, because it felt different from anything. It wasn't a euphoric swoon like, at sixteen, home in Flint, when he shot up for the first time in a pawnshop parking lot and the city narrowed to the microwaves and guitars gleaming in the window display. Then, the clamor of his thoughts shushed, his fidgeting stilled, and gone was whatever his fellow dishwasher at Ponderosa couldn't define when she said, "I guess you're kind of funny, Gus, but you're so . . ." It wasn't a too quickly falling blackness, either, like the first overdose, when his mother opened his bedroom door to release the cat scratching inside and found his lips bluing beneath his *Sgt. Pepper's* poster.

Instead, in the stall, the trout smell vanished from his fingers, the sixties soul playlist in the dining room shut off, and his heart stopped. Detroit was suddenly gone, as if one slide clicked through to another on a reel. August was standing on a grassy expanse. A flock of birds pecked around his feet, feathers a flare of copper. Beyond the birds, no houses, no people. Rolling grass and a gray sky slung with clouds.

In the next stall, a lawyer from Grosse Pointe noticed August's scuffed boot kick toward him at an unsuggestive angle. He tapped it with the toe of his oxford. Called, "You all right in there, buddy?" Bending, he saw August's white hand hanging, fingers pointing to the tiles.

"No, no idea what he took," the kitchen manager explained to the paramedics. The diners gawked from their microgreens as August was wheeled through the back door. At the front, the hostess held a finger under her bottom lashes to dam her mascara, elbow out as if she were saluting him. The kitchen manager calculated the comped meals, mourned the ensuing Yelp reviews.

"Line cook," he said. Then added, "Flint guy," as if that explained it.

* * *

Across from Henry Ford Hospital, where August, resurrected, stood smoking beside his sister, Annie, tourists snapped pictures in front of the Motown Museum's blue and white Hitsville USA sign. He'd taken Annie there just a month ago, after their mamaw's funeral luncheon. The suggestion— August's—was impulsive and probably inappropriate. Annie had disappeared to deal with Rita, who'd shown up to prove that while she still didn't love Annie, she wouldn't have ended their engagement if she knew her grandmother was about to die. Their mamaw had been a difficult person, and attendance was scarce. The potato salad rose back up August's throat each time his mother reached out from beneath her grief to repeat, "Gus is doing so well. That's something to be grateful for, isn't it?"

August couldn't pull apart what shivered in his nerves, couldn't discern what was grief and what was shame. He felt for the cigarettes and keys in his pocket and left his mother with a huddle of second cousins nakedly calculating the debt the deceased had gone into on his rehab stints.

Between the sets of doors, August collided with Annie. Her ex's taillights swung out of the lot.

With a rare wildness, she said, "Take me wherever you're going."

He was only going to sit in his car and smoke, but he was always the one who needed to be shown an escape route, and so, touched, he devised a quick plan. "Follow me back to Detroit?"

When the guide tried to coax their group into dancing

like the Temptations, August, still in his suit and tie, was the only one to acquiesce, dipping and snapping his fingers. Annie gasped with laughter. In the halls of costumes, before a shrine of Jackson Five polyester and fringe, August sang, "Annie are you okay, are you okay, Annie?" He pointed to a sequined Supremes gown. "I'm going to wear that to your wedding someday," he said. "That's my maid of honor dress."

He regretted it immediately. Her eyes were glassy with unshed tears. He braced for her to repeat that she was going to die alone and unloved.

Instead she said, "You're way too shouldery for a halter." Added, softly, "You'll have to walk me down the aisle. There isn't anyone else."

Now, August ashed into a lilac bush and Annie fussed with a defeated Kleenex. Hers was always the number he gave because, unlike their mother, she never cried in public—a skill he suspected she'd honed getting her master's in social work. By the time the call woke her, sleeping off the night shift at the women's shelter, she'd had the sixty-mile drive from Flint to cry in her Honda, and her face, puffy with breakup grief-eating, was splotchy. He hung on to this last moment before they got in her car, and he had to explain again that it was just the one time, that he didn't owe anybody any money, hadn't even pawned anything.

Annie balled up her Kleenex, dragged the back of her hand under her nose, and pulled a ChapStick out of her hoodie. After she smeared it on, she said, "Well. Did your life flash before your eyes?"

"I saw birds. Maybe they were chickens. I guess it was heaven."

"Get fucked, Gus." Not like she meant it, but like she wanted to get back in her car and cry more.

"I'm serious." He hooked a finger of his cigaretteless hand beneath his glasses to rub his eye. They'd been raised on Flint Public Library books and Joni Mitchell cassettes by an agnostic mother. They were goodish-looking, prone to solitude, and considered themselves too clever for their blue-collar lives. They weren't heaven people.

"Chickens," Annie repeated.

"I think they were eating."

"You work in a kitchen, Gus. You were probably cooking chicken right before."

"Trout. Friday fish special."

An ambulance whipped past. "Let's not tell Mom."

August bent to grind his cigarette out. He felt his sister watching him. The hospital bracelet shifted on the knot of his wrist bone. His glasses slipped to the end of his nose.

He tapped out another cigarette and let it bob from his lips unlit. "Maybe I can stay with you again."

"You want to come home?"

August couldn't tell yet whether he felt compelled to go home, or if there was just nothing to stay in Detroit for. Home was where he circled back each time he did this. There was still a copper shine of feathers in his head, and he was a little nauseous. He slid the cigarette back into the pack. "Can I?"

She turned her head, face pinched. She muttered insults to bolster her efforts in the fight against loving him. "Of course you can, you stupid idiot. You asshole." Her shoulders twitched, then her arms extended and he was in them.

He hated the tremor of his sister's chin against his shoulder, the sudden smell of her hair, blond like their mother's, and then the too-meaningful eye contact when she pulled away, one hand still gripping him as if he might float away if she let him go.

* * *

August lived in a house at John R and Baltimore with a crunchy subfloor and a few windows boarded with letters of a Tubby's Subs sign. It was owned by an EDM artist from Los Angeles who occasionally flew in to think about turning it into a studio. He charged August a modest rent in exchange for keeping scrappers from ripping out the furnace and copper wire. Across the street sat an empty Chinese restaurant shaped like a ship that had run aground, and in its parking lot pheasants sometimes strutted. Beyond, an old Fisher Body plant sagged over I-94. Further, the glass and steel towers of the General Motors headquarters glowed, an omnipresent reminder of everything August wanted to get away from.

August went to the first rehab his mamaw paid for, with yoga and a piano in the common room where one of the alcoholics kept playing "I Say a Little Prayer." Then he'd gone back to Flint, worked in kitchens and bars, and ended up in the second rehab, state-run, with bunk beds and guards selling instant coffee and cigarettes on the sly. He thought moving to Detroit established a sixty-mile-long no-man's-land between him and his mistakes. He could do better without his mother's eyes skittering to the insides of his elbows when he was just putting up the storm windows like she'd asked him to, and Annie inviting him to dinner like she could write it off on her taxes.

For a while, Detroit had been a modest success: from coney islands to the restaurant with its muraled walls and produce direct from urban farmers. There was a waitress with sleeve tattoos who invited him over every time she broke up with her boyfriend, and he played drums in a band, the Digital Displays. They thrashed through covers at the same dive bars, but it was something to do. He had a sponsor, a hippie Quaker named George who invited him to Friends meetings and kept asking him if people in Flint still talked about Grand Funk Railroad. "Underrated band. Really rockin'."

But now August had fucked up Detroit, too.

August and Annie gathered up his phone charger, a pair of ear buds with the left bud that crackled, a collection of Beatles and Who T-shirts amassed from innumerable Christmases. His Narcotics Anonymous (NA) step working guide with old work schedules and the rough tally of his IOUs to Annie, not factoring in the interest rate that he adjusted with his fluctuating guilt.

"Do we need to get a truck?" Annie asked. "Is the dresser from Mom's?"

"Leave it. A gift to the house."

She rolled her eyes. She lifted the goldfish bowl off the dresser, the little man in the diving bell alone on dry substrate. NA said an addict alone was in bad company, but the fish had been flushed months ago and August hadn't replaced him. August scanned the floor and decided the Detroit Public Library wouldn't miss that Syd Barrett biography nor that copy of *Passages Through Recovery*. His sister was saying something about the closet, but he wanted to leave so bad he couldn't hear her.

The house was the quietest place August had ever been. For a while he had liked that about it. Sound reverberated through it like a cathedral. The showerhead busted, bathwater tumbled into the tub like bells. When he played music, it pounded the walls and thudded on the floorboards, driving out his old thoughts. Since his mamaw died, though, the house's silence grew oppressive. Convinced him he could hear the blood moving in his veins. He swiped through dating apps, imagining why each girl who looked like she might be kind enough to overlook his flaws and cool enough to listen to music with deserved better, deleting message drafts. It felt like every passing car was driving through the wall.

Annie surveyed the room with a bundle of sheets under her arm. "What about the rest of it?"

"Fuck the rest of it."

August locked the door behind him, then buried the key in the mailbox beneath months of grocery circulars. He took out his phone to text his landlord—*sorry about this, man*—but a glance revealed a roll of unread texts from the restaurant, the bass player canceling practice. August's drums were in his basement. He could have them. There was a voicemail from his mother, whom Annie swore she hadn't spoken to. He shoved the phone back in his pocket.

He was too tired to tow his car out. It probably wasn't worth fixing anyway.

* * *

Waiting for the turn onto northbound I-75, August cracked the window.

"You know you can't smoke in my apartment."

"I said I can stay with Mom." He lifted his ass to dig a lighter from his back pocket. Annie's snack cake wrappers crinkled under his boots.

"That's not what I'm saying. It's in the lease. The last time you stayed with me I got fined, and things are tight enough for me right now without Rita." Then, when the light changed, "How are you feeling?"

It would seem ungrateful, to ask for a miracle greater than being raised from the dead, so August couldn't explain how he wished that, before the Narcan jump-started his heart, he'd been offered some premonition of the future he was living for. Someone's hand reaching to smooth the hair matted on the back of his neck. Anything he could want, anything he could try to be good at. He knew from rehab and counselors and NA and internet articles he read off his phone in the bathtub that after nearly ten years on and off opiates, his brain was chemically unfit for the rush of dopamine and oxytocin to want anything or anyone. Anhedonia, it was called: reduced motivation, reduced anticipatory pleasure (wanting), and reduced consummatory pleasure (liking). Three to five years, generally, for the brain to recover. He'd gotten through two years, and he didn't know now if this fuckup meant he was starting all over.

So he just said, "Tired." He tipped his forehead to the window and watched Detroit slide backward: the skyscrapers and church steeples and warehouses, the signs pointing the way toward Flint. He let the warm fuzz of the radio and the vibration of the road beneath him lull him to sleep. When he opened his eyes again they had just crossed into Genesee County, and the colossal sign for Dixie Baptist rolled before him, a sad-eyed Jesus asking, ARE YOU ON THE RIGHT ROAD? as if offering a last chance to turn around.

CHAPTER 2

From the windows of Annie's seventh-floor apartment, August could see the Citizens Bank weather ball red and blinking to signal the coming spring rain. Each hour the bells of the downtown churches clanged a few seconds apart as if in eternal argument over the time. When he lifted the window to smoke, voices and sirens and the hiss of the buses' hydraulic lifts rose up to him.

Annie's apartment was as spare and anonymous as a hotel room, the kind of place you could leave anytime and never think about again. The only picture was framed beside the TV: a black-and-white strip taken at a roller rink in the nineties, Annie's hair in a beribboned side-tail and August bowl-cut and toothless, their pretty mother squeezing them to her sides. Annie had the same pullout couch August crashed on when she was in college, the same empty refrigerator. All traces of her engagement were erased, save Rita's record player in a console pressed to the far side of the living room wall, on which August heaped what little he had.

Through August's first two weeks in Flint, he waited until

Annie left for her night shift at the women's shelter to crawl into her bed. He slept until just before she was due back, when the alarm on his phone told him to move to the couch. He'd wake again while Annie slept, walk to the gas station for cigarettes, skip through music he wasn't in the mood for, ignore his mother's calls, click through infomercials where people in spacious kitchens grilled shrimp skewers, and half watched the local news at noon repeat the story about the water switch. The emergency financial manager (EFM), installed by the governor to pull the city out of debt and dysfunction, decided to pull drinking water from the Flint River instead of piping it in from Lake Huron. On the TV he saw the same shot of the Flint River running through Chevy in the Hole, the same frowning locals saying they weren't drinking from that polluted old river. Annie had a case of bottled water beside the fridge.

In one paroxysm of loneliness, he'd texted the waitress with the tattoos—*this is the ghost of gus wondering if he can buy you dinner*—thinking maybe Annie would loan him her car and he could drive down to Detroit and take her out, make a good showing. She never responded.

He'd done the math. His last paycheck had been deposited, and if he went on not spending any of it, occasionally making Annie risottos and curries for dinner and apologizing for being such a fucking loser until she lapsed into her social work training (*Why do you say that? What can we do to change it?*), if he kept shuffling the stack of résumés she'd printed for him and moving around his Narcotics Anonymous meeting schedule, he would never have to leave this apartment ever again.

It might have worked if not for the morning he forgot to

turn on the alarm and woke in Annie's bed to the sound of her coming into the apartment. She was on the phone: her voice rose when she saw her brother wasn't on the couch. Keys clattered onto the kitchen table, then grocery bags. "Well, what would *you* do, Rita?"

Then August heard his sister say to her ex, who had always looked at him like he was about to pawn her TV and raid her medicine cabinet, "Relapse is part of recovery. That's addiction 101. Did you hear me say he was clean for *two years*? Why am I explaining this to you?"

August rolled toward the wall. Maybe she'd go straight to the shower to cry. When she came out he'd be brewing coffee, whisking French omelets, proof that Rita had them all wrong. Look at how great he was doing, and all thanks to his sister. Or he'd go back to sleep on the sofa, which wasn't hurting anybody.

But Annie said, "Forget I called. I don't know what I was thinking." A string of expletives crescendoed toward the bedroom, then stopped in the doorway.

August kept his eyes closed, his back to her tensed with excuses. But then he heard her phone hit the dresser and felt the covers move. Her weight dropped to the opposite side of the mattress. She pulled at the sheets, her legs kicking toward him and then away. He listened to her breathing close to his face.

He cracked open an eye. She was staring at him.

"You suck at fake sleeping, and my pillows smell like your cigarettey hair. I've tried to be nice, but it's been two weeks and I can't take it. You are not lying around my apartment like a moody little prince. So wash your gross hair, Jesus Christ *shave*, and go to your meeting."

August had articulated to himself all the reasons the meetings and their eternal self-flagellation was bullshit. He dreaded the interminable apologies, the intrusion of other people's feelings when he had trouble enough sorting through his own. But he fumbled to articulate this now. "You have no idea—"

"I don't. So get a therapist and tell her how no one gets it and Dad was an asshole and Mom was always at work and no one's ever suffered like you have."

She reached over and yanked a pillow from beneath his head, walling it between them.

"Martyr," he muttered on his path to the door he was going to slam. "Saint fucking Anneliese."

She expanded into the space he'd emptied. "You're welcome. Love you, too."

He threw around his pile of clothes in pursuit of a cleanish pair of pants. From their pockets fluttered the notes he'd been ignoring:

November Molloy, Can you do a load of laundry? Quarters by the door. Maybe after your meeting? Have a good day.

February Molloy: Would be cool of you to do the dishes. Meeting today? Thank you.

Gus—replace the cereal and milk you demolished TODAY thx.

And so August sat in a circle of folding chairs in the basement of St. Paul's Episcopal Church, pushing clots of non-dairy creamer through his coffee, willing strangers not to speak to him. Now that he was out of the house, he wanted to keep walking. His legs twitched, and his bootheel tapped on the tiles.

The first speaker, on whose T-shirt a guitar-strapped Johnny Cash gave the finger, introduced himself: "Crack, six years sober."

The man cleared his throat and turned his face toward the ceiling, addressing a higher audience. "Last year I started volunteering on an urban farm. I'd just got out of County. My buddy told me about these people over in Carriage Town growing vegetables in some shitty-ass house, excuse my language. I figured I'd see what that was about."

The man shook his head as he tried to explain, stunned by his own experience. "Well, fuck me, I never felt so good," he said. He raised his arms to gesture around him. He was holding a stack of papers, and they fluttered over his shoulder like fractured wings. "And that's the way this city's going. I mean, they've planted a thousand trees in Chevy in the Hole. Ain't even Chevy in the Hole anymore. Chevy Commons, they're calling it. We're living in a whole other city. A whole new place."

The NA congregants nodded respectfully, though largely unmoved; only one woman affirmed the man with a low hum. Someone behind August muttered that it was still Chevy in the Hole to her; she'd like to know who just planted some trees and decided they could rename things. August, though, stirred with vague interest. In the weeks he had been holed up in his sister's place, he had dreaded the city below: all it lacked, all the things he wished he hadn't done, and all the people he didn't want to run into. It wasn't that he was particularly moved by the trees growing in Chevy in the Hole or this farm, but that those concrete acres suddenly bloomed. It surprised him. While the man went on, trying to reconcile the sober man they saw before them with the asshole who'd stolen spark plugs off motorcycles to smoke, Flint shifted in August's mind.

August put down his coffee and rubbed the beard he'd left as a fuck-you to his sister. He closed his eyes so while the man in the Johnny Cash T-shirt lapsed into a soliloquy about hydroponic tomatoes and the mercy of their Higher Power, he could see vines snaking up from the windows of rotting houses, chickens pecking through a pawnshop lot swallowed by vines. The Flint River glittering blue, like the decades of General Motors pollution had been drained out. He opened them again when a sheaf of flyers tapped his arm. *Frontier Farm, A Nonprofit Community Garden* invited him to *Be a part of the rejuvenation of Flint!*

The man in the Johnny Cash T-shirt settled back into his seat. The woman suspicious of the name change—opiates, three months—stood to lead the last prayer. *God, I offer myself to Thee, to build with me and to do with me as Thou wilt.*

* * *

August walked the few miles to his mother's house on the west side. He cut through the old Michigan School for the Deaf campus, passed the elementary school where a few kids were kicking on the swings, bikes thrown to the dirt. On the street where he'd grown up, the bungalows were still mostly inhabited. His mother's irises crowded the porch steps.

Rose had settled into what Annie called her postmenopausal renaissance: her solitude suited her, the house brighter around her. Still, August hated being there amongst his own ghosts. On the walls and overstuffed bookshelves his image, from his chubby bowl-cut childhood to his miserable adolescence, thermals layered under band T-shirts to hide the track marks.

In the kitchen, Rose was in her after-work sweatpants, her gray-blond hair clipped atop her head, the cat crunching kibble at her feet. Finches pecked in the feeders suctioned to the window. "It's been in there long enough, but the cheese isn't bubbling at all," she despaired of the frozen lasagna. After kissing her son's cheek, she pressed a hand to her lips. "Summer beard?"

Over the last ten years Rose had delivered ultimatums, had thrown her son's stuff on the lawn, had wept and begged him not to do this to her, and now she was trying, as Annie asked her on the phone call he'd overheard, to make him feel useful.

"I told you I could make you dinner." He bent for the cat now grinding its head against his legs.

For Rose, cooking was something you did on Christmas and Thanksgiving or if someone paid you to. "Just set the table." She handed him a Diet Coke and a fork. He pushed the pile of coupons she'd been cutting from the grocery circular into a kind of centerpiece.

After Rose set down the lasagna, cheese resolutely unbubbled but melty, she pulled her son back by the shoulders, straightening his spine. "If you slump around, people won't be able to tell how handsome and smart you are. They'll think I failed you." He winced. To change the subject, he took the community garden flyer out of his pocket, the edges already soft as cloth from refolding. "I was thinking of checking this out. The dope fiends are saying Flint's going to be the Garden of Eden any day now."

"Then I'm even happier you're home. We can live in paradise together." She smoothed out the flyer beside her plate and chewed thoughtfully. "I guess this explains the deer. And God, the skunks. Do you remember skunks when you were little? Possums and raccoons digging through my trash and tearing up the garage, of course, but every morning I wake up now there's a skunk on my back porch, eating the cat food."

"What deer?" August asked, but his mother didn't hear him. She'd pulled the cat away from the lasagna, cradling it like an unhappy baby.

After dinner Rose took three carrots from the crisper drawer and led her son on a walk. The days were getting longer, the spring sun stretching into evening. They crossed Miller Road, leaving their neighborhood for the mansions built for General Motors executives on the other side. Her gaze lingered too long on him, and when he caught her, she forced a smile. "Two years is still a long time."

For the first time since he came to on the bathroom floor, he let himself have it. It *was* a long time.

When they reached an opening in the budding trees that ringed the golf course, they stood together looking across the green to the curve of I-75 and, beyond the billboards and the railroad tracks, the Truck Assembly plant, the last of the factories. It was here she'd been seeing the deer.

"One time there were three of them. You get close to them and they bolt, though. Skittish." Rose's eyes swept over the grass, through the trees, and behind her to look at the colonials set back on immaculate lawns. While they waited for a deer to emerge, August snapped a clandestine picture of his mother, carrot in hand, and sent it to his sister. It was as close as she was getting to an apology.

"I worry about them," Rose said.

"Good thing they've got so many junkies to grow vegetables for them."

"An answer to their prayers." Rose lobbed a carrot toward the trees.

His vision of heaven, or near-death experience, or whatever that was, flickered into his mind. He wondered if he should tell his mother about it. He was distracted by a text from his sister buzzing in his pocket.

There was a heart emoji and: *How's it feel out there among the living?*

On the walk home they made plans for Rose to pick him up in the morning. She'd started cleaning out his mamaw's house on the south side. The charter school on the other side of the fence had bought the house; in a few weeks they'd knock it down and expand their bus parking. Though Rose had sworn she'd take the money, pay off her property taxes, and let them bulldoze the whole mess, she'd changed her mind now that August was home.

"Maybe we can put some things together for when you get your own place? Some furniture?"

"My sobriety hope chest," August agreed. His mother, if she heard him, didn't seem to think it was funny.

"A bed frame. Table and chairs. You don't have anything, do you, sweetheart?"

* * *

Instead of taking the bus back to Annie's apartment like August insisted he was, he walked the mile down to Chevy in the Hole. A concrete bowl carved in the middle of the city with the Flint River running through it, it had once held

acres of Chevrolet assembly line. Birds tumbled from the
power lines. The skinny trees the man in the Johnny Cash
shirt mentioned struggled up from new dirt. The railroad
tracks that once huffed in car parts had been turned into a
bike path. When August was little and his father was pink-
slipped, the hill had seemed so much steeper. August remembered it lined with broken glass and twisted rebar. Now a
wire fence hemmed in acres of nothing. RECLAIMING CHEVY
IN THE HOLE, a sign on the fence said. DEMOLITION MEANS
PROGRESS. CITY OF FLINT PHYTOREMEDIATION INITIATIVE.

August turned away. All along Kearsley Street, heading
downtown, every other house was empty or burned down to
its charred foundations. An occasional car passed. His bones
felt too heavy for his skin. He'd been walking all day from
his loneliness and boredom, and now he wanted to lie down,
collapse into it.

In Annie's dark apartment, August dragged a kitchen
chair into the bathroom. On it he set up his sister's makeup
mirror and a razor. He leaned out of the tub, dragging the
razor over his face, tapping the little hairs onto the porcelain.
He avoided the reflection of his eyes. Done, he propped his
phone on the dry island of his knee. Voicemails from the
billing department of Henry Ford Hospital asked firmly but
politely for his address, and the ambulance company wanted
their thousand dollars. Texts from Annie at work reminded
him the laundry detergent was in the bathroom cupboard and
also it would be cool of him to do the dishes. He responded
only to the bass player of the Digital Displays, asking, *You
coming to practice?* He knew from the group text he hadn't
responded to that the last two had been canceled.

cant, August texted back. *died & went to hell/flint.*

He could see the flyer for Frontier Farms peeking out of the pocket of his jeans on the bathroom floor. He opened You-Tube and searched for Johnny Cash.

At the end of "Ring of Fire," autoplay took him there: Johnny Cash reading the New Testament. August dragged his fingertip over the wall to dry it, then selected it. It had sounded like a joke, but there was Johnny Cash, declaring, "This is the genealogy of Jesus the Messiah the son of David, the son of Abraham." August dropped the phone to the bath mat and let the Man in Black read.

August had tried religion a few times. The Higher Power of Narcotics Anonymous had been hazy and dissatisfying, so in Detroit he'd gone to a Buddhist meditation group, a Unitarian Universalist service, fidgeted through a silent Friends meeting beside his sponsor until he was so sure the gurgle of his gastric juices and the weird hiss of his lungs were keeping the Quakers from hearing the still, small voice of God that he had left. He was willing—relieved, even—to be told how to live, and he liked the idea of being clean slate–forgiven, but there was always something about divine love and mercy that he couldn't work out.

Johnny Cash paused for an incoming text. *Hahaha see you at 7 or for real man you working?*

Johnny Cash read while August puckered and grew cold; kept reading while August let the bath drain beneath him, skin drying, glasses unfogging. His mind moved in and out of focus, sometimes a phrase catching him—*all you who are weary and burdened.* He moved to the dark living room and curled up on the sofa without bothering to pull out the bed or untangle the sleeping bag he'd thrown to the floor. The Bible made for a pleasant kind of white noise, like familiar songs on a radio turned low: some stuff about birds and the heart and being poor.

When August woke up, his mother was crouched over him, pulling the blanket away, searching his arms, and his father was saying something stern. Only it wasn't his mother but his sister, still in the flats she wore to work, pulling the sleeping bag over him, and he was hugging himself, having fallen asleep in his glasses and his clothes. In the dark she looked so much like their mother when they were little, the same blond bun and perfumy home-from-work smell. And it wasn't his father at all but Johnny Cash on YouTube auto-playing through the New Testament.

Annie's breath was a puff of stale coffee as she whispered, "You okay, Gus?"

CHAPTER 3

1937

Chevrolet Fisher Body Plant No. 2 sat in the bowl of the Flint River valley—Chevy in the Hole, people called it. Usually, from the front windows Beatrice Molloy could see smoke pluming from the Chevy smokestacks, hear the train whistles and the trolley dinging. But after Christmas, strikers stopped the line, barricaded the doors, and announced they'd sit there until General Motors agreed to increase their wages, grant them the right to talk during lunch, and recognize the United Auto Workers (UAW). Soon the other plants followed, and then the whole automotive industry was shut down. In February, the sky over Chevy in the Hole was still a cold and starless black and Flint was quiet, holding its breath.

After Beatrice put the children to bed, she and Lewis listened to the strike updates on the radio. For weeks they listened to news of the National Guard seizing supplies, rounding up agitators. They heard of the men inside huddling together after GM turned the heat off. In interviews, men leaning out of the windows said they'd had it up to here. "They had lip readers in here seeing nobody says the word *union*. They fire you for looking at them funny." But it was different the night Beatrice and Lewis listened to the news of the Battle of Bull Run, when the police charged and the women's auxiliary brigade in their red berets fought through the truncheons and tear gas. Their men hurled hinges, wrenches, and empty bottles from the windows above. The reporter's voice floated away; Beatrice could hear the women's cries, see their boot heels raking the snow as they were dragged to the paddy wagons, adrenaline and love heating their blood.

Beatrice had spent the day worrying over the hazy map of Flint in her mind, wondering where they could go when the landlord put them out. This was the Molloys' third rental in the three years since they moved up from Detroit, on a street of paint-flaking Victorians built before the carriage factory across the river switched production to automobiles. The house was meant to be a thrifty interim before they made their entry into Woodlawn Park, where the doctors and lawyers lived. Now Lewis, who intended to make his fortune as a cookware salesman for the fast-multiplying households of Flint, had little work, they were a month behind on the rent, and she was heavy with her fourth child. She didn't know where else there was to go but this. The dingy streets just north of Buick, maybe, where soot shadowed the windows and the Black men who worked the foundries lived with their wives who cleaned houses for the executives.

"These Communists ought to wake up every morning and thank God for ol' Louie Chevrolet," Lewis scoffed.

The radio moved on to an advertisement for Chesterfield cigarettes, and Lewis pitched his head back. Stubble shadowed his jaw. She thinned the stew to broth and they hadn't had meat in weeks, but still he was portly with unemployment. "These men should go into business on their own, if their conditions are so intolerable," he said. He lifted a hand, punctuating his thought with a finger pointing at a crack in the plaster. "Or accept that a certain class of man belongs in service to the visionaries of his time.

"Imagine running through the snow to bring me bread and water. Report back to the commissar, Comrade Bea."

Beatrice considered a remark she'd never make—she mightn't make a bad revolutionary—but it was then she heard someone banging at the back door, the glass rattling. She rose to answer.

The officer's mustache reached toward his lower lip, wet with coffee and freezing into spikes. The buttons on his uniform shined like ice. "Are you Mrs. Cyril Hamper?"

The floorboards behind her creaked with Lewis's advancing weight, and the officer's hard stare rose over her head. Lewis's palm settled on her shoulder. She guarded the mound of her stomach.

"Checking in on the strikers' wives. Looks as though I've got the wrong house."

"Must be next door. Good of you to check on her. A shame they're causing you so much trouble." Beatrice recognized the forced charm in her husband's voice from all the phone calls he made when he was tired, when he'd had too much to drink, when she was in the next room with the baby who wouldn't stop crying. *Why, of course, Mrs. Jefferson, we'll get you a replacement skillet right away.*

The officer apologized for disturbing them. Lewis reached

past her to shut the door. "There's a waste of my tax dollars," he muttered, and climbed the stairs to bed.

Beatrice turned off the radio. She gathered up the Tinkertoys and folded up the newspaper, her mind still on the women running through the snow with their picket signs.

Outside a voice, high and pleading. A door slammed, an engine fired, and a car moved through the slush of the street.

Beatrice slipped out into the alley and found the woman next door huddled on her back stoop, face buried in the too-long cuffs of a man's sweater, her frizzy dark tendrils winding toward the snow.

Beatrice had never exchanged more than a *good morning* and *good night* with her neighbor. There was so little left of her, after her children and Lewis. She didn't want to be invited to anyone's church or sewing circle. Now, studying the woman's body, younger and sturdier than Beatrice's, folded small and convulsing with sobs, she was moved to comfort her but was unsure how.

"It's awfully cold," Beatrice called.

The woman smeared her eyes with the back of her hand and snorted to clear her nose. She lifted her face, soft and mottled.

"That cop says if Cy don't come home they're going to kill him in there. He said they'll put Dotty and me out to starve. This strike's gonna do nothing but make a lot of widows. That's what he told me."

The woman wiped her nose with her sweater cuff. "Ain't just me they're doing this to. Another girl I know, the police tore her house apart looking for Communist Party papers. What would I do if Cy died in there? What would I do?"

"You'd be all right." Beatrice's callousness echoed back to her.

The woman lifted her soft and mottled face.

"Your old man ain't in the shop, is he? I see him coming and going." She made a last swipe at her nose. "I'd better go check on my girl."

She turned, then reconsidered. "I'm sorry, but what's your name again? You moved in so quick after the McHenrys I can't remember."

"Beatrice."

"Well, I'm Evelyn," she said. "And you're lucky your husband don't work in the shop, Beatrice." Her door shut.

Climbing the steps to bed, Beatrice thought, *Lucky*. She thought of Cy asleep in his clothes on a nest of car seats, just a mile away. When Beatrice's first husband, Autie, died, she moved into a cheap room and gritted her teeth through the night to keep the heave of her sobs from waking Eamon. Sometimes her grief and poverty stunned her: how it stretched out interminably ahead of her. Eamon was just a few months old when his father died, and all he had of Autie was his eyes, round and blue. In the last prayers of her dwindling faith, she asked to forget what she'd lost, asked that Eamon never know who his father was, what shameful things he'd done. Her baby's name followed every plea. *Amen.*

In Beatrice's first season of widowhood, she forced herself to not think of him. She sold his clothes and his fiddle. She didn't want to go back to her parents, and if she was going to stay in Detroit, she had better not wallow.

Stepping into her nightgown, Lewis already asleep, she imagined Autie plunging out of a factory window, waving madly. Broad-shouldered, spectacles low on his nose. Beatrice elbow to elbow with the other wives, picket signs aloft, smashing into the windows when the police attacked the building with tear gas, Autie breathing the air she'd given him. That grin he had when he was singing songs around the house, swinging the baby in the air, talking about all they'd do someday, when they became hoity-toity people who went to the art museum and the symphony and the best restaurants. Her body tingled with the thought. Lewis's baby, due in the spring, kicked at the walls of her.

* * *

Lewis drove out of the city with boxes of cookware and sometimes returned in the middle of the night, the boxes gone and his breath sour. On the nights he returned late, Beatrice thought of him in those homes, shirtsleeves rolled to his elbows and an apron bowed at his back. Women in pearls cooing as he served casseroles on bone china, chandeliers dripping crystal tears above him. Their Frigidaires full. No knocking old radiators. Sometimes she tried to smell their perfumes on him when he lowered himself onto the bed beside her, pressing against her while she feigned sleep. She could only ever smell the liquor. And some nights while his hands sought her out, she thought she wouldn't mind, really, if there were some rich, bored woman with beautiful sheets to fall into, a jeweled hand to loosen his tie.

But this was the first time he'd taken Eamon with him. When Eamon came home from kindergarten, she sent him straight to the bath. She tried to get his thick hair to lay flat and told him to mind his father. And once Lewis and Eamon were gone and the baby put down, the ragged house seemed airless and the hours dragged on. She couldn't stop picturing her son made to play the charming ragamuffin, some spit-shined sales gimmick, and she wanted him home. She stepped out into the alley as if the house pushed her out.

Evelyn tumbled out her back door, too, only she was laughing, and had both thick arms wrapped around a trash can as if she'd brought it out to the alley to waltz with. Behind her was a young woman with a scarf coiled up to her nose, eyes peering out.

"Well you're up late, too," Evelyn called.

"Edith, this is my neighbor Beatrice. Her husband—oh hell, what's his name again?—he's not on the line. Me and the auxiliary gals have been making soup for the strikers. I think this whole thing's gonna be over soon. The mood down there is wonderful. You hear about that telegram Roosevelt sent to General Motors? My Cy'll be home soon."

Beatrice felt a twist of envy for Evelyn and the woman, bound together by the same furious energy.

"Oh say," Evelyn said, "you know how to drive, Beatrice? I'm supposed to give Edith a ride home and well, I . . . well, we went and got ourselves all dingy. She's only on Third Street. Crazy little thing said she'd walk, but it's colder than a well digger's ass."

"I've got my babies inside," Beatrice said.

"I'll mind 'em. Won't take you five minutes."

Beatrice turned inside to get her coat. Evelyn got Dotty out of bed and carried her sleeping to the Molloys' living room to wait.

In the Hampers' Chevy, Edith told her, "My husband said he'd be out by our anniversary. That's tomorrow, so it sure don't look like it. Seven years." She dropped her forehead into her palms and made a wounded-animal noise. "How long you been married?" she managed.

"Four years. I was married once before, though. He worked at the plant, down in Detroit. He died." It was a rare admission. She wanted the solidarity of saying she'd suffered for a man on the line. She wanted Lewis, wherever he was with her son, erased with her grief.

"Well, God bless you." Edith consoled the footboard. "Bless you, truly."

On Saginaw Street, the theater marquees spelled out the names of movie stars and the taxis and the trams crawled through the slush. A few men huddled in their coats on the steps of St. Michaels, and the icy sidewalks would be empty for a few more hours till the breadlines formed. Beatrice followed Edith's directions west until they arrived at a house with a sagging porch. She watched the woman plod to her front door and fumble with the key. Then Beatrice turned toward Chevy in the Hole.

She drove beneath the Chevrolet symbol, the factories hulking around her. A few policemen watched in squad cars, but no one was protesting, and no men leaned from the windows. The factories were dark and the river black under the bridge. Her heart sped, being so close, knowing all she did of the men asleep inside on car seats, burrowed into upholstery.

On the other side of the hole, Beatrice found their Packard in a bar parking lot. Eamon slept in the back, his coat open and his sweater twisted on his stomach. She tried the locked door.

In the back of the bar a couple of women lounged with men, their hair in shellacked finger waves and their mouths the only bright thing. Lewis was at the bar with a glass in front of him, one cigarette lit in his hand and another waiting behind his ear.

"I tell you it's sheer misery acclimating to this snow again. The missus and I just got back from Florida. We've got a place in Tampa, on the bay," Lewis said. "It's expensive down there, but try shoveling snow after you've experienced that. You'd saw off your own damn leg to be back down there on the beach."

"You're a lucky son of a bitch," the barfly said. Lewis was ringed in mirthless laughter.

"You looking for something, ma'am?" The bartender stared at her over her husband's head. She didn't say anything, and the men turned.

Though for these first years of their marriage Beatrice reconciled Lewis's failures with sympathy and gratitude, as she watched him conjure fantasies like a schoolboy boasting on a playground, he looked pathetic and small.

Lewis unrolled their money onto the bar. One of the women in the back tittered, her voice warm with sex and money.

"Just take him *home*, Lewis," she called after him. "Do whatever you like but bring my son home."

Her husband turned to face her. "He look like he's in danger to you? Did you see him driving off into the night?" He pulled the keys from his pocket. Held them so close to her face she reared back. He wasn't drunk yet, only humiliated.

Lewis dropped into the driver's seat, the door hanging open. He twisted to shake Eamon's leg. Eamon's eyes opened, big with confusion.

"What have you been doing, boy? Pick up some gals? Paint the goddamn town?"

Eamon pressed against the seat as if he could pass through it. Before she could call for him to get out, Lewis slammed the door and wheeled out of the parking lot. Behind him, where the floodlights and heaving smokestacks of Chevrolet were supposed to be, there was only darkness. Snow soaked through her shoes and stockings, and her body dropped heavily back into the driver's seat. Through the emaciated streets, the ugly city, she went home.

Beatrice made sure the children were sleeping before she slipped into her nightgown and lowered herself beside Lewis, already in a whiskey-deep snore.

After Autie died, the temporariness of her widowed life exhausted her; she was impatient for things to be whatever they were going to be. And there was Lewis, promising to take care of her and her baby, to take her to a new city. An answered prayer. Even if he was more in love with the chivalry he saw in himself than with her—the self-made man who'd rescued a shy young widow and her baby on his rise to riches—she'd been grateful he loved her enough to weave her and Eamon into his fantasies. That Eamon never had to know his father died in disgrace, body fished out of the Detroit River.

What a nice world her husband must live in, she thought, feeling the baby kick inside her, where you could sit and spin out sentences until you were someone else entirely. Florida, he said, and now the word ricocheted around her head, as absurd as if he'd said they had a second home in India, or on the moon. She tried to imagine it. The heat and the wildly colored birds and the lap of waves.

Beatrice heard movement downstairs and pulled on her dressing gown. It was probably Eamon, looking for the dinner Lewis didn't give him.

In the living room she found Evelyn, pulling back the front curtain, squinting out at the street. Her little girl was asleep on the sofa, a tumble of curls.

"I didn't hear you come in," Evelyn said, voice thick with sleep. "I was just seeing if your car was out there."

Beatrice considered her neighbor, so young, and blessed with the purity of her desire, her conviction, her sense of home.

In the dark of the house she asked Evelyn, "Could you take me with you next time?"

* * *

Beatrice gave Eamon instruction to take care of the little ones, promising to be back in time to make supper. She could feel him watching her pin her hat and buckle her boots.

In the Hampers' car, Dotty wore her mother's red beret and played with the pinafored doll in her lap. "What lovely hair your dolly has," Beatrice said. The girl blinked, as if this was hardly news.

"Cute as a bug's ear, ain't she? Looks like her daddy." Behind the girl, Beatrice saw the breadline forming on Saginaw Street.

As they neared Chevy in the Hole, the streets grew thick with cars. Police lined the perimeter, and behind them lurked onlookers and camera-strapped pressmen. Beatrice worried a loose thread on her coat sleeve and measured her quickening breath. They descended into the hole, down Chevrolet Avenue along the hulk of Fisher Body No. 2. The protestors' songs and chants grew to a din. Men waved their caps in the open windows and leaned down to accept the things that the women below offered up: blankets and sweaters; babies hatted and swaddled; cases of Vernors and beer and jugs of water; food wrapped in tea towels. Children held signs proclaiming, My Daddy Is a Union Man and Daddy Strikes for Us Tykes. They stomped circles into the snow, cheeks bright with cold.

Evelyn pushed forward into the crowd, Dotty's hand in hers. "I'm going to find Cy," she called back to Beatrice, who still had Evelyn's picket sign. Help Our Men to Win.

Beatrice wasn't standing long, though, until she was caught up in the heave of women, her feet falling into step in the protestors' circle. When she pulled herself away to rest, a tall woman in a voluminous fur held her elbow. She smiled down at Beatrice's protruding belly. "You both all right?"

Beatrice, a little breathless, said she was.

"Your man on the line? What's his name?"

"Autie," she said, and the name fell out of her mouth like a stone she'd been holding under her tongue. At the sound of her own voice stating his name, happiness rippled through her, a happiness somehow magnified by the crowd, by the heaving mass of hopeful, righteous people she was sharing it with. She felt drunk on it.

"I bet that baby will grow up to be so proud of your Autie."

Beatrice felt an arm looping through hers and turned to find Evelyn. She led Beatrice to a place farther up the sidewalk where women unloaded food from delivery trucks. Beatrice fell into the line, taking packages from a woman ahead of her and handing them down to Evelyn behind her. Crates rattling with milk bottles. Tureens of soup. Jug after jug of water. At the end of the supply line, two women hoisted their offerings up to men bending from the first-floor window to receive them.

When the food had all gone in, the women assembled in

a circle in front of the factory, raising their signs and banners aloft as they marched. They sang a song Beatrice didn't know. *Yet what force on earth is weaker than the feeble strength of one*, it asked. They circled until Beatrice heard her voice rising into the chorus, drawing into an indistinguishable mass. *Solidarity forever, for the union makes us strong.*

On the drive home, Beatrice replayed the image of all the faces and limbs plunging out of the factory. She placed Autie's grinning face in a high window, his cap flapping from his outstretched hand, the same cap he'd fling to the dresser in their Detroit apartment with the warm, familiar smell of his hair and the factory's grease layered in its fibers.

Lewis was hefting boxes of cookware from the front porch when the women arrived. The new shipment of pots and pans was stacked beside the door. Beatrice hadn't expected him to be home, and she searched for a lie to impress upon Evelyn. *Tell him we've been to church. Tell him I went with you to the doctor.* But Evelyn was opening the car door and Beatrice was a movement behind, heavy-limbed with dread.

Lewis stood on the porch, one arm holding open the screen door, the other cradling a box. Eamon was in the window with his brother.

"Hello, Autie," Evelyn called brightly.

Panic washed swiftly through her.

Lewis let the screen door slap shut. His eyes moved to Beatrice, then away. "Hello, Mrs. Hamper. I saw the cops came around the other night. Everything all right on the home front?"

"Oh, fine." Dorothy bounded past Evelyn with the doll hanging limply from her hand. "Cy told me I was going to have to be a tough girl. It'll be over soon enough."

Lewis bent to pick up another box. Beatrice watched for his face to change, to tell her what she'd done. How sorry she should be. Inside, Eamon was watching Lewis's children, and hanging out of all of the windows at Chevy in the Hole, waving and whistling and shouting and singing, were men she didn't know, and the man she loved was dead.

"Glad to hear it," he said. "I'll be glad when those fellows are home."

"You and me both." Evelyn turned to Beatrice, extending a gloved hand. Beatrice offered hers, limp, and Evelyn squeezed it. "Thanks so much for coming with me. It's swell of you, really."

Beatrice climbed the porch steps and reached to take a box from the stack, heavy with cast iron and enamel. Inside, she willed her heart to slow and called Eamon down to help with supper. While she cooked, Lewis put the radio on. She remembered him in the street outside the Harmonie Club, the night they met in Detroit, with snowflakes catching on his eyebrows. She had liked that she could stand beside him and be quiet; how he didn't seem to mind that she didn't know the dances and was too nervous to learn. The trumpets flared, and Detroit spun with money. He worked at a shipyard, he told her, unloading freighters from Canada, but he had big plans. She told him she had to go home to her son, and he asked her his name. He grinned when she said it, as though he'd always wanted a girl with a name like that.

However Lewis failed, he'd allowed her the privacy of mourning. She told him Autie died on the line at the Packard plant, and he hadn't asked her anymore. He didn't know, no one did, that Autie was laid off and mixed up with men who ran whiskey across the river from Canada and other things;

it didn't matter, he'd assured her, leaving at strange hours and sleeping into the afternoons. That they'd fished his body out of the Detroit River, and when the police came to the door, they didn't even bother to put their hats in their hands. Widows of men like that didn't deserve it, even if those men swore it was only for a while, with the baby, with the plant shut down, no one buying cars, just a temporary thing.

Eamon was done setting the table. She remembered she never had to stand outside waiting for food. There were oranges in their Christmas stockings. Lewis took her to Flint, where she could erase what pained her with imaginary truths: that this was all there was. A little table ringed in bowls for soup. Her son staring at her with his father's eyes, waiting.

"Tell your father dinner's ready."

Beatrice and Lewis wouldn't be listening to the radio when the Sit-Down Strike ended, the United Auto Workers recognized. The men in Chevy in the Hole opened the doors. A parade wound its way up the hill and downtown, the throng singing "Solidarity Forever" all the way.

CHAPTER 4

At his mamaw's house, August and his mother had only the daylight to work with; the utilities had been shut off. Overdue water bills heaped inside the door. Rose flung back the curtains, scattering a constellation of dust motes. The plan was to go through the house room by room and take whatever was worth salvaging.

August was jittery from a shitty morning, and there was no room in him for any complicated feelings about his mamaw. He'd skipped the meeting he borrowed Annie's car for and sat in the library parking lot, calling to check on the status of the résumés he'd left at every kitchen in Flint: coney islands, chains, the new gastropubs and wine bars downtown. He didn't want these jobs and was ashamed he couldn't get them.

Wracked with guilt about the meeting, he went into the library with his NA workbook and sat in the reading room. He continued his fearless and searching moral inventory in the reading room, two men playing chess at the next table. The book asked, *Over what, exactly, am I powerless? What has God given me to be grateful for today?* He answered, *God didn't stop by Flint today—check back again tomorrow*, and borrowed a line from Matthew by way of Johnny Cash, *O Flint the city that stones those who are sent to it.*

"I saw that coming," August overheard, then whispery laughter as a chess piece thunked onto the board. "That's mate."

Myrna Molloy, his mamaw, had been chronically unhappy and put upon. Rose had said she'd be relieved to be free of her, to know that her mother was finally at rest—"It's a burden, Gus, being the only child, and a daughter at that"—but here she was, cross-legged on the ancient shag because the couch was too crowded with throw pillows, a photo album splayed on her lap. Dolls and figurines gawped at them from shelves. Frame to frame on the walls were wedding portraits, Sears portraits, graduation photos, and decades of Christmases. For historical context, they were lined alongside commemorative plates of Kennedys John F. and Bobby, GM anniversaries, and the death of Princess Diana.

Rose held out a picture of his great-grandmother Beatrice. In fuzzy mid-sixties Kodak, Rose had a Beatles haircut and a troll doll in her hand; Beatrice was a thin and elderly woman in a shapeless dress. Rose and Beatrice stood in front of a big-finned Chevrolet.

"She had two dead husbands and she painted pictures of birds and she took me to see *A Hard Day's Night.* Dad took me to visit her one time, and I was just in love with her."

Rose's eyes misted. She sniffed. She twisted for the boxes of rubber gloves and the flashlight behind her. "Why don't you start on the basement? Give me a minute with my inheritance, sweetheart." August, grateful to be given an excuse to be alone, unfolded himself.

The last time August remembered being in the basement,

he'd stolen painkillers and Xanax off his mamaw's dresser, then hidden down here when he was supposed to be mowing her lawn. The time before that, he was pajamaed, nine years old. He and Annie slipped down here when Annie was supposed to be in bed with Mamaw and he was supposed to be on the sofa, beneath the avalanche of throw pillows. Their pajama pockets bulged with pilfered snack cakes and candy dish caramels. "No one's asked me how *I* feel," Annie said, licking away the cream that clung to her Banana Flip wrapper.

"I hate Dad," August said, picking the sprinkles off a cupcake. Under his pajamas his skin burned and his arm still hurt from where he'd been pulled up too fast and too hard. His head throbbed from bawling. "Dad's a mouth-breather jerk and he sucks."

The next day their mother didn't take them to school, and while she called around to find out how divorces worked, Annie showed him the closet door where their teenage mother had written lines of poetry and rock lyrics. T. S. Eliot and Sylvia Plath; Todd Rundgren and Steely Dan. Their dad's name was written down at the bottom, like a secret. Not a heart around it or an *X* through it, just his name. Gary Majewski. Gary Majewski. Gary Majewski.

After the divorce, Rose erased his name from their children, rebirthed them. August thought of his father's name still in a room above him, evidence of something shameful they'd tried to bury. When the house was gone, he thought, that'd be gone with it. He thought of the sign at Chevy in the Hole. *Demolition Means Progress*.

In the first box August opened, he found Christmas bulbs. He picked one up, swung back, and hurled it at the wall. It wasn't heavy enough to gain any momentum. The bulb shattered on the floor, too delicate to be satisfying. He tried one shaped like a Santa and managed to hit the wall. He was halfway through a set of angels, pink cheeked and holding candles, when his mother called down, "What are you doing?"

"Breaking stuff," he pitched his voice up the stairs.

She considered a moment. "I guess that's fine, isn't it." Her footsteps crossed above him.

When he was spent, he swung the flashlight beam through the basement. He pulled out a rusted, flat-tired Schwinn. Behind it a few milk crates of records were spiderwebbed to the floor.

August dragged the crates over the concrete to where a little light came in from the half-windows. He propped the flashlight, swiped his T-shirt over his glasses, and lit a cigarette.

Another voice from the top of the stairs: Annie this time. "Food's here."

"Come check this out."

Annie descended, considered the floor with a grimace, and smoothed a trash bag over the floor to kneel on. "I've got like five minutes down here before I lose the day to a Benadryl coma."

In one hand he held up an LP with the five Del-Vikings clean-cut and grinning—*They Sing . . . They Swing*—and in another, Brenda Lee in bubblegum-pink chintz. "You've got time for this."

Annie clutched her brother's arm, steadying herself against the gale of kitsch.

He handed the records over to his sister one by one, all the matching suits and pompadours: Little Anthony and the Imperials, Frankie Lymon and the Teenagers, Dion and the Belmonts. It reminded him of when he and Annie were little, and he'd arrange her Michael Jackson tapes over the carpet in order of preference. He'd open up the *Thriller* liner and fold it back so the inside image of MJ in a gleaming white suit with a tiger cub stared up at him.

August hit the back of the crate and there, a dozen records wrapped in identical brown paper. On each a yellow ring with a Detroit, Michigan, label—Engine Running Records— ringing the hole. Peter J & the Metros, "Our Turn."

"Any idea why Mamaw has a million copies of whatever this is?"

Annie leaned forward, squinting, then turned her head to sneeze. "Maybe they're Mom's."

"Maybe Mamaw was a Metro." He slid a record from its sleeve, pristine and shiny-black.

"She was too much of a diva. It'd have to be Myrna and the Metros."

"Does that turntable Rita left work? Maybe if we play one of these backward Mamaw will give us a message from the grave."

Annie sneezed again. "I was hoping to set that thing on fire in a cleansing ritual."

He gestured around them. A blow-molded Santa Claus watched them from a utility shelf, one mittened hand raised in greeting. "Mamaw left us plenty to burn."

* * *

On the dining room table, among the takeout containers, Rose had assembled a pile of pictures and decorative plaques. Rose at graduation, ass-long hair flowing from her mortarboard. August and Annie straddling an inflatable alligator in the shallows of Lake Huron. August attempted to put the milk crate of records on the table, and his mother scolded him to get that dusty thing away from the food. When she handed him his chopsticks, he used them to gesture at the crate, moved to the salvage pile at the side of the room. "Who's Peter J and the Metros?"

Rose glanced over at the records, then riffled through the takeout bag. "Who's who? You know, this table is in good shape. Are you thinking about what you might want to take? We'll have to get a truck. Anneliese, did you get duck sauce?"

"Peter J and the Metros. Some band. There's a shit ton of records. Someone in the family wasn't in the band or something?"

His mother gestured to her full mouth and shrugged. At the other end of the table Annie pulled apart another star of crab rangoon and sniffed. August started to press, but his mother had swallowed. "Gus, if we look for meaning in everything we find in this house the three of us will go insane together."

While Rose inventoried the furniture—the bed frame he could probably use, but was it strange to sleep in your grandmother's bed?—August stared at his sister until she looked up. He threw his head back in an impersonation of his own death, eyes shut, tongue lolling. Over his head he held a dusty plaque reading *BLESS THIS MESS*, a halo. Annie's grin might have split into a laugh, but she whipped her head and sneezed. Sweet-and-sour sauce shot from her nostrils and spattered the shag.

August's disused laugh started like a car backfiring. It set Annie off in turn, a variation on a pattern their mother described in which a toddler August cried whenever his sister did, so sensitive. Annie doubled over, a hand clamped over her still-full mouth, a sweet-and-sour nosebleed smearing over her fingers.

Their mother handed her a napkin, said "Bless you, Anneliese," and gazed at the accumulated chaos. "I would never leave you with a mess like this," she promised her children, who weren't paying any attention. "I would never do this to you."

In August's pocket his phone buzzed with a missed call—an unsaved local number. He stepped out to smoke and listened with equal parts hope and dread for someone in some greasy kitchen to dangle a minimum wage job in front of him. A neighbor kid with a plastic bat stared at August with a naked desire for cigarettes. In August's ear a woman said, "This is Monae Livingston, the volunteer coordinator from Frontier Farms, returning your call."

CHAPTER 5

Frontier Farms spanned two lots on a street of weathered and charred painted ladies, just south of Chevy in the Hole. Where a home used to be there was a domed hoop house and rows of budding May green. From somewhere he heard a dog growl, a woman's warning voice. He was fifteen minutes early, but he'd been so anxious he'd convinced himself the walk from Annie's was longer than it was.

He was on the sidewalk debating whether to light a cigarette, when the front door opened and a woman stood there with a third trimester bump and tattoos of flowers and birds tumbling down her pale arms. He was meeting someone named Monae, he said. She waved him in and insisted he accept a glass of kombucha she poured from one of the mason jars cluttering a dining room table. Elaine, she introduced herself.

"My partner and I bought the house at an auction last year. Paid a dollar for the adjoining lot. One dollar. Filed our 501(c)(3) and here we are. The way they burn houses down around here, I'm hoping by the time this kid"—she patted her stomach—"is in Girl Scouts the land bank will give us the block." August, unsure if he was supposed to echo her hopes that the neighborhood go up in flames, said, "Cool."

Elaine's partner came down the stairs, asking if she was ready to go. They were taking buckwheat shoots to a bistro in the suburbs. She dispatched him to the adjoining yard to find Monae, the volunteer coordinator he'd spoken with on the phone. "She's the only one out back this afternoon. We don't usually get volunteers till after Memorial Day. You're in capable hands," Elaine said. "Mo knows everything."

He found Monae behind a shipping container converted into a shed, a too-big work shirt she probably borrowed from her boyfriend knotted at the waist and rolled to the elbows.

Simultaneously he saw her, a young Black girl with late spring sun glancing off her high cheekbones and braids, and what she was doing. A shovel was raised over her head, ready to come down on a squat, muscled dog with a chicken limp in its jaws. The dog reared back snarling, ready to lunge. Behind it, the still point in a swirling nebula of feathers, was another dead chicken.

Before August could process the warring impulses to run toward her and away, Monae brought the shovel down swiftly on the dog's skull. The impact loosed the chicken from its teeth. Blood spattered over the grass like dew. She hit the dog once more and it collapsed, twitching. August took a few steps toward her as the dog lifted itself back to its feet and scuttled, whining, out of the yard.

Monae leaned on the shovel handle, surveying the carnage. She looked just old enough to buy herself a drink to unwind from the day she was having.

"Jesus Christ," August said. His chest was heaving.

She turned to him. Her face was pretty, but it was its calm that arrested him. Her honey-brown eyes. The set of her full mouth. She could've been looking up at him from a book he'd interrupted.

He extended a hand. "Gus."

She held up her hand, splaying fingers pulpy with dirt and chicken blood. "I remember," she said. "Gus from NA."

"No big deal or anything, but the *A* stands for *Anonymous*."

"You're the one who told me, and I'm the only one here." She moved past him, heading toward the house. Unsure if he was supposed to follow, he stood there with the dead chickens and their little black eyes. A few of the living clucked toward him, and he couldn't help feeling sorry for them. The breeze picked up feathers and carried them into the tomato cages.

When Monae returned, she stood uncertainly between him and the birds. "Give me just a minute. I need to take care of these and then I'll set you up."

He offered, "I worked a little while for a nose-to-tail butcher."

She looked skeptical, but she said, "Up to you."

In the shade of the shipping container she picked up a backpack, in one mesh pocket a bag of radishes, little red globes like jewels. Sweat glistened on her neck. She told him to pick up the dead birds and follow her into the house. He took up their small, stiff feet, pinching the talons.

Already she had two stockpots heating on the stove. Monae pulled a laptop from her backpack and propped it on a chair. From its speaker the kitchen filled with shimmering sitar.

He stood beside the sink, folding and unfolding his arms and pushing his glasses up his nose. Monae scrolled down the instructions. "You worked for a butcher," she repeated, without conviction.

"I quit after a couple weeks. Talk radio at five a.m. with some big dude and his knives. Wasn't for me." Steam curled up from the pots, and the smell of chicken blood bloomed in the heat. "So did you always want to be a farmer when you grew up?" he asked. "Like when you sang 'Old MacDonald' in kindergarten it really"—he thumped his heart—"for you?"

She turned from the screen. "No. I wanted to know why kids get fat on the free lunch program and the junk their mothers buy at gas stations because they've got to take two buses to get to a supermarket. Maybe it's not like that where you grew up."

In the last weeks, August had seen himself the subject of pity and frustration and occasionally scorn. He was giving his time to the farm in penance, *giving back* to Flint when he was pretty sure it was Flint that owed him, and he'd be damned if anyone mistook him for suburban. "My mom used to make a killer banana milkshake with our government surplus. Ice cubes and a banana and that weird powdered milk that came in a bag. I can't say all the poor white kids on the west side ate that, though."

He watched her reconsider him. She gave no indication of the conclusion she came to, and he was relieved not to know. He tried to form a joke about her too-big shirt—what part of town did her boyfriend come from?—but he couldn't articulate anything, and she looked so serious. He considered instead the music. "This a George Harrison bootleg?"

She got up, moving toward the pots, and ignored him. He saw on the screen Alice Coltrane, *Journey in Satchidananda*. "I think we're ready," she said.

They took up the birds by their feet and submerged them. The water grew murky with blood and down. When he swished his bird, he caught its beak and eyes in flashes. The heat fogged his glasses, and he worked beside Monae in a cloud.

Then, outside, they started with the wings, tugging downward so the skin didn't tear. Wet feathers heaped at their feet, covered the toes of his boots. The puncture of dog teeth emerged in his bird's pale skin. He wasn't sure he remembered how to cut the vent, how to release the unholy smell of it so the whole chicken wasn't inedibly fucked, and he wanted a cigarette.

Monae pulled a tarp over the picnic table and laid out the knives. He was aware of how close she stood, her body and its dirt and sunshine smell, and how intently she watched his hands. He made a joke about this being above his volunteer pay grade, and she said, flatly, that no one was paying her either. She was going into her senior year at the university, studying environmental sciences. Internship.

With a pair of shears August severed the first chicken's head. If he focused only on the quick line of the incision and didn't take in the whole bird, the vinegary taste of the kombucha went back down his throat. Hot goo gushed from the bird's neck, and August resented his sensitivity. He wanted to say something snarky to cover it up. Like, behold the pride of Narcotics Anonymous, day one and already he'd leveled up from giving back to animal sacrifice. He was surprised when Monae at his shoulder let out a little "*Oh*."

Her face, bent to the chicken head, had softened from intense concentration to mercy. She looked sorry for the poor things, too.

On reflex, he palmed the head and took it to the trash. He wanted to get it out of her sight. When he turned back to her, she was watching him. His tongue felt fat and heavy in his mouth.

She cleared her throat. "What do we do next?"

* * *

On the walk back to Annie's, August had Johnny Cash in his headphones reading Corinthians, but he couldn't hear it. A weird energy spiked his bloodstream. So he walked east, through the lot of his shuttered high school, the overgrown baseball diamond, the charred back wall where someone had unsuccessfully tried to burn it all down, the windows tagged in fuck-yous and erect dicks. She looped through his mind: Monae and the dog. Monae and Alice Coltrane. Monae and the dead birds. Monae and her confidence and her capability in a cloud of feathers. He considered that perhaps his experience of heaven or whatever that was when his heart stopped in the restaurant bathroom was actually a premonition of his future, a vision. Then he told himself that was stupid.

He thought of her again when he worked through his NA workbook on the living room floor, then moved on to the Bible he'd picked up from the literature table at the Episcopal church. He copied verses onto scraps of paper and taped them around the apartment. *"Let the water teem with living creatures, and let birds fly above the earth across the vault of the sky." "I lie awake; I have become like a bird alone on a roof."* He played Peter J & the Metros on Rita's record player, over and over. A kick of Motown-ish horns and the background singers oohing in the background. *Oh we've waited so long for our turn, honey*. Maybe he should ask Monae if she'd heard of Peter J & the Metros, if maybe the sort of twenty-two-year-old who played Alice Coltrane while she farmed abandoned city lots would know. Monae was cute and smart, but what he felt was not so much horniness as an intense curiosity.

The sensation was so odd that it wasn't until a week later that he could identify it. He'd just upended a sack of hair from the cosmetology school onto the compost heap, and Elaine called his name, waved him over. They were packing the first CSAs of the season. Monae frowned at August, looking at his chest like she'd just noticed his shirt and *The Kids Are Alright* was her least favorite Who album. She commanded, "Hold still." She plucked a clump of someone's hair still clinging to Keith Moon. Her fingers pressed to his chest, then gone. No, what he felt was not just desire but pain, a deep ache, like a space was ripping open inside himself for her.

* * *

There were more than fourteen thousand vacant lots in Flint—the highest vacancy rate of any city in the United States. As the volunteer ranks swelled around August, one and two months sober, he heard Monae repeat this on the tours and workshops and volunteer orientations she led. If that empty land was cultivated, Flint could provide all its own fresh vegetables and fruit year-round. Even where the soil was contaminated from years of industry, the possibilities were endless: raised beds made out of tires and lumber pried from rotting houses, tilapia swimming in trenches, fruit trees that sucked the industrial poisons out of the soil—*phytoremediation*, she defined it, like the sign at Chevy in the Hole said—and chickens that might've been a violation of zoning laws, but Flint had bigger problems. Just think of your neighbors, she advised, and don't get a rooster. She walked along the rows of beans and vegetables and herbs, explaining what "food desert" meant, reeling stats on diabetes, malnutrition, and obesity rates in low-income communities.

After Memorial Day, Monae was in constant movement. August made himself the last to quit for the day, hanging in her orbit. He had so little to offer, and she gave away little of herself: she didn't talk about herself, she didn't joke and seldom laughed. He tried instead to catch her with questions. Which was why, nested on his stack of folded T-shirts atop the record player, there was a book she'd loaned him. He still had the scrap of paper on which she'd written, *Hey Gus— Chapter 6 maybe answers your question about graywater?*

Alone in Annie's apartment, he hung his head over the side of the bathtub, where he kept Monae's book dry on the bath mat. Pages on which she'd drawn little boxes around the words *equitable* and *ethical* and *resilience*. From its inner chapters fluttered a pharmacy receipt and a to-do list with items underlined and crossed out and double-checked: *Mom appt 10:30 grocery store Bio 390 exam oil change return books co-op meeting @ 8 application due tomorrow*. He held the tightness of her schedule against the days he gave away to the farm or squandered in boredom and self-pity.

On the inside cover, beneath the dust jacket, was a diagram of a farm. She'd drawn the outline of it, sketched in rows and *X*s and *T*s he thought might be a squiggly orchard. A hoop house, compost heap, chicken coop, herbs, flowers. From the crude box of the main house, what was maybe a ramp. And beneath it, a rough calculation. *Lot rental soil test seeds roto tiller compost hoses water.*

A blueprint for what she wanted for herself. And a price tag.

* * *

The day camp kids from the Baptist church around the block gathered at the picnic table in their matching yellow and pink shirts with their names puff-painted on the back. On each of their chests a sun smiled above a cross on a hill. Monae left them with seeds and cut-up egg cartons and waved August over to the chicken run.

"Do you know how to pick up a chicken?" She didn't wait for the answer. She demonstrated: one hand over each wing, then the bird's body tucked under her arm, right hand slipped between the bird's dangling feet. The bird kicked and clucked, then stilled. She stroked between its wings. "So," Monae said, glancing over her shoulder at the day campers. "Your turn."

She was wearing a drab, too-big shirt with *Jay* on a patch over the breast. It had belonged to her father, August heard her explain to a volunteer who complimented her vintage style. She didn't have a boyfriend.

He got the bird in his arms. She struggled, wings beating against his face. Through the blur of feathers, before his glasses were knocked off, he saw Monae stuff a hand over her mouth. He'd at least made her laugh. He bent, swearing, and the chicken tumbled to the ground.

"She can tell I've got the blood of her sisters on my hands," he offered feebly, shoving his smudged glasses up his nose. "I've got an aura of chicken ghosts around me."

"Just do it like she should trust you."

He tried again, this time pinning the bird's wings against her body like Monae said to do. His hands sank into fluff. Monae adjusted his hand, unclenching his fingers, and he bemoaned the sweat and dirt. "There," she said, stepping back as the chicken stilled under his arm. Its little eyes blinked out over the yard.

When the kids ran over with their Kool-Aid mustaches and dirty hands, Monae gave the instructions for petting a chicken with Mr. Gus and directed some of them to the bin of cracked corn. "Gentle," she said.

August knelt, the hen in his arms. He could feel her heart beneath his hand. Monae came beside him with a second hen. The children squealed at the softness of their feathers and their dry, gremlin feet.

"What if she poops?" they wanted to know. "Will she hurt you?" "What if she lays an egg and the egg breaks?" Monae answered while he observed the sun on their parted hair and bright barrettes. Their corn-chip and blue-raspberry breath.

"I seen you before at the museum," a little girl said to Monae.

She smiled, rare and bright. "Well, I work there, so I bet you did. What'd you see there, besides me?"

"Old cars and stuff."

"That's the place," Monae said. "If you ever come back on a Saturday you be sure to say hi to me."

The chicken tumbled out of August's arms and darted back to her flock.

CHAPTER 6

1945

A mile in either direction from the Molloy house tanks rolled off the assembly lines and straight into a vat of money. Eamon's mother had a new job at AC Spark Plug and went to meetings at the UAW hall, and if he didn't find a job himself, he'd be stuck all summer with the list of girl's chores she left him: laundry, pulling weeds, returning the heavy art books she checked out of the library. The only relief he got was after the dishes were done, when he crossed the park to his friend Danny's house. Danny had a dead father and a stash of dirty magazines left by an older brother who was stationed somewhere in the Pacific, and his mother was always lying down with a migraine.

"Where do you think we can meet girls like that?" Danny held up a copy of *Beauty Parade* open to a blonde, hair tumbling from her hands, her mouth a shiny dime-store valentine. The fan in the window riffled the pages. Danny washed dishes at a Chinese restaurant, and he always smelled like chop suey and the sweat and farts of his airless attic room.

"Maybe my dad can introduce you to Billy Durant," Eamon said. "Rich guys know all the girls like that."

Danny guffawed. No one in their neighborhood was hob-nobbing with the founder of General Motors. "Yeah, tell him to introduce me to Henry Ford and Gary Cooper while he's at it."

"You read about that new bowling alley—North Flint Rec-reation Center?"

"Nope," Danny said, turning the page to a girl in garters curled on a bed.

"Well, read a newspaper once in a while. Everyone's talking about it. Billy Durant just opened it up, and he hired my dad for second-shift manager. He's there right now."

This part was true. Eamon's father had shown him the story in the *Journal*, stabbing the headline with his finger. They were sitting in an east side coney island, no boxes of pots and pans in the trunk because there was no job for them to drive to. Billy Durant, the man who'd built General Motors out of a carriage factory on the Flint River, had returned from bank-rupt obscurity to make his fortune anew with Flint's first bowl-ing alley, featuring both upscale and drive-through dining options. Eamon was sworn to secrecy—"Your mother fails to see the opportunity in things."

Eamon had been his father's assistant. On their drives together, his father taught him to converse like a man of the world: to omit philistine details of food and the gossip of the junior high halls and instead quote the poem he read in English class, to identify which of his little brothers' jokes he could repeat as charming anecdotes, how to use bits of French like *joie de vivre* and *haute cuisine* and *carpe diem*, which was actually Latin, to trick people into thinking he wasn't poor. Guiding truths about women and what a man has to protect his wife from, like worrying needlessly over an interim between jobs, or where a commission was spent.

Danny worried a pimple in his scrap of a mustache. Eamon quoted his father. "In a year the Recreation Center will be the flagship of a chain extending from coast to coast—from the shores of Lake Michigan to Lake Huron, then from the Atlantic to the Pacific. Next Christmas we'll be stringing tinsel on a palm tree." Eamon left out the part where his mother, bewildered and angry, repeated, "Billy Durant? Billy Durant isn't dead?" To Danny, he added, "I'll send you a postcard."

"Well, what's the point of all that money if you're gonna hang around Flint with a bunch of 4Fs?" He flipped to his back. "If I got a bunch of money I'd change my name to Sturmey Archer."

Eamon laughed. "Where'd you get a dumb name like that?"

"On my bicycle. On the gear thingy. I think it's British. Doesn't it just drip with money and girls?"

Eamon reached for a discarded issue of *Eyeful* and waved a bare-breasted redhead in the air above Danny's sock pile. "I'd ask her to be Mrs. Sturmey Archer, that's for sure."

* * *

Eamon knew it might be midnight before his father came home. His helping of meatloaf waited in the oven. On their nights after demonstrations, when they came in late, Eamon had seen his mother's prim handwriting reminding their father the gas bill was due, or that dinner was spaghetti again but it was the best she could do with the money he'd given her. Sometimes now his mother left her pamphlets from the Industrial Workers of the World and newspaper articles she clipped out of the paper about Walter Reuther and the UAW. She'd taken up drawing and had a pad where she sketched birds she watched through the kitchen window.

When the house quieted, Eamon crept downstairs to leave his father a note in his mother's place.

> I wanted to stay up & tell you this but mom said I have to go to bed. I decided tomorrow I'm going to the Ivanhoe to see about washing dishes with Danny. I think it would be good because like you said your boss Billy Durant started out just selling cigars on the street and now he owns General Motors and a bowling alley.

Eamon climbed the stairs, willed the floorboards not to give him away. His brothers slept head to toe in the bed and Eamon had the cot to himself. The breeze wafted in the yeasty smell of the bread factory and the acrid smell of the factories and made an undershirt slung over the footboard wave like a flag of surrender. His father said his mind was ripe enough now to appreciate the classics, and the library's copy of *Don Quixote* lay unread on the floor. He lay awake listening to his father come in, but he could tell by the weight of his footfalls, the roughness of his movements, that he shouldn't go down to him. He fell in and out of sleep.

In the morning, Eamon was the last to wake, the house empty, and the letter was still there. Eamon's grammar and spelling had been corrected. Beneath it, though, was a second sheet of school paper.

Excuse me if I'm a lousy correspondent—I am rather fatigued.

The Recreation Center is growing rapidly and in need of an army of pinboys and waitresses. I work closely with Mr. Durant, which is a great privilege. I suspect Mr. Durant would say the true reward of wealth is the respect it commands (and holidays in the South of France). As you know, once the Recreation Center expands its operations across the country I'll have my choice of locations, should I wish to transfer. Mr. Durant suggested that California is a beautiful place to raise a family, but if you like I will tell him that my oldest son is embarking on a promising career in Chinese cuisine, and I would not dream of uprooting him at this critical stage.

—L. Molloy

"Dad"

Next door his brothers and the Nelson brothers played baseball with a crumpled soup can, and for a moment everything sounded louder than normal: the crack of the bat, the birds, the trains crossing Chevy in the Hole. Eamon was so excited it hurt to swallow his toast.

He finished his chores and, because he wasn't sure when he'd be home, left a note for his mother that said, *I'm sorry I didn't take your library book back I went to get a job.* He imagined her coming in from the factory with her metallic smell and her hair tied up, pleased that her oldest son was so mature and capable.

* * *

Eamon pedaled past the smokestacked acres of Buick City. Behind the factory's wire fence a battalion of M18 Hellcats pointed their gun barrels toward the bars and coney islands

lining Industrial Avenue. He'd stolen a dab of his father's bril-
liantine and rolled the too-short sleeves of his best shirt. He
cut through one of the neighborhoods near the foundry,
where the houses were small and the windows gray with soot
and ash.

The North Flint Recreation Center with its horseshoe-
shaped restaurant attached was pristine and empty. Inside,
Eamon's father was nowhere to be seen, but he introduced
himself as Lewis Molloy's son to an angular man in a Teddy
Roosevelt pince-nez at the counter. "I would like to inquire
about a position as a pinboy." He remembered to make his
handshake firm.

The man, Al, waved him to an office, where a small, ancient
man in a neatly tailored suit sat at a desk in a bare room.
"Molloy's son," Al said, and Eamon swelled at the sound of
it. Standing, the old man extended his hand and introduced
himself. "W. C. Durant."

Eamon cleared his throat and straightened his posture like
his father taught him, though his spine wanted to slump into
a more deferential shape. He studied Durant's wrinkled face
for the younger profile he'd seen in the papers.

"I show the ropes to each one of my employees. It's my
enterprise, and I ought to know how it operates, don't you
agree? I'm eighty years old, so you'll be expected to do everything I'm showing you at about five times my speed. I like to
see my employees maintain a brisk pace."

Eamon followed Mr. Durant down to the end of a lane,
where the old man bent to place the pins in formation. A few
lanes over, two other pinboys, younger than Eamon, watched
from their perches, one's arms crossed over his chest, the other
biting his nails.

"You understand the procedure of this? The customer rolls the ball down there." Mr. Durant pointed to the end of the lane. "You will take away whatever he knocked down and send the ball back. After his second, you will set up all ten pins again. I warn you, it gets rather spirited around here in the evenings. There's no liquor on the premises, but it seems we've become a kind of rest stop between saloons for the ladies and gentlemen of Buick." Durant abandoned the pins and advanced back down the lane. "Have you seen the Queen's guards in London, young man?"

"No, sir."

"The guards stand outside Buckingham Palace, and they never speak and they never lose face—not even if you expectorate on them. This is what I require."

Eamon nodded vigorously. "Of course, sir."

Billy Durant gave Eamon's hand a firm, swift pump, and left for the night in his bowler and overcoat. Eamon lowered himself, slightly dazed, onto the stool, though Durant recommended standing for the sake of good posture and a robust constitution.

After a tedious hour, a few girls lined up their pumps on a table and stuffed their stockinged feet into rented shoes. The redhead unrolled her stockings in plain sight, and he thought of Danny's magazines. In their big shoulders and cinched waists, they giggled as the balls went thundering down the gutters. The redhead caught Eamon staring, and winked. He crossed one leg over the other to disguise a stirring in his lap.

In bed that night, Eamon tried to write a letter to his father—*Did you see me?* it asked, and *I met another pinsetter named Tony and he said he didn't know you*, and *Is Mr. Durant from somewhere different?*—but he felt childish, ineloquent.

Paper balls scattered the floor by the time Ricky and Brian were sprawling over their bed in their underwear, kicking away the sheets.

In the dark, Eamon gave up writing and returned to the image of that redhead and her stockings and savored it.

* * *

The next night, the Recreation Center was nearly deserted and his father still nowhere to be seen when Al hurried over from the desk, waving to Eamon from the end of the lane.

"Mr. Durant's not feeling well. I need someone to escort him home. Just make sure he gets to his room all right. Fetch him something to eat, aspirin," Al said. There was money in his hand. "The cab will bring you back."

Eamon's heart thudded in his chest when he opened the office door. "I'm here to help you get home, Mr. Durant," he said. Mr. Durant looked up from his desk. His face contorted, puzzled, as if searching to identify Eamon.

"Repeat that, can you?" Durant said finally. "I've got the damnedest headache."

"Al says I could make sure you get home okay."

Durant nodded. His jacket was already on, a full suit despite the heat. He moved toward the door, Eamon measuring his steps to stay a deferential pace behind him. On the way out Eamon scanned for his father, hoping to be seen with the richest man in Flint.

In the back of the cab, the tails of Durant's open jacket puddled around him.

"I'm sorry you don't feel so well, sir," Eamon said as they lurched into traffic. This close to the old man there was a curious smell around him, like powder and unwashed armpits.

"My dad says it's a real privilege working for you, sir, and I think so, too."

Mr. Durant nodded absently.

"Must be a good feeling, to see all this." Eamon gestured toward the smoking mass of the factories half obscured behind an arsenal of tanks. "General Motors builds the tanks that will win the war, they say."

Durant murmured an inaudible response. Eamon apologized and asked him to repeat himself. "I must need to clean my ears," he said.

"I never much cared for driving," Durant said. The light and smoke of the factories passed over the lenses of his spectacles, hiding his eyes.

Durant's room at the downtown hotel bearing his name was spartan. The desk was scattered with papers and toffee wrappers, pill bottles, and tissues. Over Durant's shoulder Eamon read a handwritten table of contents. *Chapter 1: My Boyhood. Chapter 5: Why Mr. Ford Was Wrong. Chapter 16: A Theory on the Arsonists That Destroyed My Son's Castle.* A photo of a young woman who could've been either his wife or his daughter, draped in fur and pinned with a fascinator, was framed on the bedside table among more bottles.

"Do you have something to eat, Mr. Durant?"

Mr. Durant sat on the edge of his bed, then stood, a hand drifting down his body as if he'd forgotten something. He lowered himself down again. "Hungry, are you, son? There's cheese and salami in the icebox."

"I mean for you, sir."

"Oh, yes. Salami. Yes." He tugged the curtains open. Below, Saginaw Street was draped in headlights and glowing windows.

"Is there anything I can get for you, sir?" He'd seen his mother kneel and unlace her children's shoes and carry them over her shoulder to bed. He felt a sudden impulse to gather the old man in his arms the same way, and wished he were bigger, more capable.

Durant fumbled in his pocket and extended a dollar bill.

In the elevator Eamon folded and refolded the money inside his coat pocket. He stretched it across his thigh while the cabdriver took him back to the Recreation Center.

The bowling alley had picked up since Eamon left, and Al asked "Is he all right?" before pushing Eamon back to his post. Down the lanes were teenagers too young to be drafted and women in trousers with their hair wrapped up in scarves or stuffed into their husbands' caps. It took a high school boy shouting "You deaf and dumb, buddy? I said we're out of scorecards" for Eamon to refocus. He climbed off his stool and crossed to the storeroom.

There was so much noise. The Andrews Sisters on the juke-box singing about rum and Coca-Cola. Clattering pins. The laughter of people blessed with money or blessed not to care about it. His father didn't hear the knob turn and the door open, but the waitress in his arms with her blouse undone and her white cotton panties exposed wrenched her mouth away from his and turned to Eamon in round-eyed panic.

"What are you doing here?" Lewis buckled his belt. The waitress grabbed a box of straws and darted past Eamon, jostling him. He accepted the blow and kept his eyes on the floor.

"I thought this was where the scorecards were at." He heard how childish his near whisper sounded.

"Don't end a sentence with a preposition," his father corrected in reflex, then yanked Eamon into the storeroom. "What in the hell are you doing here?"

"You said they needed pinboys." Eamon saw now the white apron crumpled on the floor instead of a suit jacket. Grease stains over the chest. His father wasn't the manager of anybody.

"You didn't see anything. Repeat that to me."

Eamon shook his head, eyes riveted to the floor. On the nights as his father's assistant, they went into the homes of wealthy women, aprons over their ties, and made casseroles and baked apples for rich housewives and their friends. Eamon would pretend not to notice when a woman slipped his father a phone number or led him up the stairs. In his father's old Packard, the first night they weren't really going to a demonstration in Lake Fenton, when his father said, "It's time to move on—everyone's getting filthy rich and why shouldn't we, son?" Eamon knew his father had been fired. But how much he'd wanted to believe what his father said. That the North Flint Recreation Center was a chance to start anew with Billy Durant, Flint's prodigal son. That his mother was foolish to focus on the parts of those newspaper articles that reminded the people of Flint that Billy Durant was bankrupt. The Molloys were destined for great things, VIPs.

Bowling balls hit the floor. Benny Goodman sang about going to Michigan to see a gal in Kalamazoo. Eamon dropped the scorecards on the table and sat, dazed, on his stool. In his pocket he worried the folds of Billy Durant's dollar bill and watched the clock above the front desk. His eyes were burning in his skull with tears he was too old for now. Billy Durant was an old man living off hot dogs and salami and crackers, and his dad wasn't getting rich. He wanted to swing back into that kitchen and scream the truth at him in uncouth, plebeian words. *I don't want to be nothing like you. You're nobody.*

* * *

When Eamon reported for work the next day, the lady from the closet and a blond waitress were conferring in the parking lot. One waved him over. He strode purposely toward the door, where one of the other pinboys sat with his chin on his knees.

"We're locked up till Al gets back," the blonde said. "Duke Billy's had a stroke."

"Oh," Eamon said. He looked at the blonde and the blonde only—the lady from the closet didn't exist. He'd already decided that this was going to be his last day. He'd see about washing dishes at the Ivanhoe. He was never working with his father again. "That's great. He didn't even like bowling."

"The hell is wrong with you, kid?" the lady from the closet snapped, and he saw in the fury of her thinly penciled eyebrows and pouting mouth that she remembered him. "I said Duke Billy had a stroke."

He noticed now the blonde was moving a handkerchief gingerly from one eye to the other and back, careful not to upset her makeup.

"Is he dead?"

"Wouldn't I have said that?" the lady from the closet sighed. She looked past Eamon to another waitress pedaling into the lot on her bicycle. Gripping her handlebars and slowing toward the building, thin skirt flapping, she didn't look much older than him.

While the girls spoke in hushed tones by the Horseshoe

door, Eamon imagined headlines for the *Flint Journal* and the *Detroit Free Press*. "Bankrupt Tycoon Collapses." "Duke Billy's Gutter Ball." "Sad End for the Man Who Made Flint."

He wondered if his father was gone already, on the phone with his old boss at the cookware company, negotiating a lower commission to pick up jobs farther north. His father's car sputtering in the drive, and Eamon hefting box after box of pans and casserole dishes and twine-wrapped bundles of catalogs to the trunk. His mother's disappointed silence.

Al arrived, hands shaking so bad he kept dropping the keys. The waitresses swarmed him, and he held up a hand in surrender. "Let's carry on until Mrs. Durant gets in from New York."

Alone on his stool, Eamon thought about the electric charge of Duke Billy crackling and sputtering out at the Durant Hotel. An amiable ghost, unable to stop moving through the hotel hallways. Polishing shoes left outside doors. Neatly arranging newspapers in front of doors so their headlines smiled up at the guest bending to pick them up. Tidying trays of emptied coffee cups and dinner plates.

* * *

A troop of drunk 4Fs came in from the bar after second shift at Buick, laughing and knocking each other in the back, grease on their white fingers. The smell of liquor and cigarettes and motor oil roiled through the air with them, gathering at the end of Eamon's lane.

The girl with them caught Eamon staring at her as she pulled a flask out of her brassiere. He made himself hold her gaze.

"Hey you, down there!" one of her companions shouted.

"Where's Mr. General Motors, huh, buddy? Where's Duke Billy? I got a problem with my goddamn Chevy. Maybe he can fix it."

The men flanking him snorted. The girl's red lips curled into a smirk.

"Well, maybe if I can't talk to old Billy I'll talk to you, huh? What's your name, fella? Yeah? I said what's *your* name?"

A name rose to Eamon's throat, so absurdly dripping with money he heard the silver clatter of coins in the syllables. In this doomed place, he thought, he could be anyone. No one cared.

"Sturmey Archer," he told them, his eyes on the girl as he said it, and he girded himself for their drunken, foolish laughter.

CHAPTER 7

Monae's uncle, Harold Livingston, Third Ward city councilman and twice-failed mayoral candidate, got her the job at the history museum after her father died. Besides being a way to help her mother with the many bills disability and social security wouldn't cover, the job assured she would not, frenzied with grief and hormones, sabotage her GPA, get pregnant, or do drugs. Through high school and into her first three years of college she had done her homework at the front desk in blouses and dress shoes. Every so often, she roamed the exhibits to make sure no one was touching anything in the over-air-conditioned gloom of Flint's history.

A flock of women in purple dresses and plumed and sequined red hats came in off a coach. They circled the gift shop, picking up toy cars, wondering which of their grandbabies might want them.

Zeniyah rang up souvenirs while Monae stood by to bag them and answer questions about where the bathrooms were and when the dinosaur exhibit was coming back and if they had any presidential limousines in the museum's collection, or if those were all at the Henry Ford Museum. Then Monae got a question she hadn't been asked before. Or, rather, she was reminded, "You're Cora Livingston's granddaughter."

The woman asking wore purple lipstick to match her dress and bulbous clip-on earrings shaped like bumblebees. Birthstone bracelets on her soft brown arms. The friend beside her had one hand in an oven mitt imprinted with the map of Michigan. "You don't remember me, do you? I went to church with your grandmother. I haven't seen you since your daddy's funeral. Remind me your name, baby."

Over the woman's shoulder Monae saw August from the farm, spinning the postcard rack. The sight of him was so unexpected that she wasn't sure it was him till he turned, a flush on his face like she'd caught him doing something he shouldn't.

"Monae," the woman echoed. Then, as if it had just occurred to her, "How is Regina? You know I prayed hard for you and her." To her friend with the oven mitt she explained, "Her daddy died in a car wreck. Messed up her mother bad. Her legs, wasn't it?"

"Shattered her hips," Monae said. Her eyes flicked up to August, reading the back of a postcard, eyebrows knit in a concentration its picture of Saginaw Street didn't require. "She's doing really well. Just went back to school."

"You're not still in Cora's little old house by the park?" Before Monae could affirm that they did still live there, she turned to her friend again. "Jerome cared for her, once she was on oxygen. A sweet man, after he got himself settled down. Devoted."

The woman hefted her purse onto the counter. When she pulled out her pocket book, a cascade of Carmex pots, tissues, and pictures fell after it. Monae came around the desk to help, but August was already crouched there, handing up a scattering of wallet-sized pictures in which a little girl beamed beneath a halo of heart-shaped barrettes. Monae would've thanked him, but he'd retreated into a paperback edition of *Billy Durant: Creator of General Motors*. On the back, now covering August's face, was a picture of an ancient Durant in the bowling alley he was running when he died.

After Zeniyah rang up the rest of the souvenirs, the chattering women disappeared down the hallway and August advanced, alone, toward the register. His hair reached in wet spikes toward his glasses, as if he'd dipped himself in the fountain ringing the planetarium across the street.

"Oh, hey," he said. "I forgot you said you worked here."

It struck her as a lie, but she wasn't sure what the lie was covering. A nerdiness that he thought he'd been successfully concealing, maybe, or a rendezvous with a girl—she'd come upon people kissing in dim recesses among the old Buicks and Chevrolets. Monae noticed the edge of the postcard bend in his long fingers. Zeniyah printed his ticket.

"What are you up to?" she asked.

"Learning," he said, then his mouth turned up in a funny smile, as if he was trying to make his standing there a joke. Zeniyah gave up on the window she'd expanded on the computer screen, looking from him to Monae. August thanked her and Zeniyah twice and walked off, tapping his postcard against his arm.

"Who was *that*?" Zeniyah asked.

"He volunteers at the farm."

"You're having a real day. You should check your horoscope or something."

Monae rolled her eyes and reached under the desk for her book. She had read the same paragraph twice when Zeniyah said, "I think Farmer Jack is having a nervous breakdown."

Half of the security camera blocks were voids, their cameras out of order. But in one square, August stood in the first gallery, in front of the exhibit on Flint's early settlement. He chewed a thumbnail, crossed his arms over his chest, took a few backward strides, then repeated the process.

At the farm, August stuck around longer than most of the volunteers, who often no-showed after their whim to feel good about themselves was satisfied. He didn't have the credentials or the political stances, either, of the activists and students. He made little jokes and asked people what music they liked, and on breaks he drifted around the sidewalk in front of the empty house next door, smoking alone.

She told Zeniyah she'd go check on him. "Virgo," she called over her shoulder. "Read it to me when I get back."

Monae found August standing in front of an exhibit of Jacob Smith, Flint's first white settler. From this beginning, in the museum's story, Smith's log cabin became carriage wheels, became car wheels, became a hanging question mark. In the re-creation of his cabin, the mannequin of Jacob Smith stood in his buckskin suit and beaver hat, raccoon pelts hanging from the wall among hatchets and tomahawks. Flintstones scattered over a bench. Under the spotlight, Smith's skin was bone-white, his eyes doleful under doll lashes. Silk flowers rose around his cabin, and placards planted in the foliage described the minks and beavers and foxes who'd flourished in Ojibwe territory. It now looked like the parks the city couldn't afford to maintain, wild under burned-out streetlamps.

"You all right?" Monae asked.

He gestured toward Jacob Smith. "When I was a kid I was here for a lock-in on Devil's Night, and this guy freaked me out so bad I threw up a bunch of candy corn. My mom had to come get me." His eyes skittered to hers. "Sorry, that's gross."

"Somebody cries every school tour," she assured him.

"I used to get sensitive about the weirdest shit." August raised a hand to bite his thumbnail, then thought better of it. "But that's how this town started—some creepy loner showed up and hung a hacksaw on the wall?"

She couldn't tell if he was serious. "He wasn't alone. He married an Ojibwe woman and became a translator for the French fur traders. They had kids. The exhibit is"—she paused to emphasize what she could get in trouble for naming—"incomplete."

"How'd he even know what to do? He didn't have you to loan him books."

He looked at her directly for the first time, with a wobbling smile. Maybe he was sort of handsome, but she'd preferred not to notice it. She told him to come find her if he had any questions.

She started to walk away, but he called, "So where does Flint get less creepy?"

* * *

Monae led him backward through the city's history: through a hall of old cars—1913 Chevy Classic, the '47 Fleetmaster, the '57 Riviera coupe, the '77 Phantom—and then a re-creation of the Sit-Down Strike where more white-guy mannequins chalked out the days on a car door. A few galleries away, Monae heard the red-hat women remembering which cars they'd bought with their employee discounts and how they'd seen Aretha Franklin sing "I Never Loved a Man (the Way I Love You)" at the old IMA Auditorium.

She waved August into a little dark room where the documentary *Roger & Me* played on a constant loop. He sat beside her without leaving the breathing space of a chair between them. He lightly kicked her as he crossed one leg over the other. "Sorry," he whispered.

On the screen, a man described having a panic attack as he drove away from the factory he'd just been laid off from while "Wouldn't It Be Nice" by the Beach Boys played on the radio. The camera then rolled across boarded-up businesses and kicked-in, half-burned houses with the contents of eviction heaped at the curbs. *Flint Journal* headlines announced the rising layoff numbers while the Beach Boys harmonized, *We could be married, and then we'd be happy.*

"Yeah, this is cheering me up."

Monae ignored him. For years she had slipped in here alone, watching the movie in stolen five- and ten-minute increments, shoes kicked under the chair. When she had PMS she stashed dark chocolate bars behind the television to soften them in the electronic heat. It felt like a kind of religious space, a secret altar.

Beside her, August lifted his hand, elbow knocking the back of her chair. "One time in high school I checked this out from the library on VHS to look for my dad. He worked there—I think at AC Spark Plug. I thought maybe he'd be in there. But this movie is mustache a-go-go. GM was a real dad factory."

The postcard bounced on his leg, the boots he wore despite the heat tapping. "What about you?"

"Am I looking for my father in *Roger and Me*?" She felt exposed, as if he knew somehow and was trying to trick her into confessing.

"I mean did your parents work at the mustache factory."

"I can show you where my dad worked, actually." She crouched in front of the television, skipping the DVD forward to AutoWorld, the theme park on the river that was meant to turn 1985 Flint into a tourist destination.

The scene appeared on the screen for the thousandth time: the patriotic bunting along the replica of Saginaw Street at the turn of the last century, the Ferris wheel her father worked on turning under the domed skylight. Down in the museum's archive there were boxes of AutoWorld scraps. Brochures and souvenirs, invoices and communications with the Six Flags letterhead. But on the screen was a place she could expand in her imagination and place her father.

In her father's only AutoWorld story she remembered, he wandered the park in the costume of Fred the Carriageless Horse. Kids cowered behind their mothers at this horse with its big goofy eyes and teeth. The idea of her father—the solemn face she'd inherited with his jazz records—swallowed up by a giant horse costume had seemed surreal to her.

When Monae sat back down she found August's thumb had hooked to the top of her chair, between her shoulder blades. Swiftly, all of her awareness riveted to that spot on her back, following his hand as it moved behind her, fingers splaying over her chair back. Not touching her but hovering near. An invitation. It hadn't occurred to her that this might be what he was here for.

She cleared her throat. "My dad was a mechanic. He worked on the animatronics."

"Your dad worked at AutoWorld?" he said.

"For the full ten seconds it was open."

"That's the Flintest thing I've ever heard," he said. She flushed with a rare and particular pride, and she was going to say more, but August asked, "Do you think your dad's in heaven?"

She was sure she must have misheard him.

"Not to be nosy. I heard that lady in the gift shop."

Monae was used to people telling her where her father was—that he was with her, watching her, proud of her good grades and for taking care of her mother. Her mother, when she talked about it at all, saying she didn't want to humor any fantasies or dwell in memory; he'd been gone six years now, and they had their own lives.

"I don't know," she said.

"I overdosed a couple months ago." He cleared his throat. "You know. The NA thing. I'd been clean for a couple years but, I don't know. My heart stopped for a minute—I guess you're supposed to call it near-death—and I think I saw heaven. Or somewhere."

On the screen in front of them, the AutoWorld crowd disappeared, the park failed, closed, August and Monae not even born yet. Monae stared at the familiar scene, unseeing.

"I didn't mean to weird you out." His hand slid away, dropped behind them. "Sorry."

She turned to him. He was so close. She noticed how thick his eyelashes were. A nick on his jaw from shaving. A reflection of 1985 Flint flickered across the smudged lenses of his glasses.

"What'd it look like?" she asked.

"Like a lot of open space. Grass. Weird birds."

Someone stepped in; a shadow blocked out the line of light coming in from the gallery. Zeniyah said her name, checking on her coworker who'd wandered off the security cameras with the weird farm guy.

Monae stood. "See you Monday," she called without looking back.

She didn't see him leave but through the afternoon her mind kept drawing him there, fretting about Jacob Smith alone with his hacksaw and flintstones. Her horoscope, Zeniyah said, forecast major decisions.

* * *

Every night at five thirty Monae and her mother had dinner in front of the local news. Regina had given Frankie a crouton, and he stared at her from the opposite side of the sofa, tail thumping. The emergency financial manager that Governor Snyder had sent to run the city, Flint too poor and inept to be trusted with democracy anymore, defended the city's choice to withdraw from Detroit's water system and pull its drinking water from the Flint River. The news showed again the footage from April of the EFM and the mayor at the water plant, in suits and hard hats, holding up their glasses in a cheers to Flint. He explained the new pipeline under construction that would connect Flint to the glittering expanse of Lake Huron and free them from the expensive whims of Detroit forever. On the screen a woman in a kitchen held up a glass full of water, yellow with little pieces drifting through it. Other residents, the newscaster said, had reported similar problems.

The emergency financial manager quoted test results from the Michigan Department of Environmental Quality. Any problems, he said, were from pipes in the individual consumer's home. Regina sucked her teeth in disgust every time the man spoke until Monae laughed. "Mom, *stop*." She couldn't help it, her mother said, and repeated that Monae better pick up a few more jugs of water from the grocery store.

The camera panned across a city council meeting, and Monae had a fleeting glimpse of her uncle Harold, lavender tie pinching into his neck. The newscaster reminded them that the mayor and certain members of city council had voted against the water switch.

Regina clicked it off and raised herself onto her walker. She came back with the blackberry and coconut water popsicles Monae had made.

"I wanted to show you something," she said, lowering herself beside her daughter with her laptop. Monae curled closer to her, head tipped toward her shoulder. They used to log on to her mother's online dating profile and scroll through the Tigers hats and polo shirts and bathroom mirror selfies; the slow-jam lyrics and bios in which the bachelors of the Greater Flint area described themselves as "spiritual but not religious."

"If you ever go on one of these sites," Regina had warned her, "just don't tell me. I'll never sleep again, knowing what these dogs are saying to you."

But she'd gone on a few dates with Jim, a heavy-cheeked widower with a salt-and-pepper beard, and there was a certain shift in tone when she talked about him. He worked at a credit union and had advised her on her credit score. Monae hadn't yet met him, but she knew the lilt in her mother's laugh when she was on the phone with him and how she hummed and fussed in the bathroom when she was getting ready to go out. Regina had started wearing makeup again—sweeps of bronze over her eyelids and glowy blush like she used to wear before the accident, when she worked at the jewelry counter of a department store. She'd met Monae's father there. The older man, soft-spoken and serious, done with his drinking days, who came in looking for help buying his mother something nice for Christmas.

Her mother pulled up a web page with a brick apartment complex. A man wearing chunky headphones had his wheelchair parked in front of floor-to-ceiling windows through which a sunset spilled. There was the usual text about Section 8 and a description of a shuttle that went to Walmart. The Google map in the corner put the complex just outside Flint.

Regina repeated what she wanted. No leaky basement or soft spots in the bathroom floor. No stairs. No roof in constant need of patching. No old carpet catching at her wheels. She swiped through the pictures, people on treadmills and rowing machines, sitting on picnic tables, mingling in a high-ceilinged, wood-paneled hall that looked like the kind of place where people on wedding dress shows sliced into towering cakes. She could at least get herself on the list.

"You breaking up with me and Frankie?" Monae made herself laugh.

"You've got a year of school left. I better start making my own plans."

"You think in May they'll give me a U-Haul with my cap and gown? Where do you think I'm going?"

Her mother bit the last chunk of popsicle from the stick. "You're going to want things for yourself, and maybe I don't want to be the old widow in this falling-down house anymore."

"Mom, *don't.* That's ugly. No one thinks about you like

that." She didn't say, because she didn't want to invite another argument about what a stubborn, willful little thing she'd always been, that she didn't like being told what she wanted, what was best for her. She didn't remind her mother that this falling-down house had belonged to her grandparents, had been willed to her father, and she believed it was hers.

Regina kissed her daughter's forehead, her lips popsicle-cold. "But maybe I do. I'm tired of feeling like the oldest forty-five-year-old woman alive." She gripped her walker to raise herself and got up to wash the dishes, Frankie behind her. Monae chewed her empty popsicle stick and considered the image left on the tablet screen. A bright, clean new space.

* * *

In the tiny backyard, Frankie rolled in the grass while Monae moved down the cramped rows with her watering can. She stooped to pluck a zucchini some critter had taken a few chomps from, and launched it at the compost pile.

As a little girl, when lung cancer tethered her grandma Cora to her oxygen machine and they moved in with her, Monae helped fill the window boxes, put in the zinnias after Memorial Day. She sat with her grandmother while her father trimmed the edges of the lawn and refilled the bird feeders. Cora was proud of her house and her sons and her relationship with the Lord, Monae's father said. Monae sometimes imagined the ghost of her grandmother's house beneath its repurposing. Cora's doilies where her and her mother's textbooks spread. A stone angel once marked where a pet bird was buried, and Monae now had a rain barrel in its spot. The soil turned over not for flowers but for things she and her mother could eat.

In the months between Monae's father's death and her six-teenth birthday, she'd had to do what grocery shopping she could handle alone on the bus. Nearly an hour each way, everything double-bagged to keep from spilling over the bus floor, frozen things thawing in the summer, her headphones on so she could pretend not to hear the men who asked where a cute little thing like her was going alone. In winter, when driving alone in the ice and snow scared her, she made dinner from what she could get at the corner store: cardboard-thin frozen pizzas with the price jacked up, noodles, and tinned meat.

So she started with seed packets from the dollar store and coffee cans. Now she'd expanded the garden to the yard's lim-its. Next summer, after she had her degree and a good job, she'd adopt a lot through the county land bank. On her eve-ning walks with Frankie around the perimeter of Forest Park, she staked out places among the overgrown foundations.

Monae didn't feel like going in yet, the night cool and pleasant. She went into the garage and turned on her father's little stereo. He'd always had music on when he worked, slid-ing under cars, bending into engines. She let Mary Lou Wil-liams's *Black Christ of the Andes* play low. The opening prayer to St. Martin de Porres shivered through the leaves of her plants.

Frankie passed out beside the chamomile, and Monae sat on the back stoop, hugging her knees, watching the bats swoop. She thought about August in the screening room and his vision of heaven, if that's what it was. She wanted to ask him if there were any people there, what he had felt like when he was there. She tried to imagine her father opening his eyes in the place August had described—an anywhere kind of landscape, just grass and birds—but she didn't know if he was anyone to believe, or if she was the kind of person who'd believe it.

As volunteer coordinator, Monae had everyone's number for arranging farmers market days and CSA deliveries. She had to scroll for the contacts entry she'd made two months ago: *Gus*. He was around all the time; she never needed to text him.

She considered the time and remembered his arm on the back of her chair, and she knew how this might be perceived. But she felt like telling someone how in certain moods it satisfied her, the last image of the wrecking ball crashing into the factory; that part of Flint dissolving into rubble, cleaned away, made new. She thought about this sometimes, at the farm, when she was driving around alone: time rolling backward across the landscape until the smokestacks and steamrolled factory lots and torched foundations of unwanted houses were peeled back to the soil beneath. When the city might start over green and healthy and just.

Did you watch the rest of Roger & Me? she typed, and hit send.

She heard her mother's walker clicking on the kitchen tile, approaching the screen door. Frankie roused and trotted up the back steps.

Her phone buzzed beside her.

no! does gm come back???

"What's so funny?" her mother asked.

CHAPTER 8

1953

Goldie Byrdlong fanned herself with the beauty shop's outdated *Ebony* magazine and tried to ignore the little boy wobbling on fat, dimpled legs between her and the woman in the opposite chair. He whined to be held. "Too sticky, baby," the woman repeated. Each time she shooed him off he ricocheted back into Goldie, diapered behind grazing her. She cleared her throat and recrossed her legs, feeling the sweat pooled behind her knees. Goldie tried to work up a little relief for herself, waving Eartha Kitt's face in front of her own, and watched the big-finned cars on Saginaw Street. She pretended the little boy—his grabby fingers and his tight curls and his creamy brown skin—didn't exist.

It was Goldie's thirtieth birthday and the heat unsettled her. She woke with her nightgown clinging to her and the air thick and awful, and she felt like a little girl back in Missouri. The thought of going into work at Country Fresh dairy was intolerable, so she didn't go, and it suited her just fine if they fired her—she'd treat herself to a fun weekend, and Monday she'd scan through the usual jobs listed for Black women like her: making beds at the Durant Hotel or sweeping the floors at Chevy. Her sister, Cora, would fret about it, but if it wasn't this, she'd find something else to worry about. Besides, it was Goldie's birthday and her band had a show tonight. She was determined to enjoy herself, despite Cora's fussing and this brat testing her.

"It's my birthday," Goldie announced to the manicurist as she splayed her fingers over the towel. "And if anyone's asking, I'm twenty-two."

The beautician laid out the tiny silver scissors, emery board, the nail polish Goldie selected to match her favorite lipstick, Max Factor's Coral Glow. The boy waiting with his mother squealed at something outside the window. Goldie asked the beautician to repeat herself.

"I said, Who's the fella admiring my handiwork later?"

"I look good for me." It was no one's business but her own that that wasn't strictly true.

Goldie hated the way girls acted like you were lower than the dirt if you didn't have a man making eyes at you from the moment you hooked up your bra in the morning. She'd come up to Michigan with her sister and they shared a tiny apartment on North Saginaw where the faucet was always leaking and the landlord never came. Cora was big-boned like their mother and had a habit of dropping whatever she was eating onto her blouse. Next to her picture of Jesus with his flaming heart she had a certificate from the secretarial college framed above the television set she'd bought herself and was mightily proud of, and she'd adorned the console with doilies. Beside it was her other prized possession, a squawky lovebird named Sugar that built nests out of Cora's old catalogs and lunged at Goldie's fingers when she dragged them over the bars of the cage. Cora was forever looking for someone to set her up with a man who might become her husband, and Goldie couldn't tell what for, if you were pleased already with your TV and your hateful little bird and had money of your own.

"It's the war," Cora would say sometimes, moping around in her dressing robe, mixing up her Ovaltine and offering unsalted peanuts to Sugar. "Left us all old maids."

Goldie and the beautician talked about her show that night at the Golden Leaf, what tea she drank to soothe her throat and what powder she used to keep her face from melting off under the stage lights. When she was done, Goldie admired her ringless fingers, coral polish shining.

* * *

It was just past six o'clock, and the Golden Leaf was throbbing. A jazz troupe from Chicago pretended to be Dizzy and Bird. Third shifters from Buick and Chevy greeted the weekend early. Sweat wilted the crisp lines of office girls still wearing their kitten heels and blouses, their bobby pins littering the floor. Goldie wasn't on till late. Her band—a quartet she'd found on a record shop message board, looking for a singer—wouldn't be here for hours. Goldie didn't kid herself that she was going anywhere with music, but it kept the noise out of her head. And "I'm a singer," she could say, when really she was another woman from the North End getting screwed out of her overtime at the dairy.

Goldie leaned toward the familiar Friday bartender, a thick-armed woman in a man's shirt. The rumor was that since her husband died in the Pacific she only wore his clothes and only ate the last meal he'd written to her about: SPAM and eggs. With each passing year her widowhood grew more expansive, testing the seams on the dead man's clothes.

Goldie pressed her stomach to the bar. Already her lipstick was growing smeary in the humidity. Her skin itched beneath her black dress with the gold brocade that made her bosom look more substantial and showed off her delicate legs.

"Boss in?"

The bartender cocked her head toward the office door. Goldie ordered herself a whiskey ginger and threaded into the press of bodies, cologne and perfume and sweat and cigarette smoke, letting her hips roll with the band's attempt at "A Night in Tunisia." She watched the whirlwind of the trumpet player's lungs fill his cheeks, then dissolve down the horn. The saxophonist, perspiring in his shirtsleeves, was watching her, and she held his gaze while she sipped her drink.

Goldie hadn't spoken to anyone in hours, and it made her feel peculiar—everything gone too quiet, and on your birthday of all days.

There was a hand on Goldie's shoulder. She turned, tensed to push off whichever man thought he had the right to touch her, but instead she found the owner of the Golden Leaf, Phyllis Crenshaw, standing there in a royal-blue dress brilliant against her dark skin and those big cat eyeglasses that made her look like she had the angry black eyebrows of a villain in a comic book.

"Happy birthday," Phyllis said.

It had happened as naturally as breathing: Phyllis's hand lingering too long on the small of Goldie's back while she waited to go onstage. Phyllis was nearing fifty, and not even the kind of old woman they call handsome, but Goldie liked that this was Phyllis's place, and only Phyllis's place, since her husband died. She liked the way Phyllis walked through the bar with the authority of a man, laughing and shaking hands and telling people to enjoy themselves.

When Phyllis gestured to the door, her old wedding ring caught the light. Most of the time, it wasn't the sort of thing Goldie cared to notice.

* * *

They drove with the windows down. A breeze had kicked up, and Goldie let it cool the sweat-slick on her skin. Phyllis had forgotten her pocketbook, or so she said. Goldie almost stepped out of her Cadillac at the first stoplight. Too cheap for a hotel tonight was what she meant. Phyllis untwined her fingers from Goldie's to slap at her empty pockets. "You think I'm trying to cheat you into cheese and crackers at my house? I don't even have my license on me. You seen me drive this slow?"

"You drive like an old woman," Goldie huffed. "Looks right to me."

"Remind me, Goldie—what birthday is this? Sweet sixteen?" She laughed.

They went straight down Saginaw, through the downtown blocks where people packed into theaters and bars and restaurants despite the heat of each other's bodies and the looming rain, then they crossed the river into the North End, where they could breathe easier, where Phyllis looked like a woman giving her friend a ride home.

Goldie noticed the sky spread out over the northern city limits was yellow, with clouds thick and coppery like old blood. "Sky looks funny," Goldie said.

"All that nasty smoke from the plant." Here, where the

traffic thinned, the houses newer and scattered farther apart, Phyllis found the hem of Goldie's dress, the layer of her slip, and her fingers played along Goldie's thigh. They passed a drive-in where cars snaked in to see *Invasion USA*, teenagers, Goldie thought, looking to secretly do what Phyllis was secretly doing to her now.

Phyllis lived just over the city line, in a new house small and neat and red like a child's drawing of a barn. Goldie had imagined a more stylish place for her. Instead there were floral wallpaper and floral curtains and a pink sofa, like a doll's house. On the walls pictures of her son, grown now. A brand-new television in a console so Pine-Sol fresh it would make Cora ache with envy. A record player with neat stacks of jazz and blues like she played at the Golden Leaf. Her wedding photo was on the wall, the late Mr. Crenshaw a young man in his army uniform. Goldie sometimes wanted to know if she was the first woman, if it was something Phyllis had even thought about before her, but it seemed asking might spoil what was fresh and easy between them, and fresh and easy, Goldie reminded herself, was what she wanted. The rest of it was for people like her sister, sitting at home fretting with her bird, worried about how they didn't have all the things they were supposed to have.

Goldie stood at the window, watching the gathering wind trouble the neighbor's swing set.

Phyllis's hands drifted down Goldie's back, rubbing her through the dress. Then Phyllis's breath on her neck, heating the sweat the wind had cooled.

"What about my dinner?" Goldie said.

"Wouldn't want that rain to ruin your hair." And there it was, drumming inarguably on the windows.

Goldie turned, stepping a few paces from the window, Phyllis's feet shadowing hers. Goldie let herself be kissed. She smiled into Phyllis's mouth and Phyllis's grip grew firmer, as if telling Goldie, *Pay attention.*

Phyllis had found her zipper when something struck the window. Startled, Goldie turned to find hail whipping toward her.

"Just a storm," Phyllis murmured. She peeled Goldie's dress, let it fall. Goldie felt the light in the room change behind her closed eyelids. Phyllis's fingers had met the clasp of her bra.

Through the part in the curtains Goldie saw the wind whip the shingles off a house down the road, the debris swirling in the air like feathers. A piece of hail the size of a baseball crashed through the kitchen window, and Phyllis yanked her, dress hanging around her waist, breasts loose, to the bathroom. She flung back the shower curtain and shoved Goldie into the tub.

The wind snapped and sent the house shuddering. Phyllis whimpered like a pup, gripping the plumbing, and Goldie gripped Phyllis.

First, the gunshot crack of the windows exploding. Then a deeper crack, like thunder, but beneath them. Phyllis's eyes were in front of her and then they were snatched away.

* * *

When Goldie and Cora first came up to Detroit, they both got jobs at a glove factory and lived with a girl named Stella. Stella and Goldie said they were practicing for the husbands they'd have someday, and it was new to Goldie, but it thrilled her, kissing somebody you didn't have to make promises to, who had no right to fuss at you about sleeping through church or to want to know why you weren't a better cook. Then a mob of white boys threw a woman and her baby off the Belle Isle Bridge, into the Detroit River. Fights broke out down the bridge and then across the city, fire licking down the streets to the powder keg of Sojourner Truth Housing Project, where the white people, angry enough they'd had to work alongside Blacks in the wartime labor shortage, were goddamned if they were going to have to live with them, too. They reduced the block to kindling, erasing the people they didn't want, smashing the windows of their cars. Goldie left Detroit with Cora, left Stella to figure that mess out for herself.

And Goldie thought she was back there in Detroit, in the smoking rubble. A white boy in his undershirt pulled pieces from her limbs, shucking them into the darkness. Dirt clotted her eyes and nostrils and filled her ears. The stranger slipped one arm under her knees, the other under her arms, and lifted her. She tried to protest, but she couldn't find her tongue. She bucked, kicked. Her skin screamed.

"Easy," he said.

Over the stranger's shoulder she could make out lights floating through the dark. She squinted, blinking away the grit until she could see they were flares.

She couldn't tell which way she was facing, what street she was on, where Phyllis's house had been, or how far she'd been tossed from it. Instead of the street there were pieces of it mosaicked into a senseless shape. Wood and shattered glass and crumpled pieces of upturned cars. A refrigerator door wrapped around a tree.

The man carried Goldie past an old man holding a radio

in both arms, staring at the last standing wall of his house. "Thought it was the Russians," he said.

More people emerged from the dark, stumbled out from the wreckage. It seemed to Goldie like they were walking forever, toward nothing. The man's hands felt slippery, unable to get a good grip on her. It must have been the heat, the sweat. He was only in his undershirt, and her bare breast pressed to his skin.

"Turn off those goddamn flares!" a man yelled as he jumped out of his truck. "Goddammit, there's gas lines leaking!"

Goldie and the stranger made it to the road. She could see patches of concrete beneath them, and trucks and cars that had pulled in. A priest gave last rites to a man with a piece of his house hanging out of his stomach. A woman and two children were laid out beside him.

The stranger eased Goldie into the open mouth of the ambulance. In the light, she could see hands coming away from her body, covered in blood. The ambulance door closed. The paramedic tucked a sheet under her chin to cover her breasts. She felt the ground speeding beneath her.

"Did it hit the North End?" she asked the paramedic. He was taking her pulse, frowning.

"I said how far. Did this get them in the North End?"

"Don't worry about that now, ma'am," he said.

"I just need to know how far it got," she repeated. "My sister."

"Relax, girl."

When she realized that her ears weren't ringing, that a caravan of ambulances was speeding through the dark, she remembered Phyllis and her red house she'd been flung from.

* * *

Goldie was lucky, the doctor said; she had an awful gouge on her arm, and they had to tweeze the shards of broken glass embedded into her back, but she would be fine. A few scars. A candy striper helped her pick the clods of dirt out of her hair.

The paper called the tornado "the finger of God." Over a hundred dead, plenty more missing, and seven hundred jamming the hospitals. Makeshift morgues had been set up at the armory and the IMA Auditorium. In St. Joe's, patients swaddled in casts and gauze were laid up on either side of her.

Goldie scanned through the newspaper for names of the dead. Whole households. Mothers and children. Babies plucked from their mother's arms, from their cribs. Teenagers who'd been at the drive-in theater nearby, their cars picked up and slung into trees. But the destruction had hovered there on the city limits. It didn't whip through Forest Park, didn't touch Buick City and the houses that cluttered the streets around it. Her sister would be fine.

Goldie called the Golden Leaf from the hospital corridor. When she asked for Phyllis, her stomach was rolling somewhere around her knees, and the breath between her question—"Is she in?"—and the answer felt interminable. She pressed one palm to the cold tile wall to steady herself. The halls of the hospital were full of people drowsy with shock and painkillers, with sand and rocks blown into their scraped-up skin, pocking their faces, like they were sprouting stubble all over their bodies, like they were turning into animals.

"She's in the office. Just a moment."

Goldie closed her eyes, wanting to shut out every voice, every noise, every footfall around her.

"It's me," Goldie said, as soon as Phyllis's "Yes?" came over the line. Goldie's voice was weaker than she expected; the sound of it startled her.

Before Phyllis could respond, the connection was lost. The dial tone droned in Goldie's ear. She started punching the number again, when a nurse tapped her shoulder and too politely told her that there was a line of people who needed the phone and could it be for emergencies and scheduling pickup only, please.

"Dear Heavenly Father," the woman in the bed beside her repeated. "Oh God in Heaven thank you for sparing me Jesus." The woman's leg was shattered and swelling inside her cast. They moved her into quarantine the next day for gas gangrene. Goldie hummed to herself to try to drown out the racket. She wondered if the woman would still be thanking Jesus when they sawed off her limb.

* * *

Cora came to drive her to the Golden Leaf for her car, and brought her makeup bag and the drabbest things in her closet: a pair of brown slacks, a gingham blouse, brown loafers. Goldie's long face in the mirror, even with lipstick, looked ugly and old. Her body felt tender all over, and she had to pitch forward to keep her back from pressing against the seat.

Cora had tears in her eyes as she pulled into traffic, placing Goldie back into a Flint that looked familiar, solid, like nothing had happened. "Goldie, I didn't even think you'd be out that way. I thought maybe you had a show, or, you know. I don't ask when you don't come home. If I had known—"

"Oh Lord, *don't*," Goldie said.

Goldie just wanted to see Phyllis, whole and familiar, and to drive home for the night in her own car. God knows where her pocketbook had blown and what tree trunk her keys were speared into, but Phyllis would call her a locksmith. There were ways to fix things that Phyllis would know.

But when Goldie stepped out of Cora's car, ignoring all her unsaid questions and guilt, she saw her car wasn't in the lot.

The bar was near-empty. One man nodded his head dreamily near the jukebox, playing a song Goldie didn't recognize, too much brass in it. The bartender was a man she hadn't seen before. She asked him to tell the boss that Goldie was here to see her, and he turned toward the office. When he came back he said Phyllis was busy this afternoon but to leave a message.

"Tell her Goldie would like to know where her Buick is."

"You have the yellow sedan?"

"Yes."

"Mrs. Crenshaw had that towed out yesterday."

"Go see if she's done with that phone call." The man hesitated. She must have looked strange, some dowdy woman with one forearm mummied in gauze, at a bar in the middle of the day; some wino or some pathetic thing looking for her shiftless husband. The bartender shrugged and disappeared again.

Phyllis came through the kitchen door, eyes blazing straight ahead. She'd gotten through the storm without so much as a scratch on her ugly old glasses. She snatched up Goldie's elbow without breaking stride, steering them both calmly toward the door. Goldie let herself be led. She felt both weightless and awfully heavy, like a house lifting off its foundation.

Outside the bar, Phyllis handed her a piece of paper.

"A cab is coming. This is the towing company's address."

"You thought I died out there and you had my car towed?"

"I thought that old car was junking up my lot. Which it was."

"You wicked bitch. You no-good—"

Phyllis leaned into her so Goldie could smell the midday Bombay Sapphire on her breath. "I'm a *mother*. I have a *son*," Phyllis hissed.

"That storm blow him back into town?"

Phyllis's head snapped back as if she'd been slapped.

"I lost my home—my *home*—and what was I doing in what could've been my last moment on earth? You're a sinful woman." And in a confessional whisper, she added, "What we did was unnatural."

What was the sin in that, to try to live right by your own nature? Didn't you owe yourself your own happiness first?

The cab sidled up to the curb. Phyllis stepped away from her and leaned into the cabin, handing the driver a wad of money, like a man would. When Phyllis straightened, Goldie saw she was smiling, like the driver was any other patron pulling into the lot to unwind after a long week on the line.

"I'm glad you're okay," Phyllis said to her, and turned back to the Golden Leaf.

Trembling, Goldie lowered herself into the backseat. Her bandage shifted under her blouse, and she winced as the cab's upholstery pressed against her back.

"One too many this afternoon, girl?" the driver asked. Goldie stared at the white glare of his bald spot and didn't say anything. The man laughed at her, and Goldie shut her eyes so she didn't have to see Flint lurching past the window, didn't think about the jacked-up rate the son of a bitch would surely demand for taking a Black girl back to the North End.

* * *

It must have been the tornado that inspired Cora's magnanimity, or maybe it was just that her sister had never found herself with a surplus of men: not one bachelor but two. Both of them had jobs at the Buick foundry. She'd met the one she liked, Clifton Livingston, at a church mixer. She asked Goldie if she felt up for a double date.

Goldie would have said no, ordinarily—anything Cora could've scrounged up wouldn't be her idea of a good time. But Goldie had wiped out what money she had in the bank getting her car back, and the thought of a free meal was lure enough.

Goldie's date was a little, well, *older*, Cora said. Goldie imagined the boy's father tagging along, and instead found herself at a dinner table next to a man still shy of forty. It was this town, she thought, that made a man look older.

It fascinated Goldie how smitten Cora's date, Clifton, was with her sister. His hand reaching over to brush her arm every time he laughed at one of his own jokes, and then she started echoing his laugh back to him. He brought up for the third time how impressed he was with her education. "Isn't it nice to meet a girl who knows a thing or two?"

Goldie's date turned to ask if she'd been to secretarial school, too. She plucked the maraschino cherry out of her drink. "I don't know a damn thing."

She could feel the looks ricocheting back and forth across the booth. She avoided Cora but knew she was sweating bullets over there in her pink dress, scared to death her sister was going to ruin her chance of finally impressing a man. There were two fates: finding a husband or waiting to die, alone with your no-good sister and your bird, and Cora was running out of time.

"What do you do with yourself when you're not making those cars? You like music?" Goldie asked her date. He thought a second before saying, "I listen to baseball on the radio. And I like to eat." She almost laughed. He was the sort of person other girls would call decent: a good job, a nice car. She liked how little he talked, no fussy attempts at charm. He was small, too, skinny like her. In Detroit she'd dated a boxer, but sometimes she felt panicky underneath him, thinking of the damage he could do when he got the notion to someday.

Later, after her sister had thrown the cover over the birdcage and gone to bed with her women's magazines and her devotional, Goldie would call him up and say she couldn't sleep. "That tornado just rattled my bones," she said. "Some nights all that helps is to get out and feel the ground solid under my feet, but it's just not safe alone for a gal."

She waited for him barefoot on the porch. She'd touched up her makeup and smoothed her hair. Cora put fresh bandages on her back, and the wounds were already scabbing over, toughening up. She watched him pull into the drive. She waited till he'd climbed the top porch step to stand. The lights were off, the pale outlines of the doilies on the television console and Jesus with his glowing red heart on the wall.

Goldie led him quietly to her room—just to get her shoes, she'd told him—then once he'd stepped inside, she reached behind him to shut the door.

CHAPTER 9

"Your boo again?" Zeniyah asked. Fifteen minutes to close on the first ninety-degree day of the summer, June grinding into July, the air thick and murky with impending rain; it seemed like they had stayed too late and work had become a sleepover. Like they were beginning a game of truth or dare, and Monae, elbows propped on the desk, gripping her phone, picked truth.

"He's not my boo. But all the time, yes."

Zeniyah whispered, "Is it dick pics?"

Monae rolled her eyes.

"Then what's he texting all the time?"

Monae scrolled back through the last few weeks, pretending she hadn't memorized all of these. The first few days he mostly asked her questions about the books she loaned him. That week he'd started a new job at a Mediterranean restaurant on the western edge of Flint, and so he was only at the farm once a week, shyly glancing away the few times they made eye contact over the tomato cages. But his texts accelerated, grew more inquisitive: did she always listen to jazz or was that just when she was working? Miles or Coltrane? Did she remember the guinea pigs that lived in the children's section of the Flint Public Library? He was a few years older than her—maybe they'd passed on by the time she was coming for her *Babar* and *Curious George*. They were inconsequential questions with little of himself offered to contextualize them, and no compliments, no come-ons. Not much, he said whenever she asked what he was up to. On the bus to work. Reading the Bible. Listening to some records he found at his mamaw's house.

When her parents met, her mother told her, her father had seemed like the loneliest man alive. He'd cut out all the drinking buddies he'd run around with after he got out of the army and spent his evenings fixing cars in his mother's garage. If you were shucking off an old life, you had to let go of the people who lived in it.

Monae read through the texts for Zeniyah's confirmation that he had it bad for her. From a karaoke bar where he was designated driver for his sister and her friends, he alternated recaps of the singers (*4.7 to the lady who did macarthur park*) and his count of Red Bulls.

What would you sing if you were singing?

wouldn't it be nice by the beach boys. i'd beach boys the roof off this fucker.

Flirting had never looked like this for her, but that's what it was, unmistakable.

What's stopping you?

you come up to the golden leaf & i will.

Zeniyah pressed her knuckles into the roundness of her cheek. "He's different, for sure. You like him?"

The shrug Monae gave in response was not strictly true. Two weekends in a row now she'd caught herself thinking she saw him, a T-shirt pulled across broad shoulders, bent over a Paramount Potato Chips canister in its case. She felt a twinge of disappointment each time it wasn't.

"Well, figure it out, because he sounds straight-up obsessed."

Before Monae could ask if that was a compliment or a warning, the grad student from Ann Arbor arrived to go through the AutoWorld archives. His boat shoes stopped abruptly on the tile as he told his phone, "Immediate impression: disrepair and outdated facilities." He glanced at Monae and Zeniyah. "Maybe volunteer run."

Earlier that day her boss, Caroline, had called from home, instructing Monae through a sinus infection groan: the gloves and pencils only, nothing taken from the room, the flash photography waiver if needed. He was forty-five minutes late.

"We close in fifteen minutes," Monae said, pulling her fingers out of her sleeves.

"I've communicated with a Ms. Dawson. I'm writing my dissertation on the neoliberal transformation of the Rust Belt. I have an appointment."

"Yes, I know," she said. "With me."

He looked skeptical. He consulted his phone. "I don't know what I could have done about the traffic on Twenty-Three. But sure, I can try to be quick."

Monae was still pulling down more clamshell boxes half an hour past closing time. On the table he had the incomplete finding aid from when the AutoWorld detritus was dumped in the basement. He called box numbers to her and spread trifold brochures, a felt pendant from the gift shop, and endless contracts and invoices. He took pictures and jotted notes and spoke into his phone.

Zeniyah stopped in to say she was leaving. She looked to the grad student and said a little louder, "Elise is here to clean. Here to clean because we're closed till ten o'clock tomorrow morning."

Monae called "Good night" to her, refusing the opportunity to tell the grad student to pack up. She'd been in the archives many times but never with this freedom. She pulled open boxes of souvenir T-shirts and coffee mugs. There was a mystery in the finding aid, among the souvenirs and bills of sale. *Box 111: Head.*

She recognized it from the ears jutting up from the packing peanuts. She reached down and felt the big teeth to confirm. Her heart seized in her chest.

The grad student closed his notebook. Announced, "I'll be in contact if I need more."

Monae nearly sprinted to the front door, Flint moody on the other side of its glass, and turned the lock. She could still feel the horse's teeth against her fingers.

"Is there anywhere decent to get dinner and a drink around here? Where do you go?"

She gave him the name of a café downtown she wasn't sure was open. She held the door, the humidity pressing in on the chill of air-conditioning and shock.

"When do you get off work?"

"If you could move, please, the security system is enabled."

He smirked. She was too stupid to know how flattering this was. What an opportunity for a girl like her. Monae hurried back downstairs.

She took the clamshell box down and laid the head of Fred the Carriageless Horse on the table.

There was nothing of her father in the city's annals. If he was there in *Roger & Me*, he was an anonymous figure in a crowd of disappearing people. He was a straight man in a strange and tired joke.

With her ungloved hands she traced the dulled points of its ears, its big teeth, the coarse nap of its thirty-year-old fur. She reached her fingers inside and felt the mesh of the eyeholes her father had looked from, the nostrils her father had breathed through. She tipped her forehead to Fred the Carriageless Horse's muzzle.

* * *

At the UAW hall, fans pushed stale air, and on the information table coffee mugs and snickerdoodles served as paperweights. The neighborhood association unstuck the backs of their thighs from the folding chairs and fanned themselves with agendas. Monae stood against the back wall, nodding when Uncle Harold's eyes glanced over her in his survey of those assembled. He had on the same lavender tie and wire glasses he'd been wearing her entire life, and the fluorescents glared mercilessly on his bald spot. After this he was taking her to dinner, a ritual that brought pleasure to neither of them.

Bev from Cartier Avenue held up a milk jug sloshing murky water. "I don't care what the news says, what the mayor says. This came out of my tap. You can't tell me I should be drinking this. It looks like shit. It smells like shit." Her little boy, she added, had been plagued with stomachaches all summer. Another woman pushed up the sleeve of her T-shirt to show a rash on her shoulder.

Monae's mind was still back at the museum. She felt her phone buzz in her pocket and knew it was August leaving work.

Bill from Monteith said his water was fine but he wanted to know why, when it was all supposed to be cheaper than the old Detroit water, it was so expensive. "A hundred and thirty dollars last month. It's a major financial decision every time my kids want to fill up their little pool."

Uncle Harold repeated the figures, the long-term plan of self-sufficiency, the assurance from the Michigan Department of Environmental Quality that the water, even if it was pulled from the Flint River, was made potable through a treatment process. Long term, when the new pipeline was finished, which he didn't remind them he had voted against, the city would become self-sufficient. Those bills they were paying would decrease significantly.

"I know this is asking a lot," Harold said. "I know you remember that I was with you, that I didn't want this either. But believe that this is a step toward progress."

Harold paused to survey the room. He drew a steadying breath and said he'd be happy to answer any questions.

* * *

Harold ordered cabernet for her and told her, though she hadn't asked for the first glass, that she should limit herself to one, since she was driving. He pulled a bottle of aspirin from his pocket and tipped the pills into his palm.

Uncle Harold always picked a place downtown because of the certainty that they would be interrupted: university administrators and nonprofit executives swooped into their table, clapped Harold on the back, asking him how things were at City Hall. He asked after wives and children before gesturing to Monae with the same introduction: my late brother's daughter. She's studying at the university and has a very promising career in front of her.

Where Harold was supposed to offer himself as a paternal substitute, he instead gave out professional advancements and modeled small talk. She'd been telling him off in her mind for years.

Monae made her uncle sad, she knew: she looked too much like the troubled blue-collar brother he hadn't gotten along with, the same long limbs and high cheekbones, the same poverty in the same falling-down house, the same solemn face that cracked into a smile, her mother said, in a way that made you feel you earned it.

While he talked, Monae glazed a semi-smile on her face and stared out at Saginaw Street. Across from the wine bar were statues of David Dunbar Buick and Louis Chevrolet and Billy Durant, fathers of Flint's auto industry; the city had recently erected them in baffling nostalgia. In the waning day, still threatening rain, they looked like loiterers on the sidewalk, no place better to go.

When the chair of the history department had moved on, Harold asked, spearing a cherry from his Michigan salad, how her mother was. Because she knew it would make him even more uncomfortable than it made her, she said, "She's dating. His name's Jim and he has a van and they go to Tigers games."

He dabbed at his mouth unnecessarily and nodded. "It's healthy to move on." She held back the urge to make him explain from whom and toward what one might move.

A crack of thunder reminded her this dinner was more

than the standing reminder of their kinship: Monae had to ask him for money. By the time the rain came in the fall, the crack in the foundation would turn the basement into a pool. She'd attacked the growing mold with bleach, moved the lower storage boxes into plastic totes. She needed the wine to hit her before she could do it.

After a few fortifying bites of her entrée, she told him she'd seen the AutoWorld archives. She kept the thrill of Fred the Carriageless Horse to herself. "Why do they keep that stuff?" she asked him. "It's been sitting down there for what, thirty years?"

"Twenty," he corrected her, rolling his shoulders down his back and refolding the napkin in his lap. "They wanted to make an entire exhibit about it. As if this city needs another shrine to failure. What was that man from Ann Arbor writing on?"

"I was wondering if Dad might've worked with some of that stuff, though."

Harold took a sip of water. "I'm sure anything valuable was auctioned off. It's just flotsam down there. Debris."

It was checkmate. She didn't want to admit to wanting a piece of trash when already she had to beg for money.

After a board member from the art institute said something about a Jacob Lawrence piece on loan, Harold resumed. "You should be preparing your grad school applications this summer. Studying for the GRE."

They'd been over this. "I can't leave Mom."

"Excellent nonprofit administration program here. You have the museum as an outstanding reference."

She excused herself. In the empty bathroom, she leaned against the tile with her phone. Zeniyah asked if she wanted to go to a movie that weekend. Her mother reminded her to pick up another case of water bottles on the way home. A string of unread messages from August. She ignored them and pulled up a picture of the horse head. She expanded the image with her fingertips. Natty fur, teeth, nostrils, ears. Kept expanding until just its eye filled her phone screen. All-seeing, calm, a serene blank.

When she sat back down, Harold had his usual gin, neat, in front of him and he'd taken the liberty of ordering her a bowl of ice cream. He polished his glasses, rubbing the same small circle. He frowned down at the smear he couldn't get off. Outside, it had finally started to rain, fat drops sparking on the bricks of Saginaw Street.

Her dad used to make fun of Harold. In his stories, as they drove to pick up a car part or takeout from the Mexican place he liked, he'd talk about Uncle Harold at twelve, sci-fi obsessed and nerdy as all get-out. He mimicked Harold's big-word speeches, but never cruelly, somehow, as if her uncle was funny in the way her mother was funny, whom he teased for her squeaky sneeze or her singing voice till she was blushing, eyes watering, and she swatted at him, begging, "Oh Jay, *stop*." Monae couldn't find what it was her father thought was funny about Harold, but the thought comforted her.

She'd ask him for the money next time.

* * *

Monae drove home beneath stitches of lightning. By the time she got inside, a wall of rain sealed the house. Her mother went to bed early with her painkillers and cold packs on her hips. Monae turned down the television and stretched across the couch, the bottom of the screen scrolling the names of

Michigan counties, the mitten of the Lower Peninsula flaring red and yellow. She pulled up the horse head pictures again. If she stared hard enough and touched her fingertips to the old upholstery, she could pretend she had it again. The wind rattled the open windows in their panes. From the bathroom, Frankie whimpered in the place he wedged himself between the bathtub and the toilet every time it thundered. She answered August's texts in order.

Nina Simone Pastel Blues. Mingus Plays Piano.

Over easy, wheat toast, a little hot sauce.

I can't moonwalk. Can you?

A mist of rain puffed through the screen behind her. Her phone hummed below her ribs.

no tho i practiced a lot in 3rd grade.

Then, *the shitty band i used to play w/ in detroit is playing downtown thursday you want to go maybe?* Then, *9.* Then, *i will not moonwalk or try to moonwalk.*

Monae rolled onto her side, a throw pillow pushed under her face. "Oh, please *hush*," her mother called to Frankie.

It'd been a while since Monae had any romance. For much of sophomore year she thought she'd been in love with a political science major who went to the same food security lectures and alternative spring break neighborhood cleanups, but he'd made her feel frivolous when she couldn't afford to take off work and protest the water shutoffs in Detroit with him. When he broke up with her, she was first devastated, then relieved. Before him, there was a birthday party at Skateland where a friend's brother stuck his Tahitian Treat–sugared tongue in her mouth and she'd let him because he was kind and she felt sorry for him, with his bad skin and hissing laugh. Mostly, though, even if Monae felt lonesome, she didn't have time for romance; had scheduled it for next year when she was done with classes and internships and the museum and could work one good job and take care of the house. She'd have time, then, for things of her own.

But still. It was June. Most of the summer was left. And since he never asked her questions about her family, never asked if she believed in God like he seemed to, never told her about how he ended up in NA on his sister's couch, it couldn't be anything so serious.

What if I want to dance?

CHAPTER 10

August walked downtown to meet Monae, the cigarette smell shampooed out of his hair, teeth brushed till he spat blood. From two blocks away he spotted her on the sidewalk in a blue dress, her hair tied in a scarf. She was talking to a girl in a long paisley skirt. College kids and hipsters lit cigarettes and wove around each other, opening and then obscuring his view of her. He kept waving, and not seeing if she waved back.

As the day had crawled interminably by, August imagined himself at the bar first. Because he'd convinced himself it was all low stakes, that they were just buddies hanging out, coworkers at a job where neither of them got paid, he gave her a loose, one-armed hug, then casually told her she looked nice, then ordered her a drink and coffee for himself, which annoyed the bartender but looked more sophisticated than pop. It was all easy, and he'd know if he should ask her out for real next time, so there was no need to get weird about it. In reality, after waving like a one-man parade down Saginaw Street, he stopped a few feet from her with his heart jackhammering. He waited until the girl in the skirt headed back into the bar and Monae finally turned to him. Her pretty face, as always, was serenely inscrutable.

"Fuck, I'm late, I'm sorry."

"I'm early." Her lips were shiny with gloss: evidence of a girl who'd readied herself for a date. They weren't just hanging out as friends.

There was nowhere to sit, so August left Monae standing along the wall and waited an eternity while the bartender brewed coffee, though August leaned over the bar to tell him to forget it, man, just give him a Vernors. Nineties hip-hop pulsed from the speakers. By the time he returned, with a vodka tonic Monae drank through the stirrer before eating the ice cubes, she'd been pulled into the crowd by the girl in the skirt. A guy in a Michigan hoodie and a fade swooped in to hug her, and it occurred to August the volume of men she must know who were not volunteers from NA sleeping on their sister's couches. He couldn't hear anything over them, just when Monae said, "Gus works with me over at Frontier," brushing his arm so that the knot inside him momentarily slackened. He dipped away to buy her a second drink.

In his mental rehearsal of the evening, when the band came out with their new drummer, he knelt into her, lips brushing her ear to say funny, disparaging things about the band. He was the one who picked their name from a Ready for the World song, which she would appreciate as the secret Flint homage he intended. He danced with her in an isn't-this-ridiculous way that made her laugh and permitted him to graze her shoulder, her hips. Instead his mind was a blank panic. On stage, some guy he didn't know was banging on a drum set nicer than the one he'd abandoned and with more skill than he had. Their cover of "Search and Destroy" didn't even sound that bad.

Monae lifted onto her toes to yell into his ear. "Is this weird for you?" she asked. She'd been eating the ice cubes and her breath puffed cold against his face.

"No, drinking always made me sad, and my brain can do that on its own."

"I meant seeing your band."

He excused himself to buy her a third drink, hating himself with a familiar violence.

After the set she followed him out to the sidewalk, where he fished his cigarettes out of his pocket. For two weeks he'd texted her from his shitty new job, from the bus, from his sister's sofa, from his grandparents' emptying house, and had felt himself gaining momentum, had congratulated himself on a performance that verged on charming. She hadn't asked anything that forced him to spoil the whole thing, how he came to be a junkie volunteering away his empty days at a farm, and he'd felt himself grow more confident. He'd won this evening and wrecked it, and he was considering making an excuse and parting ways. Then the Digital Displays and their new drummer came out the side door to load up.

"It's wild seeing you here, man," the lead guitarist said. "I heard about what happened at the restaurant. *Fuck*."

"This is Mo," he said. He was supposed to tell her the names of the band members, but he caught the grin the guitar player threw past her to August, and he regretted not saying his *friend* Monae. But when the singer asked Monae what she did, August recognized in the uncharacteristic hesitance and inexactitude of her answer—"Oh. A lot of stuff"—and the way she was rocking slightly, rising out of her sandals, that he had bought her too many drinks.

They told August they were playing at some after-party on the east side, he and Monae should come along. With a promise to text the address, they went back into the bar, leaving August and Monae on the sidewalk.

"Do you want to go back in? I'll get you some water."

Monae blinked up at him. They were alone. It was the longest he'd felt permitted to look at her.

She seemed to be deliberating something. Then she looked past him at the stupid statues of Billy Durant, Louis Chevrolet, and David Dunbar Buick, moonlight on the backs of their bronzed heads. "Maybe I should've eaten more," she said.

"There's a coney island open on Court Street. I can get you something." Then corrected, because it seemed to be a thing with her, "We'll both get something but we'll eat it together."

No, she said, she wasn't drunk and she wasn't hungry and she didn't want to go to that party either. She pulled her keys out of her bag and told him where she wanted to go. Yes, she was serious. She pressed her keys into his hand. She just needed to run in and grab something.

* * *

Monae told him to circle the museum, not to wait outside the back door where she'd directed him, but the parking lot was deserted and he stepped out to smoke. In the back of the car was the book he'd given back to her, CD jewel cases scattered over the seat. He recognized Alice Coltrane with her robe and dangling earrings on the cover of *Journey in Satchidananda*.

Monae came back, hefting a gray clamshell box in both arms. "I asked you *not* to wait here."

He dashed his cigarette to the sidewalk and moved forward to help her. When she ignored his outstretched hands, he opened the back door.

"Drive away regular," she instructed.

"Did you just hustle me into being your accomplice?"

"Drive, please."

At the first red light he twisted in his seat to the gray box, then turned to her. "Did you steal a tire off a Model T?"

"They stole something from me, and they don't even remember they have it, so I took it back. They won't even notice it's gone. And the museum doesn't have a Model T, they made those in Detroit. What are you so worried about? Do you not have a license?"

"Do you not see this great getaway driving I'm doing? And I have a car, by the way. Has some electrical problems."

"Oh sure," she said. Her shiny mouth a half-smirk. "It's just that usually when the light's green, you keep driving."

But the street was deserted, the library and the music school dark, the Jell-O mold of the planetarium shadowed.

"You haven't told me where we're delivering the goods."

She said, "How about your place?"

* * *

Had August anticipated the evening would progress this far, he would have folded up the pullout, stashed away the sleeping bag, and maybe burned his meditation guide asking, *In what ways did I compulsively avoid sex?* And, *In my relationship with my family, do I sometimes feel as though we're locked into repeating the same patterns over and over without any hope of change?* He might have pulled the Bible verses off the refrigerator door and the bathroom mirror. His sister, after he assured her the farm wasn't a Jesus freak commune thing, said it looked like he was studying a foreign language, like God was a test he needed to pass.

Monae scanned the bare walls. "Your sister just move in?"

She had not allowed him to take the box from her after they parked, nor in the elevator. While he bent at the record player she asked, "Where's the bathroom?" and disappeared with it.

He put on one of his mamaw's records, the air filling with honeys and sweethearts he hoped sounded bright and goofy, like they were at a fifties diner without the milkshakes and pictures of Elvis. He poured Monae a glass of green tea from the pitcher in the fridge and waited for her to come out. He was debating whether he had time enough to fold up his bed when he heard her murmuring to herself. He went to the open bathroom door.

Monae was standing before the mirror with a giant horse head resting on her shoulders. It had a toothy, grinning mouth and the napped fur of a teddy bear that had been tied to a lamppost in a memorial. With the horse head at the center, the bathroom smelled like chemicals, a preservative burn layered over dust. The box she'd brought it in lay open on the floor.

"Jesus Christ," he whispered.

He watched her trace the horse head's big ears and teeth with her fingertips. Her breath was loud inside of it. She sounded like she was crying, and when she pulled off the head, inhaling as if she'd been submerged underwater, he saw she was. She dragged the side of her face against her shoulder to stop the tears tracking to her jaw. On the mirror, beneath her reflected face, was a piece of taped paper, and his handwriting. John 4:48: *"Unless you people see signs and wonders,"* Jesus told him, *"you will never believe."*

She handed the head to him and bent to rip off toilet paper for her nose. He followed her out of the bathroom, sitting the horse head on the coffee table as if on an altar.

They sat shoulder to shoulder on the pullout, legs extended over the unmade sheets, with her iced tea. She wasn't crying anymore, and he couldn't tell if it was inappropriate to put his arm around her, especially since they weren't even sitting like decent people but had gone straight to his squalid bed. The horse head watched them.

"What the hell is that?" he asked.

"My dad wore it sometimes when he worked at AutoWorld. He was a mechanic, but they had to take turns doing the character stuff." She slipped off her sandals and folded her legs beneath her, rearranging her skirt on her lap. Her kneecap dug into his thigh. "They've had it in a closet for twenty years. They won't even know it's gone. His name's Fred the Carriage-less Horse."

August murmured a few expletives in appreciation of this.

She put her tea down next to it, touched its fur. The Crew Cuts sang about a girl named Martha who made them melt like butter on toast. August considered that no matter how he messed this up, he would still have the smell of Monae on his sheets when he went to bed, and his anxiety eased.

"I want to ask you something," she said.

"It's a shitty Saturn, the car you don't think I have."

"I'm serious."

"Sorry."

"Did you see anybody in heaven?"

"I didn't really have time. I was just sort of dropping by. You know when you're just starting to dream and your alarm goes off? It was like that. Just a second."

"You really think heaven is what it was, though?" Her lashes were shiny black from crying.

"That or a combination of low oxygen and abnormal activity in my temporal lobe, according to the internet." He met the big, empty eyes of the carriageless horse, considered the heat of the body beside him. He had the sense he'd been let in on something holy. "But it felt bigger than that."

He was weighing the pros and cons of resting a hand on the knee digging into him when she asked, "What's with this corny music?"

He swung off the bed. "My family heirlooms aren't as cool as yours."

"Oh, your grandma. Right."

He raised a record sleeve heavenward. "RIP, Mamaw." He sifted through the evening dresses and pompadours and matching suits for one of the paper-wrapped 45s. "This one's different. Have you heard of Peter J and the Metros? Some local band."

He dropped the needle. The now-familiar kick of drums and fanfare trumpets. He could see on her face she didn't hate it. Her buzz seemed to have worn off, and she looked dreamily pleased.

"I did the tour at the Motown Museum once—you ever been there?"

She shook her head. She had her chin in her hand and the tumbler of tea on her knee. He calculated the distance between them, he at the console, she on the sofa, and the sequence of movements he might will his bones and muscles through to kiss her.

The girls singing backup cooed into the chorus.

"I'll take you when I fix my car. The tour guide showed us

how basically every Temptations dance is just this one move."
He hinged slightly sideways at the hip, both arms bent. "You
just pretend you're shoveling snow." Though he might have
been too sober for this ordinarily, the clamor in his mind too
loud, he was emboldened by the miracle of the evening landing them here. He had to try. He demonstrated, shuffling
around the living room, glasses slipping with his enthusiasm.
"You just channel your experience of Michigan winters. You
don't even have to have rhythm."

"So I see."

He threw some finger snaps in. Peter J & the Metros' trumpet player wailed in ecstasy. The singer repeated, *Oh we've
waited so long for our turn, honey*, and Monae looked miracu-
lous, cross-legged on his bed.

"You can do it, too, Mo. I've seen you with a shovel."

"You said there'd be no dancing."

"I said there'd be no moonwalking. Moonwalking was
Motown Twenty-Five. This is like Motown One."

"Have you even Googled Peter and the whoevers?"

"For what, their Myspace page?"

Monae's mouth twitched in a near smile. She didn't accept
his hand, but she stood and moved into position, gripping
an invisible snow shovel. She moved a half step forward and
stopped, one hand pressed to her mouth.

August changed direction and swung a hip at her, landing a bump. "Gimme a do-over," she said, and they crossed
the carpet shoveling the same endless invisible snow. He
threw his shoulders in, emboldened. He bumped her again
and she didn't laugh, and because he badly wanted her to, he
attempted a Jackson 5–ish forward dip, hands rolling left over
right over left, and she turned midshovel. They collided. The

song was over. Her bare feet were on his shoes, an elbow in his stomach. He steadied her against him, his hand on her arm. She blinked at him a moment, as she had on the sidewalk outside the bar, as if she were thinking through an offer that had presented itself.

She lifted onto her toes and kissed him. Her mouth light, lips slightly parted. It lasted just a second. He kissed back to see if she meant it. Her hand fluttered up to his ear.

He waltzed her backward to the couch, pulled her down with him, where she half straddled him, one foot still on the floor. He'd kissed off all her lip gloss and all the green tea, and what was left was just her mouth and her tongue. Her hands braced against his chest as if she were restarting his heart, until his hand slid over her breast, then she was just holding him at a distance, no longer kissing him. He apologized reflexively, but her bare thighs were still over his, and her lovely, serious face was in front of his, her eyes bright and close.

She slid his glasses off his face and onto her own. It felt intimate, as if she'd turned the lights off, the edges of everything softer. His hands drifted down to where her dress bunched on her thighs. He followed the flex of her thigh muscle until his hand was just inside the hem.

She adjusted the glasses. "You're blind."

"I know, I'm sorry," he said, and finally she laughed. Maybe, he thought, because now that she was here, she knew it was the least of all the things he had to apologize for. She knew the things that he was eternally sorry for, ashamed of: he the fatherless, homeless junkie on his sister's sofa. She looped her arms around his neck and kissed him. His thumb reached the elastic of her panties. She sighed into his mouth, signaling, he hoped, that he had no need to feel guilty or sad or inept. On rare nights he believed God had jettisoned him back from death for something, and his brain glowed with the idea that perhaps this was that something. When Monae said, "*God*," right into his mouth, he might have concurred, "*Yes*," if his mouth wasn't on her neck and he wasn't so focused on her bra hooks. But she rolled off him, dug her buzzing phone out of her bag, and tapped its glowing screen. Her mom, she said.

He admired her in the underwear he had not removed, the light from the street on the slope of her stomach. He had what he wanted, and he couldn't see it clearly: she still had his glasses on.

"Can I come back for this?" She was looking at her horse head. "I don't know where I can put it yet. You can take care of it for a day or two?" Then, "Promise."

He drew a cross over his heart. Hope to die.

In the elevator he was grinning, stupid, watching the numbers light in the countdown to the lobby. He felt her look at him, then felt her fretting. "Tell your mother a god-fearing man with a clean driving record and no tattoos didn't snitch on you for B and E."

"Forget you," she said, but she'd given him his glasses back and he could see she was smiling.

Outside, he was surprised to see the same city. The church bells clanging two a.m.

Before he could kiss her good night, she'd turned and both her arms were around him. He tensed: every other time he'd been held this tightly it was by someone he'd just made cry.

"Take care of my Fred," Monae said, and dropped into her car.

August walked around the block, smoking and composing text messages to her in his mind, things he might have said if it all didn't sound so dumb—*you're very pretty, i had a really nice night*—until his heartbeat slowed, and it was nearly four a.m., and she must have gone to bed. He rode the elevator back to his sister's apartment, trying to smell her still on the sofa, on his hands, his shirt. The horse head, which he swaddled carefully in a towel and tucked into a closet behind his sister's suitcase, was the only assurance he hadn't hallucinated the whole thing.

Alone again, August put the needle down on his mamaw's record.

Per Monae's advice, he typed "Peter J and the Metros" into the search bar, expecting a dead end. Instead, the first link was a YouTube video with thirty-five thousand views. The record with its yellow Engine Running Records logo the thumbnail image. The familiar kick of trumpets. The singer ready to propose to his girl. The backup singers' lovestruck *oooh*.

August scrolled through the comments.

I WANT THIS SOOOOOOOO BAD! £2k+ I don't think it will be coming my way any time soon *sniff, wipes eyes and nose*

This is 100% ENERGY FLOOR-FILLER!

Gonna buy this when I win the lottery lol

August opened eBay in another window. One listing appeared, the current bid at seven thousand dollars. RARE NORTHERN SOUL RECORD, MINT CONDITION. Twenty-five were watching the listing.

A vibration ran through August, and he couldn't quite feel his tongue in his mouth. He pitched toward the screen to make sure he hadn't overlooked the pinpoint of a decimal. Clicked back to the YouTube page to verify: 34,989 views. A Google search pulled up music forums, DJ message boards, and fan sites gushing praise and verifying the auction numbers. *What a tune*, the Brits said, unanimous.

After a call to Annie went straight to voicemail, August ransacked his corner of the apartment, digging in pockets. He held up his notebook, NA workbook, and Bible for the many bits of paper in which she instructed September October November Molloy to take out the trash and replace her granola. Through the chaos in his brain he remembered he could Google the shelter number also.

"*Hey*," he panted as soon as her voice came on the line wishing him good evening and asking how she could help. She paused and gave him the spiel, adding, "If this is an emergency, please hang up and dial 911."

His jump-started heart felt like it was going to beat through his rib cage and shatter his body. His brain was still lit up from Monae and the bright chaos of all this information. In the monastic solitude of his sister's apartment, back home in Flint, of all places, there was a holy horse head belonging to a girl who might be in love with him and a crate of records worth thousands of dollars. He was only just trusted with borrowing his sister's car for the meetings he'd secretly stopped going to because he'd made his inventory and he'd given back and never had he and the Higher Power gotten so close. His mother glanced over at his phone each time he pulled it from his pocket. "Who are you talking to, Gus?"

This could be his and his alone. Money he'd never make cooking. Money enough to do what he wanted.

"Hello?" his sister repeated in her work voice.

He hung up. He worked through the math in his mind. British pounds to American dollars, multiplied by twelve. He pulled up the photos on his phone, swiping for the picture he'd taken of Monae's farm blueprint, her calculations. There were four thousand abandoned houses in the city of Flint, she told visitors to Frontier Farms. To get started, you really just needed a soil test and some seeds.

The sun was rising over downtown Flint when August had calmed enough to lie down on the rumpled sheets where Monae had just been, and he thought of all the things he could do to prove he deserved her.

CHAPTER 11

1967

The first day of Detroit's uprising, twelve-year-old Harold sat on the sofa with his mother, Cora, and his big brother, Jerome, their plates of pasta on TV trays, tea towels under their feet to protect the carpet. Their cat, Mr. Green Jeans, swished his tail in the window overlooking the street that was calm despite everything the television was telling them.

The *Star Trek* rerun Harold looked forward to had been interrupted. They watched instead the smoking skyline of Detroit. Early that morning the police had raided a blind pig. A crowd gathered to protest the arrests—Black men, home from Vietnam—and *tensions escalated* between the crowd and the police, the reporter explained over an image of a broken shop window, and then a boy running down a street littered in glass and ash.

But the news wasn't broadcasting from Detroit: on the TV now, white people were fleeing Flint, northbound I-75 clotted with station wagons. West side grocery store shelves were picked clean of nonperishables. A man with tufts of chest hair escaping his collar explained from a Hamady Brothers parking lot, "It's a matter of hours before they burn Flint to the ground."

Jerome snickered. Harold wasn't sure at what. Their mother turned to him, her hand gripping the parmesan canister and her mouth tight. Jerome was a teenager now, thirteen and sullen behind the Stevie Wonder sunglasses he wore even in the house until their father told him to take them off, and he wanted people to call him Jay. The more Jerome misbehaved, the more their mother fretted, gave him chores, held him to a curfew, and warned him against the boys running around this neighborhood and the cops who circled it. Everything had changed this summer, Harold felt, and it seemed Jerome was at the center of it. When she came home from her job at General Motors Institute, answering phones and filing papers for young white men who were going to become engineers, Cora no longer asked after Harold first. Harold felt himself disappearing into the wallpaper, reduced to a shrimpy, bookwormy little brother, his good behavior unpraised, unnoticed.

The news anchor announced it had just been reported that about fifty Negroes were now gathered at the corner of Saginaw and Leith. Harold took the images he'd seen of Detroit's broken, flaming windows and upended cars and rearranged them in his mind over those familiar cross streets. Mayor McCree was on the screen, sweat-shiny, but Harold couldn't hear him over his own speeding mind. He looked to Jerome, smirking inscrutably. He strained for the peal of sirens.

But the evening took on its usual quiet. Front doors locked. Curtains closed. Abandoned dolls slept on front lawns. The spaces between the trees of Forest Park across the street deepened in shadow. Buick grinded into third shift.

* * *

Harold had a hard time sleeping that summer. His bones ached in their slow stretch to adulthood, and the words in his science fiction novels seemed out of focus. Sometimes he slipped out to the tiny backyard with his telescope and waited for someone to notice he was missing, to stand in the back door ushering him in. Jerome was never sleeping either, and sometimes he told bedtime stories of easy girls with big tits and guys who went to jail as regularly as old ladies went to the hairdresser. He said he knew guys who sold stolen televisions and the same guns soldiers used to kill people in Vietnam. Harold was starting to doubt him, since he'd spent most of the summer hogging the television and nobody ever called the house asking for Jay.

Jerome's plan was to get a job and save up till he could buy enough grass and pills to supply the shoprats at Buick. That's all they did in the plants—got stoned and fucked each other. Their dad probably had another woman there. All men did. When Harold went quiet, Jerome's laugh floated down from the upper bunk. "Oh shit, man—you surprised?"

Harold was. A chasm opened between what he had thought was true and what he was just learning. Where he could go and where he couldn't. Whom he should be scared of and who was scared of him.

That night, the house took longer to settle. Harold stared at his glow-in-the-dark stars and listened to his mother on the telephone in the next room, her voice thick. "I just wanted to make sure you were okay," she said, and then she hung up the phone, blew into a handkerchief, and closed her bedroom door.

Jerome's feet descended from the upper bunk. He stuffed his feet into sneakers and hissed into Harold's ear, "I know you're awake. You coming or not?"

They dropped down into their mother's black-eyed Susans and cut across the street, through the church parking lot, past houses dark save the occasional blue television glow. A few blocks away, a plume of smoke rose—not the familiar haze from Buick's smokestacks but black and serious tendrils—and with it came a crescendo of voices, the sound of shattering glass. Jerome broke into a sprint, Harold following. By the time Saginaw Street opened in front of him, Jerome had disappeared, and Harold's scaredy-cat body refused to take him farther than the sidewalk.

A crowd swelled in front of the little grocer their mother said was too high, the chop suey place, the secondhand bookshop where Harold bought paperbacks with his birthday money. The silhouettes of boys darted in and out of the streetlamps clutching pop bottles with rags twisted into flaming wicks. A telephone pole burned, and the electric hiss and bitter stench of burning wire filled the street. A woman behind Harold prayed. He'd lost sight of Jerome.

Beyond the busted store windows, boys hurled Molotov cocktails at a row of houses. Harold already knew that on the fast-disappearing windows were notices announcing that the houses were slated for demolition, their occupants already relocated to projects near the river. Construction of the new expressway was underway, and soon these houses would be carved away to make it easier for white people to get out of Flint. The boys were destroying what the city was already taking.

Sirens swung onto the street, so loud Harold clapped his hands over his ears. The police came out of their squad cars with guns drawn. Some of the boys scattered. Others advanced, shoulders thrown back, screaming taunts. A cloud of multi-colored housedresses and thin summer sheaths puffed around Harold.

Then Harold saw Jerome in a pool of light from a squad car headlight, a cheek to the cement, a uniformed knee pinned between his shoulder blades. Harold searched his brother's face for anger or fear and found nothing. Calm even as the officers yanked him up and pushed him toward the wagon where the other boys seethed or stared out limp and mournful.

Harold ran home, pulling himself back in through the bedroom window. His heart still hadn't slowed when the phone rang. His mother had told them stories about what police did to boys in their neighborhood, boys caught out at certain hours, on certain streets.

Harold had seen their mother slipping pictures of Jerome into thick envelopes. At Christmas she sent her family in Missouri pictures of both of them in front of the tree in their matching sweaters, Mr. Green Jeans twisting in Jerome's arms. But she loved Jerome more. Harold had seen her writing out the dates and details on the backs of photos of just Jerome, his school portraits and church pictures. Someone was getting photos and news of him like he had a fan club. To someone, she was declaring, *This is the one I love most.* Ordinarily this hurt. But paralyzed with fear in his bed, listening to the police whip through the neighborhood, thinking of what they might do to Jerome, he felt dizzy and hot with fear and what might be love. They were brothers, after all.

When his father flung open the door and ripped the sheet from Jerome's empty bunk, Harold was relieved to hear him vow, "I'm going to kill that boy."

* * *

Governor Romney declared a state of emergency; from Flint and Detroit the uprisings spread to Lansing and Grand Rapids, Pontiac and Saginaw. The NAACP and the Community Civic League issued statements invoking Dr. King and disavowing destruction. Liquor sales were banned. Gasoline sales stopped at seven and were forbidden to anyone looking to fill anything smaller than a Chevelle. On the boarded windows of Saginaw Street shops placards declared THIS STORE OWNED AND OPERATED BY NEGROES. BLACK POWER. SOUL BROTHER. Gun-strapped National Guardsmen patrolled empty sidewalks. Tanks assembled in a border between the North End and the rest of Flint.

Mayor McCree released the rioters on the condition they helped patrol their neighborhoods and maintain peace. Jerome was assigned to Bethel AME to help with the lock-in. "Better enjoy the walk there," their father told him; "the next time you walk out of that door it will be to mow this damn lawn." Their mother dispatched him with Harold.

"I didn't snitch and you owe me," Jerome said on the walk. Jail gave his sunglasses a new gravity. "You were there same as I was."

The church basement was quilted in sleeping bags. Girls huddled together with magazines and bottles of nail polish. A coed game of Monopoly was underway, paper money and deed cards fanned across the floor. On the walls waxy Jesuses held up smiling fish delighted to feed the multitudes.

Jerome and Harold were welcomed by Pastor Douglas, a short, thickset man with white hair ringing a bald patch. He pumped their hands and said, "God bless you for volunteering," as if it were a choice. He dispatched Jerome to the kitchen to help serve hot dogs, and Harold followed. They made it two strides before Jerome turned, his eyes shooting down to his brother's. "Where you going?"

"I think we're all set back there, son," Pastor Douglas said, and encouraged Harold to join the fun; there would be Pink Panther cartoons after dinner.

Humiliated, Harold found the stairs and climbed them with the hope of getting as far as he could from Jerome and the little kids and their cartoons.

At the top of the staircase, a voice floated toward him. The tones were bass-heavy and authoritative, but the words weren't from the Bible.

"Did they trick you into thinking Flint was progressive because our mayor is Black?" the voice asked. "Did you know you are sitting in the most segregated city in the north?"

Harold followed the voice to the open sanctuary door. A young man in glasses, his shirt buttoned up despite the heat, was addressing the few dozen teenagers in the pews.

"Last night I stood in the front door of a house on the west side with a shotgun. The neighbors had hung an effigy from the porch rafters. When the man of the house came out this morning, he had tears in his eyes. He told me, 'Freddy, this isn't worth it.' And you know, he's right. We can't buy houses under the names of our white allies and guard them like a militia. We can't burn down the streets, either. The equal opportunity housing ordinance is the only solution. If they can't recognize our humanity, they'll have to recognize the law."

Harold, hugging the doorway, was transfixed. It didn't all make sense to him, but he sensed the man was explaining what his mother fretted over, what ensnared Jerome, why the white people on the news were scared.

By the time Freddy urged them to join him next week, to flood city council with letters in support of Mayor McCree's equal opportunity housing ordinance, and mentioned Black men Harold vaguely knew from the news, he had a glimpse of who he might like to be. Not his father, taking too long to wash his Cadillac in the driveway because he wanted the neighbors to notice, then falling asleep on the sofa with his hand in a bag of pork rinds and the baseball game on. Certainly not Jerome.

Afterward, he hung around in the crowd of teenagers, shifting his weight from one high-top to the other, thinking of something he could say to introduce himself to Freddy. He burned with self-consciousness as Freddy came toward him. "I don't think we've met, brother."

"Harold, sir." Freddy's hand felt big and warm over his own.

"What did you think of what you heard in there, Harold?" Up close, the man's smile was wide, disarming after the gravity of his speech in the sanctuary.

"I don't know."

Freddy laughed at him, but without mockery. "Keep coming and we'll figure it out."

* * *

Across Michigan the smoke cleared and the tanks rolled out, and the dead and the damage were tallied. On the news, Harold and his mother watched the reporters walk through the wreckage in Detroit and ask the survivors how they felt. At the city seal, the mayor mourned, "Today, we stand amidst the ashes of our hopes." Jerome listened to records in his room and pushed the mower over the tiny backyard.

Believing the devil found work for idle hands, one of Flint's philanthropic foundations put the rioters to work for the city. Jerome manned the concession stand at a public pool. His nose burned and flaked shreds of skin. From his bunk he whispered to Harold about the curves of a bikinied girl named Venita who'd bought barbecue potato chips. "Guess where she kept that dime." Jerome showed the back of a CPR graphic where she'd written her name and number, then stuffed it under his mattress.

Harold sat on the front stoop reading the copy of *Why We Can't Wait* Freddy had given him. He had been riding his bike to the meetings for three weeks. Each time Freddy spoke to him, seeking him out in the crowd of teenagers to ask what he thought, to praise his insights, Harold felt himself expanding into the space in the air where the man's words lingered.

Which is why, when Jerome stepped through the screen door with a glass of Tang, his arms sweat-shiny from his daily push-ups, and said he wanted to go to the meetings, Harold's heartbeat rose to a panicked clamor.

"Why?" Harold asked.

"I heard you telling Mom about it, and it sounds pretty cool." He turned back inside.

It shouldn't have surprised Harold when Jerome stopped at the corner and said he'd meet him back here in two hours.

"You tell them I didn't go to your meeting and I'll tell her that her Goody Two-shoes son was with me that night. I'll tell her it was your idea."

Harold walked toward the warm light of the church, relieved that these hours with Freddy and the righteous future of Flint were still his own.

* * *

In August, city commissioners voted down the equal opportunity housing ordinance five to three. Mayor McCree announced that he would no longer be used by the city commission as a false front of racial equality and threatened to resign. Freddy told them Mayor McCree was in the hospital.

"Stomach ulcers," Freddy explained. "This man is so sick with what his city's doing he's laid up in a hospital bed. So tonight, I'm asking you: how do we help him?" Freddy's eyes swung slowly over the assembled teenagers. Freddy, though, was not soliciting ideas. He'd already searched himself long and hard, he said, until he remembered that this was Flint. They all knew the story of the Sit-Down Strike: how thirty years ago, General Motors workers stopped the line and sat down. They occupied the plants for six weeks, sleeping in their clothes on a factory floor, resisting the police and the tear gas waiting outside until the executives recognized the United Auto Workers.

So they'd take their sleeping bags and picket signs and camp on the lawn of City Hall until their plea was heard, Freddy said. "Let's show Flint we know our history."

Harold, who had only dimly known of this story before, waited to feel the thrill that seemed to be moving through the teenagers around him.

"They may turn the sprinklers on you," Freddy warned. They will say hateful things to you. You might have to call your mothers and fathers from the county jail."

Harold pulled his shoulders back, felt his chest expand and, within it, his lungs and his heart pulling wide with courage.

* * *

On the day of the protest, Harold and thirty other teenagers stepped off the church bus, Freddy behind them with a bullhorn. They scattered across the lawn of City Hall, raising the signs they'd painted in Bethel's basement: OUR CITY WANTS TO KEEP ITS NEIGHBORHOODS LILY WHITE. EQUAL OPPORTUNITY & HUMAN DIGNITY. END SEGREGATION NOW.

Faces gathered in office windows, secretaries with their arms crossed over their bosoms, city commissioners with their shirtsleeves rolled up and sweat spreading in half-moons from their armpits. A cop stepped out of the front doors with his hands on his hips, watching the kids stomp slow circles over the grass, chanting along with Freddy's bullhorn.

Harold and Jerome had left a note on the kitchen counter while their parents were at work. Harold wrote it: *We're going downtown with the church for a protest about equal opportunity housing.* He added in the postscript, *Don't get mad at us, please.* Jerome said he'd find Harold downtown by sunset, camp out with him on the grass. "Real big brother–little brother shit," Jerome said.

Jerome didn't appear, but as the day waned the protestors were hemmed in by a line of police cars and reinforced by a band of white hippie kids with their own homemade signs: a peace symbol drawn on a broken-down cardboard box, a crude drawing of MLK. A teenage girl with hair swinging down her back held a sign proclaiming BLACK AND WHITES TOGETHER NOW!

Passing cars laid on their horns. Someone screamed a slur from a rolled-down window, and Harold watched a white girl lunge forward, the veins in her neck straining as she screamed, "Fuck *you*! Fuck *you*!" at the dissolving taillights.

The girl beside him turned to Harold and shook her head. "A lot of white people don't get it. Even my old man. Sits at dinner complaining 'the coloreds' this and 'the coloreds' that."

"I'm sorry," Harold said.

She looked at him, bewildered. "Don't apologize to *me*, man."

At sundown the protestors sat cross-legged atop their sleeping bags. Harold's feet were sore from stamping the cement walkway; sweat gathered behind his knees and at the small of his back. He found himself with three boys passing a bag of potato chips between themselves, sucking the grease and salt off their fingertips. Two girls, Valerie and Letitia, looked at magazines in the dim light thrown by a streetlamp. Valerie swore, "When I get my license, I'm gonna drive down to Detroit and see if Marvin Gaye will marry me. I'm prettier than Anna Gordy any day of the week."

"Better be careful down there," Letitia said. "My cousin knows this boy who got shot by the National Guard." One boy, Leonard, said he wished he'd known about the uprising in Flint. "It's a good thing I didn't, you know. But I was so angry no one would've been able to stop me."

Harold said, "I was there." For weeks he had moved invisibly through the meetings, the runt of the group, needing only the encouragement of Freddy's attention. Now faces swiveled toward him. Leonard crossed his arms over his chest. Valerie looked impressed, but Letitia appraised him, lips pursed. "*You* were there?"

Harold felt as though he was momentarily hovering over his body, observing his skinny limbs and high, sweaty forehead. He swallowed and nodded. "We snuck out. My brother and me. We were there when the fires started." He reached for the descriptions from Heinlein and Asimov. "The whole street glowed like plutonium."

"It what?" Valerie said, but Letitia interjected before he had to answer. "But you didn't get arrested."

"I ran. I'm pretty fast."

"How old are you?"

He was grateful Valerie pressed in. "I think you're brave," she said. The smile she beamed at him probably didn't hold a tenth of the passion she'd bestow upon Marvin Gaye when the time came, but he was grateful for it.

That night, in his sleeping bag, Harold listened to the occasional car honk as it passed, whether in support or intimidation he didn't know. If he turned his head even slightly, the stench of his own armpits flooded his nose. The kid at his left tossed, legs bucking against the constraint of the sleeping bag in the throes of a dream. Harold walked toward the downtown buildings, the lights on in the highest buildings, the weather ball atop Citizens Bank bright red, promising a hotter day ahead, the unfinished lines of the new Genesee Towers. Harold searched himself for the revolutionary zeal he'd felt earlier that day, imagining all the people in Flint and how much better it would be because of their sleep-in, just like the men at General Motors thirty years ago. He tried to ignore how much he wanted to be in his own bed, the cat treading

on his legs while he read, Jerome above him repeating jokes
from boys he wasn't supposed to be running around with.

* * *

Harold was woken by a man yelling for someone to get him
a comb. The reporters were back on the City Hall lawn,
cables snaking over the grass to their vans at the curb. An
anchor, suited and coiffed, extended his microphone to the
protestors. "Tell us why you're angry," he said. "Why are you
out here?" Harold milled near the reporters, rehearsing his
answers, but the reporters reached toward older boys who
spoke about job opportunities and college applications.

In the afternoon the bus returned from the church with
women holding sacks of food. Harold saw, above the heads in
front of him, his mother in her pink shirt with the daisies on
it, talking to one of the women handing out sandwiches and
cans of Faygo red pop.

On reflex, Harold retreated one step backward. His shoulder blades connected with the chest of the kid behind him,
and he was given a "Watch it" in return.

His mother's eyes were already on him. Across the lawn,
he couldn't make out her face, but he believed she was proud
of him, moved by his self-sacrifice. He wanted to tell her everything Freddy had said, everything he'd learned that he'd been
keeping to himself all summer. She crossed the grass, and he
stepped out of line to meet her.

Then she asked, "Where is Jerome?"

Unwashed teenagers finished their sandwiches and watched
Harold as he was yanked to her old Bel Air, parked behind
the church bus. Through his embarrassed, useless tears the city

blurred around him; the City Hall lawn and the grass and the tall downtown buildings rising ahead of him, cars reduced to blurs of light color. Harold couldn't see Freddy, but he could feel his disappointed eyes all the same.

* * *

Harold's mother drove him to the recreation center, made him go with her as she asked if anyone had seen Jerome, if anyone knew where he might be or whom he might be with. They rolled through their neighborhood, past the empty lots of houses that had burned the night of Flint's quickly extinguished uprising. Sweat gathered in his unwashed armpits. His feet ached in their high-tops. They walked through Forest Park, not speaking, anticipating Jerome at every bend in the path, stopping every teenage boy they encountered, who stared back at them incredulous or hurried off, anticipating trouble.

She stopped at a pay phone. She called home, just in case, called Clifton at work, and called someone who made her cry. "Goldie, I don't *know*," she said, tilting her head back and thumbing away a tear.

Soon the streetlamps were on, the park closed. Down the street, the windows of houses were lit by televisions eulogizing a summer when boys were shot in looted pawnshops and women were picked off by snipers as they tried to drive their husbands and sons away from chaos.

His mother spoke to him for the first time in the driveway. Her eyes burned on the tiger lilies at the end of the driveway. "Don't fool yourself into thinking you're doing a thing for anyone," she said, "sleeping on the grass, making a spectacle of your own discomfort, when you're too selfish to look out for your own brother."

Inside, Jerome was there, watching television with Mr. Green Jeans purring on his feet and an empty bag of barbecue potato chips on the coffee table. Looking up, he said, "Some lady called looking for me."

Beside him, Harold's mother sagged against the closed door. "Who?" she asked, breathless.

"She wouldn't say. I asked how she knew my name. She hung up on me."

"Both of you go to your room. When I want to hear where on earth you've been, I'll ask you."

On their way down the hall, Jerome threw a grin over his shoulder. "Remember Venita with the bikini?" he whispered.

* * *

Harold and Jerome were both grounded for what was left of the summer. Jerome's punishment would last until he'd paid off their father's gun in yard work and help in the garage, but Harold was granted a one-day break for the rally at City Hall. On Saginaw Street, a crowd had formed, thickening as Harold threaded past the shops and bars. As he neared City Hall, the crowd became a shoulder-to-shoulder swell. On the lawn of City Hall, where Harold had stomped over the grass, a platform had been erected. A white man in a suit addressed the crowd.

Harold strained forward on the rubber toes of his high-tops to see over the shoulders hemming him in. Floyd McCree, his wife, Leeberta, and their daughters were seated on the stage. Harold searched the crowd for the familiar faces and Afro puffs of the youth groups and the affirmation of Freddy's slight but satisfied smile, but everyone he knew had dissolved into the mass of thousands.

The speaker announced they had a special visitor from Lansing. Governor Romney strode forward.

A woman to Harold's left gasped, "My Lord, it must be serious if Governor Romney's out on the Sabbath." In the sun the lenses of his thick glasses blurred the eyes behind them until he looked otherworldly—a man who was realer on television.

"I stand with you against injustice in Flint, and everywhere in the great state of Michigan," Governor Romney said. The crowd applauded. The governor turned to Mayor McCree. From so far away, Harold couldn't see what looks passed between the men.

Harold braced himself for a thrill of triumph or bitterness and came up with nothing. He wasn't sure if this meant that they had won, and he couldn't find Freddy's face in the crowd to tell him what to believe. There was the same gnawing of incompleteness, the same ache in his bones he felt at night while his body stretched with nothing yet to fill the new space of himself.

CHAPTER 12

August's car had been sitting in the driveway in Detroit for four months. Probably the landlord had sold it to a junk-yard, or the windshield was a mosaic of fines, a litter of kittens mewing in the recesses of the engine, the tires black puddles. But if it was still there, he had the money now to tow it out, and his mother would wait with him for the estimate.

Before Rose drove him to Detroit, though, she wanted him to go with her to confirm that his mamaw's house was truly gone. Rose had sold a few things on Craigslist, and a scrapper paid her to gut the house for copper and scrap metal. They'd hauled out August's sobriety hope chest: kitchen table, book-cases, and a set of dishes now in Rose's basement. All he needed for the apartment he said he was looking for. They'd left the house for the last time without ceremony, but Rose knew the demolition date had passed. "I can't bear it by myself," she said.

When they pulled onto the street, the absence of his mamaw's house announced itself immediately. The fence was gone, along with the house it had hemmed in. The foundation had been filled in, smoothed. Rose pulled up to the curb and cut the engine. "Let's sit a minute," she said. "I'm never coming down this street again."

August rolled down the window to smoke. His mother's labored exhales threatened to burst into sobs. Though he had felt guilty for not being sadder about his mamaw's death, he thanked her now for his secret inheritance. If he was still writing in his NA workbook, he'd have had a list of things he was grateful for. There was a kind of glow to things lately. He had a rare momentum behind him; he wanted very much to turn the radio on to cover up his mother's heavy quiet and keep driving.

Beside him, Rose fumbled in her purse for Kleenex. "It's a strange feeling, isn't it, when something you didn't even want gets taken from you." She didn't cry, but she blew her nose. "Tell me something nice."

August stared at the vacant lot, considering. He wanted to tell her he was in love, but they'd had their fair share of family counseling and support groups, and she would know this was frowned upon in the first year of sobriety. You were supposed to focus on yourself lest you, an emotional grenade with the pin half pulled, blast to smithereens someone else's life. This was a point of recovery he had never tested because he'd never had what he'd call a girlfriend, just stirrings he seldom pursued and occasional hookups. And anyway, he didn't want to open up any conversation about his alcoholic father, his alcoholic grandfather, the guilt she'd carry forever for passing on their genes, the Molloy legacy of failed and miserable marriages.

For the last month they'd been dating, though it wasn't a labeled thing. She came over a few nights a week after Annie left for work, and he reworked recipes from the better restaurants he'd worked at. "You're going through a lot of coconut milk and chickpeas for someone who used to live off Pop-Tarts," his sister said, and maybe she'd raised an eyebrow when she came in and he was playing Alice Coltrane instead of Johnny Cash reading the Bible, but if she had any suspicions, the leftovers overpowered them.

He could've told his mother about the records. No one but Monae knew he had a PayPal account fat with eBay money, and even she cocked an eyebrow every time he brought it up. He'd been paying off his IOU to Annie in modest increments to avoid suspicion. At the post office he'd filled out custom slips and insurance forms bound for the United Kingdom, France, Canada. He swaddled the records in bubble wrap and sealed them into padded envelopes. Tucked inside, postcards from the museum on which he'd scrawled, *Hi from Flint, MI. Enjoy the jam.*

But maybe that, too, would become another occasion for fretting, another intervention with his sister the social worker asking questions. The last thing a newly sober man needed was a wad of easy money.

He wanted to grip it all tightly, white-knuckle, because he finally had something rare and gleaming with potential: Monae and her blueprint and his secret money.

"I thought we came here to be sad about Mamaw," he said. "Shouldn't we just feel bad and go?"

"I've never wanted you to feel bad," his mother said. "Never."

"I know," he began around another cigarette. This conversation was hurtling toward him, and he was pinned there in his seat belt.

"My whole life," she said. "I was always messing something up and all I did was hurt her. You know, the night she told your grandfather she wanted a divorce, she'd just yelled at me for cutting my hair like a boy? She had to work so much overtime to keep us in this house, to buy me school clothes. She couldn't meet a man because of me, because she was a mother. I don't want you to ever feel like that. Responsible for my happiness."

August lied and said he never had.

Rose sniffed in something like defiance and put her turn signal on though the street was empty. "You're right. I've felt bad, and now we can go."

* * *

In Detroit, August's car still sat in the driveway. No fines from the city were secured under the windshield wipers. When he kicked the tires, they were firm. In the back still a blue thrift store cardigan, food wrappers, and crumpled cigarette packs.

"And you tried jumping it already," his mother repeated.

"It made a noise, I turned the stereo up because the noise was annoying, then the stereo died, then the car didn't start. It's fucked."

"Just humor me," Rose said. She bent into the hood with the cables: red to red and black to black. Each of them got back behind their respective wheels, August with his door open and one boot still on the concrete.

But his engine sputtered, then hummed. The stereo came on, striking into the middle of *What's Going On*, bought in the Motown Museum gift shop, while Annie behind him in her funeral dress said, "Who still buys CDs?" The tank was three-quarters full, and Marvin's voice floated out of "God Is Love" and dropped with the struck piano chords of "Mercy Mercy Me."

His mother rolled down her window. "I should've been a better father to you," Rose said. "You're stupid about cars." She frowned up again at the house that had sheltered a more wretched version of her son and asked if they could please never come down this street again either.

Once she was on I-75 heading back to Flint and August and his new battery were supposed to be behind her, he dug in the mailbox for the keys he'd buried four months before, gathering up the grocery circulars as they fell. No one had been in this house since he'd left it.

In his old room he picked up the pop bottles and food wrappers and crumpled cigarette packs from the floor. He took his razor and a dried-up bar of soap from the bathroom. He gathered up the library books to return, bookmarking a ten-dollar bill in one for the fine.

He stretched out on his mattress on the floor, fingers beating out a rhythm on his breastbone. He started to consider the person he'd been four months ago, then pulled up his phone to check his email. Re: parcel number 212. Re: 3 bedroom 1 bath. Re: auction ending 10/1/14.

He found listed on eBay and Craigslist hundreds of houses, acres of land. He was looking for a house where, if you looked at it askance, you could see the boards on the windows peeled away, the weeds and overgrown yard cut back, lights inside.

In another tab he kept open the results for the search *what does the Bible say happens when you die?* He'd ended up on an unpacking of the Gospel of John and the word *abide. Jesus answered and said unto him, If a man loves me, he will keep my words: and my Father will love him, and we will come unto him, and make our abode with him.* The word *abode*, the blogger said, is the Greek word *monē*, meaning "dwelling place" or "abiding spot." *Abide in me.* Come home.

He considered sending Monae a picture of his dismal old room, the view of the Chinese buffet across the street and the crumbling factory beyond, and didn't. She never asked him to explain anything. She asked him about her horse head, in its clamshell box at the back of a closet beside Annie's winter boots. When her boss caught her on the security camera leaving the museum in the middle of the night, she asked him if he thought her lie was convincing, that she'd forgotten her books and it was a paper-writing all-nighter emergency. She asked him if he would make that thing with the beets and smoked goat cheese again. She made him promise to wake her if she fell asleep. She felt like permission to let the godless, unloved motherfucker he'd been die forever on that bathroom floor. All his bad decisions buried, done with, forgiven. RIP August Molloy 1988–2014. Long live August Molloy 2014–.

my car's not fucked, he texted her instead.

Looking through pictures of houses, he imagined presenting himself to Monae like a man with a dowry. *If you'll have me, I offer you a half acre of urban prairie and my unconditional love.*

Monae's days at the farm were winding down, and he wondered what she'd smell like if not its dirt and sunshine smell. He'd miss her hissing, "I'm at *work*," when he knelt too close to her among the raspberry bushes, then sneaking him one of the shipping containers, still redolent from the morning volunteers who'd hotboxed it.

So you do have a car, she texted back.

He gathered up his library books and paused in the kitchen to pull down a box of stale Cheez-Its he could throw to the pheasants in the lot across the street.

CHAPTER 13

August still seemed shy around Monae every time she got into the passenger seat. He asked her too many times how she was and what she'd been up to, though usually he'd been texting her all day, following her from school to work and on her errands. His eyes flicked over to her at the first few stoplights. He drove, and Monae put her dad's CDs into his stereo. Nina Simone for the industrial boulevards near Buick City and Chevy in the Hole. Dorothy Ashby through streets that time was picking clean: the houses General Motors built for the rush of autoworkers in Civic Park and Chevrolet Park now dollhouse frames, glassless front windows you could see straight through to the backyard. Monae told him General Motors refused to sell houses to their Black employees, pointed out the ghosts of neighborhoods pulled up to make room for the expressways, told him what she remembered of her grandma Cora's stories about the sooty, leaky little apartment near the Buick foundry she paid through the nose for when she first moved to the city. "*Damn*," he said, or "That's fucked"; then he wondered aloud at how little he knew, and how much she did.

August was looking to buy a house, he said. He still worked in a kitchen and they were still messing around on his sister's couch, and so she was skeptical of the money he claimed to have. And he didn't seem to understand that if you bought a long-empty house from an online auction, there were the repairs and the taxes and winter gas bills. These drives seemed to Monae a kind of dreaming out loud, but she liked being with him. He had an abundance of time for her, and he always wanted more of her. She liked pointing out the places where she used to go with her father, liked thinking of how these spaces could be used for the farm she'd start someday.

The GPS guided them to each address August had saved. If there were no neighbors, August pulled open garage doors and lifted on the toes of his boots to peer into windows. Sometimes, if a door gave way beneath his shoulder, they went into rooms empty, or scattered with toys and clothes and dead birds. They turned away if the walls were ripped open for wires, matted carpet scattered with bits of tinfoil and burnt spoons. In basements they swung the flashlights of their phones, looking for evidence of cracked foundations, asbestos, rotting roofs. They had met possums and sleeping bats and found evidence of rats along baseboards.

Then, on the river, just north of the old farmers market and the armory, they visited a blue house. It was a quarter mile from the main intersection and a few miles from downtown, but because of the river's quiet, they felt as if they'd left town. The blue house sat back from the road, its walkway scattered with maple leaves. Boarded windows faced the river. In the front yard, a weeping willow tree. On the other side of the river, the silver pylons and power grid. The trail that followed the river all the way past the white bulb of the water plant and out of the city to Genesee Lake.

They climbed up the front porch, tried the locked doors, and ended in the backyard, which swept so far you could call it a field.

The arm that wasn't circling Monae gestured to the back door. "Could put a ramp on the back. For your mom."

She made a noncommittal hum. Her mom didn't know August existed. She'd kept the university library schedule magneted to the fridge as evidence, should her mother question her. Her mother was out with Jim more in the evenings, or she was working on her online classes, and they had become more like roommates. Her mother liked Jim's good job at the bank, his flowers and dinners out; she wouldn't like that August lived with his sister, wouldn't understand the two or three evenings a week she spent with him, dinner and sex and abandoned houses. She'd ask so many questions about him that Monae couldn't answer because she hadn't asked them herself, hadn't wanted it all to be spoiled. It was easy because August seemed to hover in a place somewhere between the present and the near future, everything before this summer discarded. Everything an incomplete plan for something better.

"Show me the pictures again," she said. He pulled up the listing, swiped through. Three bedrooms. No falling plaster, no ripped-out wires, no water damage. "This might be the Graceland of bandos," he said. "You might just call this a house, even."

"You could do so much with this," she agreed.

"Tell me what."

She plotted out the rows with her finger. A hoop house, a chicken run. All the things she'd do if she wasn't with her mother in that tiny, crumbling house with its tiny yard and so little time for herself.

She was very aware of the hand that had slipped inside her sweater and its bitten nails dragging over her low back.

"What would you call it?" he asked.

"Carriageless Horse Farms."

"That's fucking *perfect*."

She had a paper on food systems to finish that night, and she needed to pick up a case of water and her mother's prescriptions. If this was fantasy, foreplay, that was fine, but sometimes he needed help getting to the point. "You should buy it," she said. "Maybe it's your house." She gestured at the grass sweeping around them. "You can play music as loud as you want."

"Maybe it's our house," he said.

She lifted her mouth to his. Behind the garage, his breath shuddered into her mouth, and the smell of his cigarettes and shaving cream kept the dusty, animal smell of this empty space out of her nose. She liked the stubble he'd missed on the angle of his jaw and the salt of it. She liked the fading daylight and how it obscured the open need in his face, which sometimes touched and sometimes alarmed her.

* * *

Monae was trying to listen to music on her headphones, but Sun Ra kept getting interrupted by August's incoming texts. Since they'd been to the blue house a few weeks before, he'd sent pictures of it, repeating the details. *do you want to go to the habitat for humanity store & look at stoves?* She was in the basement with a rented wet vac and didn't have time for him.

A rainy autumn had widened the crack in the foundation. The slow leak in the basement was a deluge. Her shoulders burned from hauling buckets of water up and down the stairs. Frankie whined at her from the steps.

Before her were all the soggy, collapsed boxes of things she'd gathered up and hauled out right after the accident, before her mother came home from the hospital. Papers with the ink washed out. Clothes sour with mold. She found a box with a rusted electric razor and a can of Barbasol and a comb: useless things she had thrown into boxes because it didn't make sense yet that her father wasn't coming back, wouldn't need them. And deeper, the Christmas decorations, linens, old crockery, and church cookbooks from her grandma Cora, when the house had another life entirely.

Monae gathered what was unsalvageable into garbage bags and brought up the rest. She fed the dog, put the kettle on for tea, and sat at the table with her wrecked heirlooms around her. She hugged herself, massaging her sore arms and shoulders, and her nose dripped the gunky black dust she'd inhaled all day. She waited for the kettle to whistle before she summoned the nerve to dip a hand into one of those dry boxes.

Pictures. Christmas cards. Several copies of her grandmother's obituary. Bound in rubber bands were letters someone in Detroit named G sent to him when he was in the army.

The envelopes were long gone, no return address, and the letters were brief. She tilted them to make out the loose, faded handwriting. *Jay*, they all began, without greeting.

Trying to quit smoking. I'm tired of hearing about how it's going to kill me.

Can't afford anything but spaghetti at the moment.

Monk's Brilliant Corners. Listen when it's so hot you can't stand your own skin.

Frankie ran barking from the room; her mother was home. Her phone chimed again with photos of the blue house on the river. He'd gotten inside somehow. In an empty room, a ceiling sloughed off plaster like old skin. Linoleum tile bubbled up around the toilet. *i can probably fix that*, he texted.

"Oh God, what mess is that?"

Monae put the phone screen against the tabletop, but it was the soggy detritus of the house's old life that her mother was staring at. She rummaged for space in the fridge among Monae's preserves for a takeout box. Monae ignored her exasperated sigh and the clinking of mason jars.

"We need to get someone over to look at the basement," Monae told her mother's back. She smelled like warm vanilla and was wearing a bright new blouse. A memory of her mother before the accident flickered back, when she'd come home late from work, kicking her heels under the kitchen table and unhooking her earrings, undoing the day's glamor.

Her mother sighed. This time not for the clutter of mason jars, but for her. She settled at the table. Between them a photo of her grandmother with a birdcage behind her and a baby, her father or Harold, against her breast. "We've gone through this time and time again. I'm not throwing any more money at this raggedy house."

"But there's mold down there."

"Smells like it," she agreed.

"So we're just going to wait until it makes us both sick?"

"Honey, are you listening to me?"

Monae's text notification chimed again, and she turned the ringer off. "Listening to what?"

Her mother laughed, breathy and incredulous. "To what I keep telling you about *moving*, Mo. You want to wait till we're the last house on the block and the city shuts off the street-lights? What about when you want a family of your own but you have to come over and take my clothes down to the washer? For the water bill and the insurance and the property taxes and the hundred things we need to fix, we could get a place of our own. We could do better than this."

Monae bit the insides of her cheeks. She hated her mother's eyes on her. Hated, too, her perfume and her blouse and her takeout. What did *better* mean? she wanted to know. What could be more their own than this place.

First her vibrating phone distracted her, then Frankie stretching himself onto her leg, little claws hooking into her jeans, reminding her he needed to be taken out for his walk. She kicked him away. "Calm down," her mother said. When Monae looked across the table to her, the pity on her mother's face was excruciating.

"No one's making you go anywhere right now. I'm saying long term, we need to make new plans. I'm sure your father would be very proud of you for taking care of things, but he wouldn't want this burden for you."

The phone kept buzzing and buzzing. The screen lit with another picture. She gripped the phone in her hand, letting it pulse against her palm. Her eyes burned.

"Sell it to me, then, if it's just the money. What's this place worth—a thousand dollars? Two? I'll get a loan next semester. You can go live with your boyfriend anytime."

"I don't know what's gotten into you, but you need to watch your tone."

All that Monae did, all that she carried, and she could still be reduced to the smallest thing. Fix your face. Go to your room.

"And get that out of here," her mother said, a finger stabbed at the pictures and letters scattered over the table. "I don't want all that in my face."

CHAPTER 14

"I'm hoping you can explain this to me again." Caroline's door was closed, her monitor swiveled to face Monae. On the screen saver, her pink-cheeked daughter on a suburban lawn. Then the girl disappeared, and on Caroline's screen was the security camera grid.

Monae woke that morning from a dream that she and her father were driving through Buick City. She got out of the car to see the same family of turkeys she and August had come upon once after an encounter in the backseat, on a Sunday looking at houses. The turkeys darted into the bushes, and when she turned back, the car was empty, her father gone. Alone in bed she tried to gather the fleeting details, text them to Gus: The sound of her father's voice. The shirt he was wearing. The Tigers playing the Cardinals on the radio. But it all slipped away, and what persisted instead was the loss. All day her thoughts had fuzzed and blurred, and she'd felt as if she couldn't quite catch her breath.

On the screen was arranged the black squares of busted cameras. In the center, though, was the museum's external surveillance and on it a time stamp from July. The clock running past eleven p.m. Caroline sped it up, the minutes moving like seconds. Then she stopped. One of the black boxes illuminated with a grainy image of the back stairwell, and Monae slipped by in a summer dress.

She remembered the buzz of alcohol and the security code and the slap of her sandals echoing through the dark. How she moved by muscle memory and the red light of the exit sign. Didn't need to flick on the light, didn't need to search along the shelves of gray clamshell boxes for the right label. She'd pulled the box down to a lower shelf weeks before so she didn't have to drag over the ladder every time she wanted to pay tribute to what really belonged to her.

Caroline clicked the video forward. Monae already knew what for: the return of her own grainy figure. She hurried past, but there was the unmistakable bulk of the box in her arms. Caroline had shown her this before, and bought her apology that she needed to come and get a book she'd left in the break room—a paper due. But then another box lit with August's thin figure, leaning against her car. The bright speck of his cigarette. Caroline paused the video in the gap of time before Monae disappeared from one box and walked into another.

"I told you I left some things here I needed for school. Some books. My friend"—she pointed to the image frozen on the screen—"came to help me. My car was getting fixed, and my friend works late. I had a paper to finish, so I had to ask him—"

"As you perhaps didn't know, the interns have been auditing the archives, and a box came up missing. And it appears to be one of our boxes you're carrying."

Monae reached one hand to her burning cheek and then pinned it between her knees to steady it. "What even is gone?" she asked, because she had seen the slapdash finding aid and she held on to this: Caroline wouldn't know what *Box 111: Head* held. "Why do you think I'd want it?"

"Monae, I don't want to make a scene about this. Out of respect to your uncle. But we're going to have to let you go. If you return whatever this is, we'll keep this between us."

"I didn't take anything," she said. "It was just my stuff."

Caroline looked not so much disappointed as disgusted, as if she'd always known this would happen, had just been waiting for the councilman's niece from the bad part of town to show her true self.

* * *

Monae crossed the street to the pool surrounding the planetarium's green dome and sat refolding her arms—first over her breasts, then when that didn't make her feel any more solid and safe, her stomach. When it seemed she'd been there too long, that the kids coming off the school bus were staring at her, she crossed the grass to the public library and drifted into a chair in the main reading room, where two men played chess by the windows. Waves of indignation and shame assailed her, so violent she thought she might throw up. She hugged her knees on the floor of the women's room and tipped her head back against the tile. She stayed there till August texted, *outside*.

"Had to return something," she said. He kissed her cheek, and the cigarettes and coffee riding on his breath irritated her. Had she been able to think at all, she realized, she would've gone home already.

"You cold?" She was shaking. He twisted to grab a scratchy blue sweater from the backseat.

He was taking her to see the blue house on the river again, though she'd seen it already and he'd been texting about it for weeks. Half an acre. Room to expand all around him. No neighbors for a block. He repeated the details as he steered them onto the street running parallel with the river. They arrived at the blue house with its boarded windows.

He pulled into the drive. "This is it," he announced. "My spooky-ass Jacob Smith cabin on the river."

She was supposed to laugh or voice her approval, and she did neither. She pulled her fists up into his sweater sleeves and strode away from him. August squinted into the garage window. "How many raccoons do you think I'll have to evict?" he asked, and she didn't answer. He kept coming too close, crowding into the moat she wanted circling her.

She stared at the blank face of the house, and it seemed indistinguishable from every other house he'd shown her, every house she'd grown up around, seen torched, seen flake shingles and siding and paint buckle under their own weight, trees shooting up from their split roofs and broken windows. It was nearly six o'clock, and she couldn't say there was anything left at home for her mother to make for dinner, if her mother was even home. They were barely speaking. She had a midterm the next day. She needed to go over to Uncle Harold's and beg for money, or a job, or all of the above. She had no space for this shabby blue house, and she wanted to get away from August and his dreaming.

But he fished a set of keys from his pocket. He held them up. "Bought it," he said. He looked delighted with himself. "Got a soil test, even."

She didn't have to respond. He had her hand, and he led her up the back steps, which they could turn into a ramp so her mother could visit, no problem. He pushed open the door and swung the flashlight on his phone over the dusty floor. "Utilities get turned on soon," he said.

She wanted to sit down—not in here but back outside, gulping fresh air—but his hand was still there, and the stairs were creaking beneath them. With the hand that wasn't holding hers, August felt his way down the hallway to a room with windows that, if they weren't boarded, would look west.

"We'll watch the sun rise over the Flint River," he said.

The circle of flashlight hovered there on the dirty toes of his boots, everything else invisible. *We* banged around her brain. His warm, sweat-slick palm.

Then, in the dark, he said, a little too fast, like he'd been holding it on his tongue, "I love you. I think you should come live with me. I think we should get married."

In the dark, a ring. A flicker of gold.

It slammed into her sternum, and then her eyes watered. She opened her mouth, but the air was too thick and stale to draw into her lungs.

There were supposed to be so many things before this. This was no kind of proposal. You couldn't just drag someone out to the edge of nowhere and impose yourself upon them like this. Not when there was so much else to worry over, so much else she had to fix. She wasn't even his girlfriend, not really. They'd never agreed on any terms.

August unstuck himself from her. The house's stale air widening between them. "No," she said, then couldn't stop. "No. No. No."

"What do you mean, no? No, what?" She moved toward

where she thought the door was, because, she would tell herself later, it wasn't that she didn't want what he was offering, or that she hadn't thought about it herself on all the Sunday evenings they parted and she was in bed with the foundation crumbling underneath her, the taste of his kiss still in her mouth and something funny he'd said looping through her memory, it was just that the day was all wrong, and she wanted to be done with it. "This is way too soon," she said, "this is absurd," and still he protested, kept saying her name, demanded to know what was wrong, he'd asked a dozen times if she liked this place and she said yes, it was ideal, she could do everything she wanted here, and he loved her, even if that wasn't a thing they'd said before he knew she knew it, and finally, when he asked, again, what was wrong, what was she thinking, she said, "I think you're a junkie who wants to play house with a bunch of money he didn't earn and a girl he thinks will do the work for him."

August was standing close enough and there was light enough to see his face slacken into a curious blankness. He blinked a moment, as if some formerly irrefutable, foundational fact had been proven false. It was not October. Barack Obama was not the president. His heart hadn't jump-started on the floor of that fancy restaurant in Detroit, and this was the dark solitude of whatever came next. "That's not true," he said. But his voice was too low, and there was too much confused space between the words, because even this registered as impossible—that she knew so much was the reason he'd started trailing her around the farm and sending her a thousand questions a day in the first place.

In the car she didn't turn to see what anger, or hurt, looked like on him. In her drawing of boundaries—two or three nights a week, just dinner and sex and old houses—there had been no space for fights.

They drove back along the river, passed again the empty market, then he turned toward the museum. Her car was the last in the lot. When she got out, she was still wearing his sweater, and she was still trembling despite it.

* * *

August texted her the next day. *are you ok? idk how i fucked this up but im sorry.* Then a few hours later, *ive been really happy & that never happens to me & I got impatient or greedy about it.* Then, *maybe you can call me?* And, *i know youre busy.*

Then he sent her a picture. On a piece of notebook paper in her handwriting there was the blueprint of a farm. She'd drawn slight variations of it in the back of so many books and notebooks she couldn't say where he'd gotten it. Below, a rough estimate of what it would take to get started. She sat staring at her own handwriting, gnawing a knuckle.

On a walk with Frankie, she started to text him. *I'm sorry*, she began, but it felt overly simple, neither untrue nor entirely dishonest. She hadn't yet sorted through her thoughts for what she wanted. She resented that there was so much to think through, and so much she didn't know. What he was thinking about, for instance, when they drove through the city and he tensed at certain intersections, said he didn't want to go down certain streets.

But she ached for him. Some rehearsed joke while he tensed to see if she liked the dinner he'd made her. His heartbeat under her ear. His "What's this?" when she put on another song.

She waited for him to text again. She checked her phone

while she circled campus, where none of the libraries or the recreation center were hiring midsemester, while her thoughts knotted and frayed in class, and while she hauled out the rest of the soaked and molded boxes from the basement, throwing away the remnants of her father, waving away Jim while her mother said, "Oh, don't even bother with Miss Independence over there. She's not happy unless she's working herself to death." She thought about texting him as she drove along the west side big-box stores, hoping for a seasonal Christmas job that would get her through to next semester; as she passed a house she thought she recognized from his endless pictures; when a couple kissed on TV in a jewelry commercial; when Zeniyah texted her, *omg you quit????* But she hadn't decided yet what she would say to him.

* * *

It had been a week since she'd seen him. She was swallowing her anticorporate vitriol and had just explained to the manager of Starbucks what qualified her to be a barista when he texted again. She was in her car with a complimentary ghost-shaped cookie she didn't want, staring at the screen.

There were no words, but a picture of Fred the Carriage-less Horse, sitting on a table in a room she didn't recognize, big eyes staring through the phone.

I can pick it up tomorrow probably? she said. *Been busy.*

ok, he answered, a word on its lonesome without punctuation or tone.

She drove to Uncle Harold's house, her father's letters smoothed into a hollowed-out notebook on the passenger seat. She'd texted him the warning that she was putting him down as a reference on new job applications; she didn't work at the museum anymore, she said, and was relieved when he didn't ask for an explanation. Uncle Harold lived in a neighborhood ringing the golf course on the far west side of town, where once General Motors executives lived in Tudors and colonials and columned houses with swimming pools and big yards. When she was a little girl, her parents brought her here for trick-or-treating. The houses were so spread out you had to run between them, but the people gave out full-size candy bars, even the old white people who hesitated and asked, "Do you live in this neighborhood, little girl?"

Her uncle unlocked the door and gestured with his phone-free hand for her to come in. When she handed him the ghost cookie, he looked offended. He reached for her coat, repeating to whoever was on the other end of the line, "This is the information we have. We're in contact with Lansing and the EFM is in conversation with the governor. But GM is shipping in its *own water*—are you listening to me?—and I'm asking you why? They want the engine plant totally taken off Flint water, that it's too expensive. Who do you know?"

He went upstairs to continue belittling whomever in private. Monae made herself coffee and sat in his living room, feet pulled up onto the sectional. She held the letters on her lap. The television played a *Star Trek* episode on mute. She listened to him pace above her, the unintelligible bass of his voice coming down from the ceiling. She knew when Uncle Harold was ready to lacerate someone, the way his words were issued slow and precise. A city of incompetent, foolish people in love with a rosy myth of its past. Everything in need of fixing, tearing down, making right again.

It took a moment for her to realize, after Harold stepped back into the living room, phone hanging from his hand, that his anger wasn't boiling over from whoever had been on the other end of his call, but was a separate anger exclusively for her.

"Monae, I've tried to help you. I do everything I can for you and your mother, I know you don't appreciate me, and now it's starkly evident you also don't respect me." He said then what she already knew. "Caroline Dawson and I had a very uncomfortable meeting this morning, on occasion of which she informed me my niece had been fired for what the law and I would define as breaking and entering. I said surely there was some mistake, that my niece is a conscientious, bright young woman. But no, she told me, she had you on video. Told me you admitted to it."

Monae held out her chin.

"She said you were with a man. White. Glasses. Smoking. Who's that?"

Unblemished driving record. God-fearing. No tattoos. "Just a friend."

"He's no friend if he lets you do stupid things like this. He put you up to this? I suppose he has whatever you stole."

"I just went in to get some books. It's not breaking and entering when you have the keys, and it's not stealing when you're taking your own things."

He shoved his wire glasses up his nose and stared at her like he couldn't believe they were blood. "What belongings of yours are archived in the history museum, Monae?"

"You said yourself it's all trash down there. Just flotsam and debris. That sounds like me, doesn't it?"

Once, after her father was gone and her mother was just home from rehab, sleeping in a cocoon of drugs her weeping sometimes woke her from, Harold took Monae to the mall. He'd gotten her the job at the museum and she needed appropriate clothes. He gave her his Visa and waited with a newspaper in the food court. When she came back, he made her pull each piece from the bag and hold it up. The top was all wrong: too bright, too many flowers. He frowned all the way to Macy's and then told a saleswoman, as if Monae wasn't standing there, she needed help finding something less *juvenile*. In the dressing room she'd said to the closed door, never knowing if he heard her on the other side, "I wish it'd been you."

Harold shook his head. "You're creating a difficult world for yourself. You're just making things harder."

Her eyes stung. She wanted to ask, "How could it possibly get harder than this?" But Harold's phone rang again. He grimaced. "I have to take this." She remembered she could get up and walk out.

She only drove a few blocks before she decided to pull over by the golf course. She cracked the windows and took a gulp of brisk air. She closed her eyes and held her next breath until her lungs burned. When she exhaled she saw the deer grazing in the yard. A buck with one antler and a doe, both of them sleek with white puffs of tail. They swiveled their heads in unison, and then they bolted across the street, disappearing into the stand of trees.

* * *

On Halloween, Monae dumped all the little boxes of raisins into a mixing bowl and flicked on the porch light. She'd seen the kids stepping off the bus earlier, faces streaked with crusting zombie paint and fake blood, plastic fangs popped into their mouths. They'd be coming through soon with their pillowcases, mothers on the sidewalk reminding them to say thank you.

By sunset, Jim came over with a pizza and a two-liter of pop. Frankie, sporting a black and orange bow tie, yapped at his feet. Monae had agreed to this evening in an uneasy détente.

"I got spinach and mushroom. Your mother said you like vegetables."

"I'm vegan," she lied, since her mother wasn't in the room to catch it. "But thank you." She intended to spend the evening politely present, reading between trick-or-treaters while they watched television on the sofa.

Regina came in with paper plates on her lap. Jim bent to kiss her cheek and told her she looked, as perhaps a ghost might say, boo-tiful. Monae thought her mother laughed longer and louder than the corny joke merited, until she realized her mother was looking past Jim to the smiling Sunmaids beside the door.

"Oh, Mo. That's what you bought?"

Monae bristled, ready to repeat the sermon she had delivered a thousand times about inculcating healthy community eating habits and the association of good food with pleasure. Her mother, intuiting this, said, "We all deserve a little joy, don't we? Can't happiness be enough sometimes?"

Monae considered this.

"I like raisins," Jim said.

"Well, you can have them," her mother said. She told her daughter to get ten dollars from her purse and run up to the store.

Monae ignored her mother's money and went to get her jacket and her purse. When she closed the front door behind her, Jim had an arm draped around her mother, both of them with plates of pizza in their laps, eyes on the TV.

What startled her was how little it hurt. Her mother would leave this little falling-down house with its little yard, and so would she. There was nothing left to salvage.

The street was dark, but no trick-or-treaters were out yet. Many families here drove or took the bus over to the parts of town where the occupied houses clustered closer together, or to Uncle Harold's neighborhood, where the people were wealthier and the treats bigger. She sat in her car, digging through the CD cases scattered over the backseat. The leaves were gone, and the snow hadn't come yet to cover things. All the city's emptiness accentuated, all the concrete grayer, the streetlamps black bones. The park across the street stretching on for a desolate eternity.

She slid *A Love Supreme* into the stereo, but it was irritating, repetitive. She shut it off. Silence felt wrong, too.

She made it two blocks, then, at the first stop sign, pulled her phone from her pocket. *Hey. Are you home?*

A princess in a puffy coat and a vampire with a vinyl cape crossed the sidewalk in front of a burned-out bungalow. Her phone chimed with an address, as if she wouldn't remember his new blue house on the river. As if there were any other houses on the block, or in all of Flint, she might now confuse it with.

* * *

August's car wasn't in the driveway, but the boards on the windows had been pulled away. Uncurtained windows looked into dark rooms. She knocked and knocked, and just as she turned to go he pulled into the driveway behind her. He

stepped out with a grocery bag in his arms. She didn't recognize the unsmiling way he was striding toward her, thrift
store overcoat hanging open, a shirt the gray-blue of dirty
water underneath, boots crunching on the unraked leaves.

He stepped past her and unlocked the door, holding it
open for her with his boot. "No costume?" he asked, a joke
delivered like an unfortunate diagnosis.

She had his sweater in her arms. "I'm going as you. I came
to borrow your glasses."

She baited him the opportunity to tease her. He didn't
take it.

He flicked on the light, opening into a living room with
the sofa he'd salvaged from his grandmother's bulldozed house,
a bookcase with shelves still empty, and the record player
from his sister's apartment. The windows bare, the floors
gritty underneath her shoes.

She followed him into the kitchen, where the horse head
was in its gray clamshell box atop the refrigerator. Around it
were the herbs he'd started from Frontier seeds in his sister's
apartment. On the fridge were new Bible quotes on scrap
paper in his scratchy handwriting—1 Peter 4:8: *Above all,
love each other deeply, because love covers over a multitude of
sins*—and an NA schedule, though she thought he'd stopped
going to meetings.

The windows looked over the backyard, moonlight on
fallen leaves. It was so quiet. There was so much space.

From the grocery bag on the counter he pulled out a box
of the tea he used to keep for her at his sister's, after milk and
peanut butter and dish soap and a box of matches. He held
it up over his head without turning to her. "Sure," she said.

After he filled the kettle, she watched him shuck his coat

onto the opposite chair so the gash in the lining faced her like a funny smile. He stood beside the stove, arms folded. The dull light of the kitchen made him look older.

Whenever she thought of August, there was music on and his voice in her head. Always questions. What did she think about. What did she know about. She didn't know what to do with this quiet, unlike the silence after sex or just before, drowsy and companionable, or the quiet in his car, driving between houses they imagined him living in. It wasn't accompanied by the little ache she got when she couldn't let herself fall asleep, had to get up and drive back to her mother's, nor a silence fraught in the way it sometimes was when she felt her chest blooming with tenderness for him and she made herself remember all that was wrong with him, how far he was from even the obscure outline of the man she imagined for herself, someday, when she had the time. Silence now, waiting for the kettle to whistle, filled the space around them in a new way. Words clotted in her throat.

Her phone buzzed. *Where'd you go?*

While August made tea, she chewed the insides of her cheeks and confessed, *I've been seeing someone. I'll tell you later. Tell Jim please leave me some raisins.*

The mug of tea thunked in front of her, and he sat in the opposite chair. His bitten fingernails drummed on the table between them. A steady tap tap tap like water from a leaking faucet. On reflex she reached across the table to still him, and then she was gripping his wrist.

"I got fired from the museum. The day we came to look at this house. The museum caught us on the surveillance camera. I thought they were all down." She stopped. She tugged her hand back. This wasn't what she wanted to talk about at all; this didn't matter. "I didn't mean what I said. I don't think about you like that."

Her phone again. *I know baby. Nobody spends that much time at the library. Tell me about him when you get home.*

She could feel him watching her, and she couldn't control her face the way she wanted. Her features wobbled, her mouth loose and wavering. Her eyes pricked with tears though she never cried, and she liked that about herself when she didn't feel there was much about her to like at all: she worked hard. She had her father's quiet grit and loyalty.

"You just," she started. She'd explained this to him in her mind so many times. He'd come on too strong. He'd put too much pressure on her. He was asking for so much, was skipping the many logical and appropriate steps she knew must go between making out to corny old records on someone else's sofa and getting married.

She studied his hand on the table, then the dark yard through the window behind him. A stand of naked silver maples with the reflection of his empty kitchen superimposed on it. She wanted him to apologize, for them to go on like before, but her words had tangled and he wasn't talking. She grew embarrassed; maybe he'd just wanted her to take her stolen trash from the museum and leave, and here she was, pitiful.

"I just wanted you to have what you wanted," he said.

"I don't need you to get it for me." Indignation was easier to bear. She stood, knocking the chair over behind her. She pulled the horse head down from the fridge, an awkward baby bundled in her arms, and left.

His car was parked behind hers, blocking her in, but she couldn't go back in crying. She put the carriageless horse head in the backseat and sat gripping the steering wheel. Over the river the silver pylons. Bony tree limbs bent toward the river. She was still in the city, her father's house and her stupid raisins a few miles away, but there was no one opening a front door and flicking on the television, no headlights flashing through the dark on someone's drive home. It felt like the Flint the newspapers projected someday, when there was no one left in the city but her, canning vegetables for the winter, catching the monstrous carp that finned through the submerged cars in the Flint River. Alone in the city her father had left her.

There was a knock on her passenger-side window. August stood there with moonlight on the tops of his glasses and the buttons of his jacket. He was pointing to the lock, asking to be let in.

* * *

Monae woke with one of August's arms bracing her against him, the other under her head. Her eyes adjusted to the dark. A scatter of books, and a lamp with its cord snaking over the floor. A chair with her coat hung over the back, and on the dresser an empty fishbowl.

She eased herself from under him and pulled a sweatshirt from the floor. She moved through rooms that had sat so long unwanted, that smelled peculiarly of paint and dust and desiccated bugs scattered over windowsills, and something sharp and cold, like glass. He had so little to make this a home.

There was no rush, they'd agreed hours before. They could go on like before but in this new place, with a door to close and a proper to bed to lie down in together and none of the church bells and buses of his old penitential space. They'd talk about the drug thing, she'd tell him more about her family, everything they were supposed to talk about. They'd do all the things they were supposed to do, in the right order, at a sensible, mutually intentional pace.

She pulled open empty closets, cabinets, a medicine cabinet with nothing but a plastic comb and a razor. On the mirror, from Lamentations: *I remember my affliction and my wandering, the bitterness and the gall.* From Philippians: *I have learned the secret of being content in any and every situation, whether well fed or hungry, whether living in plenty or in want.* There was no attribution to *Serenity is what we get when we quit hoping for a better past.*

"We've only known each other a couple months," she'd said in her parked car, hiccupping still after explaining the basement and her father's ruined things and her mother's new life and her uncle who hated her.

"Six months," he corrected. "I came home in May. I saw heaven and then you."

In the bedroom looking out from the front of the house at the street and the river, she eased August, still sleeping, onto his back. He stirred, drew in a funny breath. She settled into him until his heart beat under her ear and the rhythm of it filled her head. Her fingers traced the dry, studded skin of a rash above his heart that she'd noticed when they were undressing. From the shower, he'd said. The water smelled rotten. It was just that the pipes had sat so long, all the silt and gunk still moving through them. It'd clear out.

"Leaving?" he murmured, breath against her forehead. An arm anchored her back into him. She wasn't.

He made a pleased little hum. "Morning," he began, then a sighing exhale. "We'll have." He slipped back into sleep before he could name what was theirs.

She stayed up a while, finishing the sentence for him. A house as quiet and empty as theirs you could fill with anything you wanted.

PART 2

CHAPTER 15

2016

August had returned to Detroit as a personal guest of Aretha Franklin, and if he wanted to monopolize Moonwalker until this shitty arcade bar closed, then no one was stopping him. The hipsters with their craft IPAs at the Mortal Kombat machine could go on clearing their throats; they could read aloud, again, the sign that said you weren't supposed to hog the machines, and they could ask "You done yet, dude?" as if he owed them anything. August was vibrating out of his skin, and certainly these Mortal Kombat assholes whining over his shoulder with their quarters knew nothing of that. He wanted nothing to exist beyond the pixelated Michael Jackson in his "Smooth Criminal" suit running through the underworld with Bubbles the chimp at his heels. He couldn't stop even to shrug his coat off: sweat soured his T-shirt. The hole in his boot had let the snow in, and his wet foot itched.

Though Aretha gifted them the suite at the Holiday Inn and a per diem at the coney island across the street, she was not paying their mortgage or insurance, and so August drove back up to Flint for work each day. He'd clocked out of the restaurant at seven, made the hour drive back down to Detroit, and now it was nearly midnight. He'd parked the car at the Holiday Inn and went down the parking structure stairs to the street below.

He blamed traffic, the miserable winter dragging into March. He pretended that he was checking in on the house, because she didn't know how its emptiness spooked him. Her car sat in need of a new transmission behind the house, chickens pecked through the pine shavings, and his shame filled up all the dark rooms. He couldn't explain to Monae that he needed to wear himself out so he could rest beside her. He'd bought the house on a poisoned river, and he didn't know now, when Aretha's charity bottomed out, what they could do or how he could fix it.

MJ spun into Game Over. August pushed his hands into his coat pockets for more change, but his fingers met his cigarettes instead and he realized he wanted one. It was close enough to midnight anyway.

"You done?" Mortal Kombat asked.

Without answer, August turned to the door. His shoulder connected with Mortal Kombat, pushing into the space he'd waited to claim. "Watch it," Mortal Kombat said. August tensed for sudden hands on his back, a hard shove. "Dick," Mortal Kombat called after him, barely audible in the bullshit pop music.

August strode into the plumes of smoke rising from manhole covers. A few blocks away, the towers of the General Motors headquarters rose like a middle finger over the city. Around him was a blur of cars and last buses. He fumbled in his pockets for cigarettes. His lighter sputtered in the wind sheering off the river.

His phone vibrated in his pocket. Monae asked, *Where are you?*

took me forever to find that stuff you wanted, he said. *heading out*. He climbed the escalator of the People Mover station, dropped seventy-five cents into the turnstile, and stood on the deserted platform, shifting from foot to foot.

When are you coming back?

The train rattled in, and he boarded an empty car. *in a little bit*, he texted back. The train lurched along the Detroit River, snaked between the buildings. He saw his reflection superimposed over the fleeting windows of dark skyscrapers and turned his gaze back to his phone. He scrolled back to a selfie Monae had taken in the mirror over the hotel bureau. It was a double portrait: Monae cross-legged on the hotel bed and their daughter, Beatrice Jae Molloy, against her breast. *Hurry back tonight and see the roll forming on this precious and perfect thigh*. He pulled at the picture with his fingers, held the phone up to the tip of his nose. He couldn't be sure he saw what she was showing him. His daughter snapped into a fresh onesie, nearly four months old. She looked so fragile and small.

The feeling was akin to detox. His whole body hurt, like all his muscles had atrophied. An alarm rang over and over in his head. It was one thing to fuck things up for himself, but he'd ruined his wife's life, created a whole other life that was sick and bound to suffer alongside him in ways he couldn't fix.

*　　　　　　　　　　　　　　　　　　　　　　　　* * * *

It was Monae who proposed the second time, the one that mattered, and August who said yes. He circled back to this often: She'd asked to marry him. She loved him. She'd wanted him.

It was their first winter, when she didn't live with him but never slept anywhere else and her plans for Carriageless Horse Farms spread across the kitchen table. He'd been in the bath, reading Ecclesiastes off his phone, ashing into a soap dish, the window open despite the snow. She appeared in the doorway.

He extinguished his cigarette and extended an invitation. "You'd be a sucker not to get in on this."

She didn't hesitate. She stepped out of her jeans and gathered her braids. He pulled his knees up to make space for her. She lowered herself into the opposite end, extending her legs around him. He had not yet gotten over the wonder of her intelligent and lovely face, that he could see it all the time.

"Wholesome fun," he pronounced.

She said, "It would be more wholesome if we were married."

"Probably we're just brining in sin. In our metaphysical and physical filth."

"So marry me."

The wound of her rejection was still fresh. He squeezed the pads of her toes under the water.

"I want children," she said. "I'm not taking your name. You need to quit smoking."

So they'd married at the farm after Monae graduated, with a sparkling grape juice reception on the back porch. Soul and jazz from a laptop, extension cord snaking through the screen door. Both their mothers cried, and her uncle Harold stared at him with polite skepticism.

Bea was a multiplying cluster of cells as they honeymooned through the boil advisories. Around the house, pots and kettles of boiling tap water cooled on trivets. The fridge was stocked with pitchers, bottles refilled beside their toothbrushes and prenatal vitamins. Monae soaked her swollen breasts in the tub and brewed cup after cup of ginger tea for her morning sickness.

By the fall, when Monae was in her second trimester and the farm's first season was winding down, the state still said the water was fine. But the pediatrician from the city hospital got on the local news and said that children were showing elevated lead levels in their blood. She explained that this could mean impaired brain development of fetuses and children. Reduced physical development. Anemia, hearing impairment, cardio-vascular disease, behavioral problems. She said, *Irreversible neurotoxin*. In pregnant women, lead poisoning was linked to stillbirths and miscarriage. That, too, was showing up in Flint's data. Monae kept refreshing the clip on the internet. She made August repeat the doctor's words back to her. "Tell me what she's saying." By then Bea could hear her mother's heartbeat accelerate in panic, absorbed her mother's cortisol. She could hear her father lamely insisting that they would be fine.

The state of emergency was declared just before Christmas, when it was clear the city of Flint had been drinking toxic water for the last year and a half. Monae, nearing her due date, panicked at every discomfort. To distract them both, August said, "Let's come up with nicknames. Do you think she'll be a pumpkin or a sweetheart or a honey or something else?" He tried to turn chapters of *What to Expect When You're Expecting* into bets. *Come on, fifteen bucks says her first word is Mama. Twenty says she's smart as hell like you and she's saying it by six months.*

But Monae'd shut her eyes against him. "They're going to take this from me," she said. *Don't say that*, he told her, but she kept saying it. He'd pulled the comforter over their heads

like tragedy was a boogeyman they could hide from. He'd figure it out, he'd said. He'd keep them safe. As if there was
anything he could do. Anything in his control.

Bea arrived a little early and a little small while the National
Guard and the Red Cross rolled through Flint's neighborhoods, unloading cases of bottled water. While their families
admired her long eyelashes and her sweetness, brought food
for her parents and more clothes and toys she'd grow into,
Flint Lives Matter protestors marched down to the water
plant, and her uncle Harold organized buses to the state cap-
itol and to DC. Poisoning the water supply, he said, was a
war crime. Women staged die-ins on the lawn of City Hall,
white jumpsuits splashed in red paint at the stomach and
crotch to represent the stillbirths and miscarriages. Billboards
warned in English and Spanish that BOILING WATER DOES NOT
REMOVE LEAD—yellow letters on black backgrounds, a slash
through a running faucet. Governor Snyder folded his hands
on television and said he was sorry and that he'd fix it.

In the kitchen where August still worked, because it'd be
years before they could make enough money off the farm
to live on and already they were sliding into debt from
the equipment the farm needed and the repairs the house
demanded, they kept the news on. Commentators compared
it to Chernobyl—the city destroyed, generations poisoned,
nothing left but to evacuate—and Hurricane Katrina's cata-
clysm of white supremacy and negligence. Environmental
racism, they pronounced. Bureaucratic incompetence. Capi-
talism and a bottom line: it was cheaper to bury some people.
"Can we fucking turn this off?" August snapped, and one of
the dishwashers reached for the power button.

Most celebrities sent money and water, but Aretha Franklin donated hotel rooms with a per diem at the coney island across the street. Two months after Bea was born, August took the note from the pediatrician down to Bethel Baptist to ask for Aretha's charity. There was lead in her bloodstream. The Flint River was the amniotic fluid she had somersaulted in. There was no way of knowing what would happen to her, the particular ways she would suffer, or who she could've been.

* * *

August got off the train in Greektown and went into a church hulking between casinos and the red glow of signs pointing to valet parking. It was a few minutes to midnight. There was an NA meeting in the basement, and he remembered which door was unlocked. This had been his after-work meeting once. Down the stairs, he heard voices, folding chairs dragged over tile.

Once he was inside, though, he didn't go to the basement but to a door down the hall, past a table of prayer cards and leaflets and an empty coatrack. It was unlocked. The vaulted sanctuary was empty, shadowed. He dropped into the pew. Stained glass saints watched him. He worried the corners of a tract and stared at his boots, bleeding snow all over the floor beneath him. His breathing, the rustle of his clothes, the squeak of his wet, busted-up soles—all of it ricocheted around the silence, too much of him.

For much of the last two years, August had found himself a man of joyous if inchoate faith. He'd been brought back from the dead and he'd given himself to someone smarter, more deserving, more capable. He'd felt a gratitude he was sure must be what people meant by *blessed*. But now he felt swindled and bereft.

If he could form a prayer, it might be: God, if you exist, if you're not a superstition, a weird dream I had when the oxygen stopped moving to my brain, don't let her be sick. Instead, what came to him were the bits of verse he copied down. "Abide in me," he mumbled. Carried low on his breath. "Abide. Abide."

He lay down on the plank of the pew, shoulder blades digging into the wood. A narrow man on a narrow board, as if in a coffin. He pushed his fingers under his glasses and covered his eyes. The sound of his own trembling exhalations throbbed in his ears like someone was holding him upside down and all the blood had rushed to his head.

He imagined the walk back to the Holiday Inn. In rehab his therapist showed him this: to rehearse the situation he was anxious about. Practice it. See what the worst thing that could happen was, and feel ready for it.

So he'd walk back. Round the corner onto Washington Boulevard, the statue of Casimir Pulaski they could see from their window. In the trunk of their car, there were boxes he had to bring in for her. Four months into the state of emergency, no one in jail, just the Red Cross trucks and the astronomical quotes for the new pipes that needed to snake under the city, a conspiracy theory circulated that Flint was just waiting to be evacuated. The city would be junked like an old car; it cost more to fix than it was worth. No one was going to put new pipes in a city already half-empty. An email from the Michigan Department of Environmental Quality had leaked: "I don't think this is a city we want to go out on a limb for," someone at a desk in Lansing said.

A friend who texted Monae to congratulate her on the baby told her there was going to be nothing to come back to. She'd be waiting a long time if she thought she was waiting for the water to get fixed. Monae, alone and underslept with the baby, had sent him a text earlier that day. *Bring my dad's stuff. The boxes in the back bedroom.*

what about your tinfoil hat? He felt like an asshole as soon as he hit send.

Bea's birth certificate. Top drawer of my desk.

He brought them, shifting in the back beside the car seat. In them the loose jingle of dog tags and the rustle of paper. Some water-stained photographs. How little she had, and how little he'd given her.

But he'd get them out of the trunk. Cross the hotel parking structure and pass the chlorine smell of the pool glittering quiet and then the elevator up to their room. He'd get a little flutter in the base of his stomach once he reached their floor, because he loved them, had missed them through the week, and it would be so nice to see the baby, kiss his wife. The word still felt fresh. *Wife.* But then the door would click open and she'd be curled on the bed in one of his T-shirts, the baby asleep beside her. He'd catch her eyes slipping into the crook of his arm when he took off his coat. He knew she searched his pockets when he was in the shower, scrolled through his phone. Shame would kick into him, so swift and vicious that he'd just want to put her sad boxes down and turn around.

August stayed in the pew until the bell above tolled midnight and he knew the meeting had started and no one would see him leave. He pulled his body back into shape, knees knocking into the Bibles and hymnals on the pew back. What he wanted to ask was, was it so wrong to think that if he could release the buzzing in his blood he could return to them less furious at what had been done to him and what he'd done to them? Weren't there exceptions to sobriety in cases like his, so far beyond the NA bounds? His NA book said, *We continued to take personal inventory and when we were wrong promptly admitted it.* He'd been wrong. He was constantly searching for a way to make his amends with her, and there was only one way that kept returning to him.

CHAPTER 16

1967

Eamon's new Chevy rolled through Tennessee, the rock 'n' roll Rose liked on the radio. On her lap rested a pink-haired troll doll and a *Tiger Beat* magazine from a gas station in Ohio, open over an atlas Eamon didn't need: I-75 shot out of Flint and arrowed down the country till it hit the bull's-eye of Tampa. "Are we still on Seventy-Five?" he asked her.

Rose paused, drawing stars and sunbursts around the Beatles in their new Sgt. Pepper suits, to squint at the map. "I think we are, yes," she said. A pair of sunglasses with heart-shaped lenses held back the flipped bob her mother fussed over. At her feet, a vinyl purse held nothing.

"Good. By midnight there should be an exit that says Grandma Snowbird. Tell me when we're getting close, though, so I know to watch for alligators. I hear they jump out in the road like the deer do."

Rose was old enough to recognize when she was being lied to and smart enough to appreciate the care her father took in crafting these embellishments. When he told her they'd bring a flamingo home, and they'd eat oranges until they cried orange juice tears, she was delighted. His wife, Myrna, had once been amused, too, but lately called it bullshitting, diagnosed it as another flaw inherited from his drunk, womanizing father.

Rose sat in the passenger seat because Myrna decided that morning that she wasn't coming to Florida. Someone had to stay home, she said. The riots down in Detroit and the brief sputtering of unrest in Flint convinced her every backfiring car was a gunshot. If they left their house empty, those people from the North End would march up Saginaw Street, steal the pale pink sofa he was forbidden from putting his feet on and the figurines of delicate women in ball gowns that lined the television console, then burn it all down.

Myrna spoke only to Rose that morning while he loaded the car. "I packed your dress with the flowers in case your grandmother takes you somewhere nice. Try and eat whatever she feeds you." She took up a fistful of hair ribbons and despaired, "What sort of a mother am I, letting you out of the house like this. I should've had you at the beauty shop weeks ago."

"I'll get her a haircut," Eamon said. But Myrna had unpacked the Coppertone and was brandishing it at her daughter.

Eamon hadn't seen his mother since his father hit a patch of black ice on the drive home from the bar and launched himself through the window. Beatrice took the life insurance payout and moved to Florida. She had not been back to meet his wife and children. She sent cards she painted herself, of little birds and palm fronds. In 1964 she sent campaign literature for Eric Hass and the transcript of a sermon on racial justice at the Unitarian Universalist church.

There was a strange fluttering within Eamon when he thought of seeing her. An excitement that quickly plummeted. He was bracing for bad news. She'd never invited them down to stay with her before.

Rose twisted out of her seat belt for a Vernors from the cooler. Myrna had packed them tuna sandwiches and bags of cherries and celery sticks, but with the *Tiger Beat* Eamon bought her the Banana Flip she wanted. A blob of cream crusted on her chin.

"Will Grandma Snowbird like me?" she asked.

Sometimes, when Eamon was with his brothers and the night stretched long enough, they couldn't agree on who their mother was, or who she had been. She was melancholy. No, she was only worn out, raising all those children and putting up with their father. She was smart. She wasn't a very good cook. She made a beautiful chop suey. She was born in Detroit. She was born in Fort Wayne.

"More than anyone's ever liked anyone, flower," he promised.

All through Kentucky they fantasized about Florida and their inevitable alligator-related deaths. They drafted their obituaries. Rose Molloy, 1959–1967. Avid reader, excellent drawer of cats, wife of George Harrison. Eamon Molloy, 1932–1967. World traveler, Chevrolet foreman, husband and father, eldest son of Beatrice Molloy.

* * *

They arrived in Tampa in the dark, palm trees silhouetted in the streetlamps. Before Eamon was certain he was circling the right apartment complex, a light came on. The door opened, and there was his mother on the landing above. He hadn't seen her in ten years, and still in the dark that was the unmistakable line of her. Narrower, perhaps. Whittled down to something more essential.

His hand trembled when he woke his daughter. "We found Grandma Snowbird," he whispered.

Beatrice descended the stairs, stepped into their dissolving headlights. Her dress skimmed her bony shins, and her shoes looked too clunky for the Florida humidity.

Eamon couldn't quite move. He anchored an arm around his daughter, pressing her into him.

In his mother's apartment was a faded love seat and a little table with two chairs. Beside the phone, a pad with a doctor's appointment written in her familiar hand. There was a shelf of books with all the spines tapped in line, a clock, and a pencil sketch of a woman crouching alone on the beach, her old housedress gathered and bunched in one hand while the other reached for a bottle that had washed ashore, a message on a white slip of paper scrolled inside. With the woman's face bent to the ground and her hat securing her hair, you couldn't tell how she felt.

It was late. Beatrice offered them something to eat, showed them where the towels and blankets were, and excused herself.

* * *

While Rose showered and put herself to bed, Eamon slipped out. There was a liquor store he'd noted between his mother's apartment and the expressway. He bought gin, took a few drinks in the car, and stared at the pay phone. In his wallet was a phone number, and if he dialed it, there was a chance he'd hear the woman's voice, husky with sleep, for a few moments before her husband wanted to know who was calling. He didn't have the change for that kind of long distance, so he dialed through the radio instead and thought of her and her big laugh, cracking up in the break room at Chevy, asking him what book he was carrying around her. Her hot mouth, and how, like the other women on the line, she tasted like stale coffee and cold metal and smoke.

He expected Rose asleep in the sleeping bag he'd unfurled for her, but instead her blond hair rolled over the pillow. She squeaked her tongue against her clean teeth. The troll doll propped on the other side of the pillow her blond hair splashed across.

"Can't sleep, Dad," she whispered.

"Me neither," he said, stretched out beside her. "You got any bedtime stories?"

Rose nosed her head off her pillow and against his arm. "It's my birthday and Mamaw and Papa are there and Grandma Beatrice and the Beatles are all coming. Mom makes a chocolate cake." Her words space. In her breaths, Eamon is aware of the air-conditioning and his mother coughing on the other side of the wall. No cars outside, no one leaving for third shift, no trains huffing car parts to General Motors. "Ice cream?" he whispers.

She can't hear him. "Mom invites the man with the trumpet. They're gonna." She's mumbling now. "Song."

"What man?" Eamon asked, but her peppermint breath buzzed in his arm hair. She'd fallen asleep and left him with his thoughts.

* * *

In the morning, Eamon let Rose continue to believe that no one saw her dropping pieces of the toast with its too-tart marmalade off the balcony to the gulls below. She'd dressed and attempted to look nice for her grandmother: a bow hung limp by her ear. Eamon pulled his cigarettes from his breast pocket.

"I don't remember you smoking," Beatrice said. In the fullness of the sun, the loose collar of her dress hung from the ridge of her collarbone. A scarf wrapped her hair.

"Dad's influence," he said. "Good thing he didn't live to see me like this, huh? Married to a woman from that unwashed southern horde, working for Chevy like any other schmuck." He forced a smile. "I was thinking you could show Rose pictures of the old place, of her grandfather. All I've got are the letters he used to send back to me when I was in the service. You remember?" He turned to his daughter. "I wrote home from Morocco and Spain and France telling everyone I was having the time of my life, and he sent them back with my grammar corrected. I was supposed to be studying Shakespeare at Harvard, I guess."

"Where, Daddy?" Rose said.

"I don't have any," Beatrice said. She dabbed at the line of her mouth.

"Photographs," Eamon clarified. She must have misheard.

"There was so much to move and I have so little space here. I'm sure your brothers have them." She stood and gathered up the dishes, relieving Rose of the burden of marmalade and wheat. Her fingers were knots of bone. "I think it's healthy to let things go." To Rose she said, "Would you like to see the city?"

* * *

Along the bay, Rose gasped at birds. Beatrice drew lines in the air between the bird and its illustration in her guidebook. Cormorant. Ibis. Spoonbill. After Rose whispered to her father that she was starving, they had hot dogs and watched for dolphins. They walked through the grounds of the domed and spired Tampa Bay Hotel, where Teddy Roosevelt and the Rough Riders had stayed and where John F. Kennedy had spoken four days before he was shot in Dallas, God rest his soul. Beatrice, who needed to stop at the occasional bench and rest and waved Eamon off each time he asked if she was all right, if she wanted him to go get the car, said she'd like to come here and paint it someday, when she was more advanced in the classes she took at the community center.

By the time they were back in the car, the air had thickened. Sweat slickened Eamon's back, and his cigarette pack wilted in his pocket. His mother directed him to a neighborhood with curling wrought iron lampposts, cluttered with cigar shops and tattoo parlors and Cuban cafés. She declined the extravagance, but Eamon was a foreman at Chevy now, and he wanted his mother to guide him to the best meal in town.

In a restaurant with big open windows and walls covered in blue and white tiles, Eamon ordered a pitcher of sangria. When the waitress poured his mother's glass, she cleared her throat and politely asked for an iced tea. He watched her tip pills into her palm from a vial in her purse. She pretended not to hear him over the music when he asked what she was taking.

Gazpacho and shrimp and yellow rice soon spread over the table. Drowsy from the sun and underslept, he found the second glass of sangria to be punishingly sweet. He signaled the waitress for a beer. He let Rose have a hunk of orange from the sangria pitcher and decided not to scold her when she picked fibers of it from her teeth while she answered her grandmother's questions about school and what books she liked.

"Maybe we could get you a cat, Mom," Eamon said. "Must get lonely down here."

"We have a cat," Rose said, endorsing the idea. "I could help."

"I'm content with my own company." His mother raised a neat forkful of salad. He wanted to make a joke about the birds they'd seen. *You eat like a spoonbill. Let's ask the waitress for clean spoonbills for dessert.* On his third beer, he was growing drowsy and unclever.

"But are you happy, Mom?" Eamon asked. "You must miss us down here."

She answered immediately. "I'm the happiest I've ever been."

Rose reached for the plate of olives at the center of the table. Dazed, Eamon watched as she licked the brine from her fingers and slipped the pit into her palm. His mother put aside her fork and coughed discreetly into a handkerchief.

"Well, that's really something," Eamon managed. "Not many people can say that, can they."

On the walk back to the car, they passed a salon with pictures of beautiful dark-haired, dark-eyed women painted on its side. Between two of them there was a poster with the

Beatles on it, wearing suits and running down a dreary London street. *A Hard Day's Night* was playing at the cinema, one day only. Rose clutched a fistful of her father's madras shirt and pointed to it.

"Well, why don't we ask your grandmother if she has a few hours to spare for us tomorrow. You got a favorite Beatle, Mom?" His voice came out a sneer. Disliking himself, he turned to his daughter. "What do you want to do right now, Rosie? Whatever you want to do, flower. Anything you like."

* * *

In their sleeping bags that night, Rose still smelled of chlorine and Coppertone. Till the sun went down he'd watched her cannonball into the pool and pull herself out, calling for her father to watch each time. Old women in their floral suits and sunglasses ringed the pool on the deck chairs, their thighs soft and wrinkled. Beatrice, though, had stayed in the apartment.

He told Rose a story. She liked best when he described the Barbary apes in the square in Marrakech, their little vests and how their handlers flung them onto their shoulders. Was their fur soft, Rose wanted to know? Had he given them bananas or candy or maybe something else?

After she fell asleep, Eamon drank in the car. His father used to send back the letters, corrected. But he remembered his mother never wrote back at all.

* * *

For their last day in Florida, Rose requested the haircut they'd promised her mother. At Salon Elegante bright music played, the singers trilling their *r*'s. Rose brought her *Tiger Beat* with a spread on Beatles haircuts: teenage girls in Beatles wigs. She held it up to the woman at the front desk, a tower of hair and thick eyeliner. Rose pointed at George Harrison in a picture from back when the Beatles all had the same hair.

"Ah—Beatle." The woman nodded and made a note on the guest sign-in. She caught Eamon looking at her. "Little girl pretty like your wife?" the shock of her lipstick asked him.

Eamon slumped down into a chair on one side of his daughter. His mother was on the other, swallowed by the pale flowers on her dress. "Look at these Cuban gals. Stunners, all of them. These women know what they're doing. After this, when you're looking gorgeous, I'll buy you and your grand-mother big fat Cuban cigars and we'll go see your movie."

Rose pulled at the ends of her hair, dragging out the flip, testing its length.

"I used to cut your father's hair," Beatrice said. "I cut all my children's hair, didn't I, Eamon?"

Rose stared at her, her little mouth parting. The maga-zine shook on her lap. Eamon noticed she'd used his pen to draw birds in the margins of an article on the Beach Boys, their beaks too big and their eyes dots. Maybe his mother had tried to show her how.

"In the backyard, with a butcher knife." He stood, announc-ing he was going to buy cigarettes down the street. Instead he slipped into the car and drank a beer, sweating in his shirt, watching women twitch by in their thin dresses.

When he returned to the salon, his mother watched Rose's reflection across the room. The hairdresser gathered the flipped bob into a ponytail and lopped it off. The sudden apparition of her neck, whiter where the sun hadn't hit it all summer.

"I've been wanting to talk to you." And that was it. He was floating too far from himself to feel dread, to try to stave this off. They were in the car. She was behind the wheel. He didn't remember giving her the keys. The engine wasn't running, but his mother's bony hands on the steering wheel looked steady, authoritative. She looked like she could drive him anywhere he wanted to go, and he'd be safe.

And then it seemed to roll out like a song on a radio playing in another room, a song someone else had requested, meaningful to some stranger. It was cancer. In her breasts. There might not be another time to tell him that Lewis wasn't his father at all. She'd been married before. He died. That was his real father. Not Lewis, who was also dead. His father died. Somewhere in Detroit. Not his father who had died, but another father, before.

It was all static, her words scrambled by the pulse of his headache. The sidewalk thinned so he could see a man on an upturned bucket playing a trumpet down the street, and he remembered what Rose had said, about the man who came to visit Myrna. It suddenly seemed so important that he know where Myrna was. So he'd cheated, but didn't all men.

"I imagine you have questions," he heard his mother say. From between the pages of the paperback in her purse she pulled out a photograph, a brittle black-and-white.

He didn't want to see it, so he swung out of the car.

Back in Salon Elegante, Rose bounded toward him with her shorn head, beaming. He managed, "Well, you look like a real rock and roller, flower."

The woman at the desk watched while Rose ran back to grab the trail of frilly things she'd left behind her, the ribbon and the little empty purse.

* * *

On the drive to the movie theater, Beatrice asked Rose why she liked the Beatles. Eamon's head swam. Behind him, his daughter puffed with importance. The information sloshed in his head. Not your father. Your father died in Detroit. This man you've grown into was not your father.

In the dark theater, Eamon slumped down into his seat, and Beatrice and Rose watched the Beatles on a train chugging across England. Paul McCartney sat beside an old man in a hat and spectacles, reading the newspaper. Ringo and John sat on the other side of the compartment, staring. "Who's that little old man?" they asked Paul.

"That's my grandfather," Paul repeated.

"That's not your grandfather," they said. Paul insisted he was.

The audience tittered. Beside Eamon, a noise like a creaking door came out of his mother.

He knew Rose didn't understand what was funny about it, but she laughed because the Beatles ran and joked and no one ever told them to stop it or fussed over their hair. They never stopped moving: Beatles on trains. Beatles throwing themselves on the grass and rolling around. Beatles thundering down stairs and sprinting across sidewalks and flinging themselves into phone booths and train compartments. Beatles staring straight into the camera eye, waggling their eyebrows and curling their lips and giving smart-alecky answers and singing with unpretty voices and arguing with strangers and flirting with girls.

He stepped outside and called his wife collect. In his empty house the phone rang and rang. His fingers shook too badly to light his cigarette. He'd left his father's funeral luncheon with a relief that shamed him. He'd never liked the son of a bitch, and now he didn't have to try to impress him. He was just home from the service, hadn't even unpacked his ruck-sack. He could do anything. He knocked back a few whis-keys at a bar near the funeral home, then took himself to the diner next door. Lovely blonde with the last traces of a Ten-nessee accent dissolving into a midwestern honk. There was something in the curl of her ugly name embroidered over her breast, the disappointed line of her pretty mouth, that struck him as funny. "When's your day off?" he said over the chicken and dumplings she slid in front of him. "I'll take you wher-ever you want to go."

Back in the theater, he dropped back into the seat beside his shorn daughter. On the other side of her, his mother the solitary snowbird, the artist alone with her secrets, seemed caught in a rare delight.

* * *

Once the aspirin kicked in, Eamon let Rose do what her heart desired with the radio. She stopped on "Good Vibrations" and "Heat Wave" and "Mrs. Brown You've Got a Lovely Daugh-ter." She kept pulling down the visor to admire her haircut, feeling the ends with her fingers. Eamon had loaded their suitcases while Rose burst into tears and threw herself at her grandmother's legs, promising to send pictures. He couldn't tell if the last look Beatrice gave him was pity or disappoint-ment.

At a rest stop in Tennessee, on a picnic table beneath a tree, Eamon and Rose shared a bag of boiled peanuts, sucking the salt off their fingers.

Eamon felt miserable, that if he was left alone and sober with his thoughts a moment longer he'd explode in tears. Sometimes when he didn't like himself he thought, the apple doesn't fall far from the tree. Only to find out that wasn't his tree at all. "We didn't see a single solitary alligator," he said.

Rose considered this. "We never talked about my grandpa Lewis, either."

"Well, to be frank, darling," he said. "He was a drunk and a son of a bitch, excuse my French, but you don't need to worry about it because he wasn't your grandfather anyway."

Eamon gave her the photo his mother had given him. It was a black-and-white picture of a man, his face crinkled up in a laugh so the eyes behind his wire glasses disappeared. Behind him a shingled house and the fender of a giant car, a midwestern anywhere. Thomas August, the back said in his mother's curly handwriting.

"Thomas," Eamon read. He pressed a cold Coke bottle between his eyes. "This is your grandfather, God rest his luckless soul."

Rose pressed into his shoulder, her Beatles hair tickling him. "It says Thomas August, Dad."

"I think that's the date, flower. Thomas comma August. The photo's just a hundred years old. The comma's faded out."

"But you have to put a year on for a date." As if a sheet of lined paper materialized in the air, she wrote in its upper right corner with her finger. "The month and the day and the year."

It was a good point. "Well, what kind of name is August? Augustus, maybe. Augustine, like the saint."

"It sounds fancy," Rose said.

He didn't tell her his body had been fished out of the

Detroit River. Bootlegging. The fog of his hangover had lifted enough for that to return to him: "For years I hated him for getting mixed up in that awful business, dying in the way he did," Beatrice had said in the car. "But he died trying to make things better for us with the means he had." Eamon had laughed at her, stunned and sputtering. She'd looked so disappointed.

"We should ask Grandma Snowbird," Rose said.

So when they rolled up the drive and he carried Rose, asleep, to bed, he considered the picture of his father curled on the coffee table beside the doilies and candy dish and called long-distance. He let it ring and ring until his mother woke and padded to the living room and her croaking hello came down the line.

"We made it. We're home."

Her voice held sleep and questions in it. "Okay," she said. He was going to tell her that he should've told her she could stay with him, that he'd care for her even though he didn't know how and the thought of it scared him. He could sleep and drive back the next day and get her. "Well, don't run up your long distance. We'll talk soon," Beatrice began, but he heard Myrna screaming above him and then Rose crying out.

In Rose's room, bent in the dark at the bed, hands moving down the side of her face, patting her daughter's back and shoulders like her hair could be hidden in a secret pocket of the cotton dress splotched in ketchup and chocolate. She pushed past Eamon, turned the light on, and gasped.

"What did you do?" Myrna demanded. "Oh my God. It was the prettiest thing about you." Rose tried to bury her head in the pillow to hide what had been done. On the wall above her, there were pictures of the Beatles and a hand-painted card with a bright fat bird on a railing, palm fronds unfurling behind it. *Granddaughter*, it said in black script among the leaves.

"Oh, for Christ's sake, Myrna, it's just hair."

"Just hair? Just hair? She has *my* hair. She has beautiful hair and look at you squandering it," Myrna said. "She's a beautiful girl and you've ruined her." Her eyes were frantic, and her breath came out in shudders. Eamon felt an old reflex to reach for her, to still her against him, but he could see, by the way her body shuddered as it lifted from their daughter's bed, it was all futile. He listened through the wall as she fell into a bed that was now hers alone, in a house filling up with her sobs.

CHAPTER 17

On the white comforter in front of Monae, a camel and her knock-kneed, underbitey calf stared up from a touch-and-feel book of animals from Bible stories. Monae and Bea had bleated with sheep and whistled with birds, but she realized she had no idea what sounds camels made.

She heard August's key card click in the door. Then his boots unzipped, kicked against the wall of the adjoining room of their suite.

Monae kissed Bea's head and lifted her voice toward him. "Daddy can tell us what sound camels make after he fixes your bottle."

The minifridge opened, the microwave dinged. August, in from wherever he went when he said he was stepping out to smoke and returned hours later, had a burp cloth over his shoulder and snow dusted in his hair. He dragged the chair next to the bed, his back to the television, and stretched his legs out. His big toe winked through a hole in his sock.

He rolled his jaw, mimed spitting. "Camel," he said. Then he reached for their baby.

Once, before they married, Annie told Monae what relapse had looked like for August. He'd grow quiet, angry with himself, sleeping strange hours, skinny and broke, always with vague excuses for wherever he'd disappeared to. That it was so difficult to imagine him this way had assured her that his addiction was past tense. His sister had said nothing about this, though: how, when he returned from wherever it was he disappeared to, he had a look in his eyes like he'd been focusing hard on something inside himself and was having a hard time coming back out. He came back to their hotel suite with his vague excuses, but it was difficult to tell if it was the righteous anger and grief of what had been done to them, what had been taken from them, or if this was what self-annihilation looked like.

"What?" he asked.

"I didn't say anything." She handed him the baby.

Monae picked up the remote from where it rested beside a speckled banana. One banana more and the housekeepers would call CPS, August had warned. They'd been here long enough now that Monae knew all the housekeepers—as well as the staff who laid out the breakfast buffet, the valet drivers, the night-shift front-desk girls who asked if they could hold the baby—and told August that she had no fear of judgment from Tenisha nor Kat nor Hiba.

While Bea sucked and grunted, blinking up at her father, Monae clicked through the channels. On the twenty-four-hour news outlets, Flint was becoming harder to find, and even on the local channels the nightly updates skimmed past Flint. Monae wanted so badly to go home, but if the water wasn't news anymore, then it wasn't going to be fixed, the pipes weren't going to be replaced, there would be no justice, and they'd be forgotten. The conspiracies that panicked her when her mind was fogged with hormones and sleeplessness and fear would prove true: they'd never be able to go home.

It relieved her when she clicked onto the rerun of an interview with Michael Moore, jowly in his baseball cap, hands folded on a desk. It was comforting, the familiar image of him.

"There's not, like, a show about animals or people making elaborate cakes or something?" August asked. To Bea he whispered, "Auntie Re-Re didn't give us this room so Mommy could watch that, did she?"

"If she stops by, I'll change the channel." Monae hugged a pillow. "Also, being married to me doesn't mean you get to call her auntie. We've discussed this."

"It just sounds so nice. Warm." He added to Bea, "I didn't get an Aretha and an Annie. Auntless and auntieless, your poor dad."

On the television the usual footage of Flint reeled as the newscaster reminded the audience why Michael Moore was their guest. There was the water tower. Broken houses in snow. Fourteen thousand abandoned properties, Monae always added while they reeled off the statistics on race and poverty. Enough vacant land to raise food to feed every person in the city. Enough corroded pipes snaking untreated river water with enough neurotoxins and bacteria to kill them.

Bea was starting to fuss. "Not much appetite tonight? Can I get you a to-go box, honeybee?" Her mouth tightened in refusal. He stretched behind him to put the bottle on the dresser. He moved her to his shoulder, his palm moving a slow circle on her back. The only time he seemed to settle back within himself was with her.

In Moore's beleaguered hometown that's already suffered

massive depopulation, the newscaster said, only the poorest people would be left.

"Oh, they've been saying that since I was born," August dismissed. To Bea he soothed, "When you're older I'll show you *Roger and Me* and tell you how your mother led me into a dark room at the history museum to make you."

It bewildered Monae that this had become the joke: love at first sight and whirlwind romance. Star-crossed farmers. In her mother's version of the story, she sent her daughter out for Halloween candy and she came back with a husband and a baby. Monae alone seemed to remember the compromise and consideration. August was a decision she made. Motherhood was a decision she made. Everything had felt deliberate until this hotel room.

Bea—crying now—was likely conceived in their newly erected hoop house still strung with lights from their backyard wedding. A citronella candle, a blanket spread over the dandelions. August was a year sober. She had her degree. The maple and beeches gathered thick and lush, the river a fleeting blue between their branches. Elaine from Frontier Farm, forgetting how August had found the farm in the first place, brought a bottle of cherry mead to their wedding. With no corkscrew, Monae pulled the cork out with a hammer and nail. She drank it from the bottle, syrup-thick and sweet. When she woke, shivering, the dregs of the wine spilled into the grass like blood and she shook August to go inside with her.

The thought of it now, climbing the stairs to their bed and curling cold and sleepy against him, hurt.

Bea scrabbled at her father's chin with her tiny nails. He put her hands to his mouth, kissed them while she howled. "Michael Moore stresses a lot of people out."

Monae turned off the television and reached for her.

In the next room she tried the pacifier, an array of pastel animals with stitched eyes, a rattle. She zagged a path between play mat, crib, and sofa. She put Bea on her mat and pushed aside the boxes he'd brought in last night with her father's letters and pictures to reach under the sofa for a toy. She turned on the white noise. When she looked up, she saw August through the open door, still sitting in the chair, turned toward the window. He tugged his hair as if he could scalp himself.

For the first week, the hotel suite had seemed like a birthday party with no guests. August drove to Banglatown for takeout, and they had curry in bed and watched mindless TV while the baby slept. He made up names for the YouTube videos of white noise they played to soothe her. *It Takes a Nation of Millions to Hold Babies Back. Electric Babyland.* His mother and sister came, then Regina and Jim stayed a night so she and August could go on a date and maybe *bond*, as the blogs she read called it. She'd done the pelvic floor exercises and postnatal yoga YouTube videos. But Monae was too tired to care about jackfruit barbecue, and August repeatedly failed to parallel park, the snow heaped at the curb throwing off his depth perception, and he ranted about how much he fucking hated Detroit, until he made her so nervous she'd told him to calm down. It shook her when he snapped, "Wouldn't I, if I could?" and they hadn't *bonded*.

She'd hoped when he went back to Flint during the weeks it might feel a little like dating: texting in bed and the anticipation of him. It afforded him an opportunity for the grand gestures he liked: showing up late to spend the night with them, bringing back things she liked. Instead, when the baby

couldn't be consoled, her spasms of fear and ineptitude deepened. When he didn't respond immediately to the picture she
sent of Bea, to her *What are you doing?*, when he worked dou-
bles and stayed in Flint overnight and answered FaceTime in
the dark and she couldn't see if he was there, in their house,
stretched across their bed, her mind moved with all the places
he could be, all the things he could be doing when he wasn't
with them.

Monae turned the white noise on, eased Bea into her crib,
and sat back on the bed. Still, Bea howled. "I can," August
started, and Monae snapped, "You can what?"

"Do whatever you want."

She sipped in a breath. She'd go get dinner. She took his
overcoat from the back of the chair and stepped into her
shoes. Down the hall she listened to her daughter's cries dissolve into murmurs of televisions behind closed doors, the
humming ice machine.

Some nights, when August was gone, she and Bea walked
up and down these closed doors. It was a strange and dreamy
sort of floating, like she was in a long corridor that connected
who she was to someone else. If she pulled open doors, they
might each lead into another time, like rooms in a museum,
or other versions of herself, who told her parents not to get in
the car and so were never hit by the drunk careening through
an intersection, who took her degree and her husband and
moved somewhere else with a baby who had her own infinite
selves. All the articles and news segments and information
from the pediatrician said the same thing: with lead poisoning, there was no way of knowing who Bea might have been
or would be instead. There was no way of knowing how this

would shape her body, the ranges of her moods, her intelligence.

While Monae waited at the coney island, she emptied his coat pockets onto a table. The tangle of his earbuds. Car keys. A lighter. A pamphlet from the Jehovah's Witnesses about the approach of Armageddon. Gas station and party store receipts for cigarettes and chips and coffee. Wrappers from front desk peppermints. On his phone she scrolled through texts: *hey four eyes* and *how's Detroit, September Molloy?* from his sister and *how's my grandbaby?* from his mother.

"Two Lent specials," the man called for her at the counter. She picked up the fried fish she didn't want.

Back in their suite, August was in bed, his shirt balled on the floor and Bea's head under his chin. He was humming "I Say a Little Prayer for You." The baby slept against the vibration of his vocal cords. He lifted a hand from Bea's butt and wiggled his fingers at her. She couldn't tell if it was just the lamplight: the line of his collarbone seemed in sharper relief.

Monae sometimes tried to harden against him so that it might hurt less when it became clear they weren't going to get through this. But he looked so pleased with himself, and she pressed her thumb through the hole in his sock to the callus beneath.

"She likes my chest hair," he whispered. "I was thinking we could shave it off and glue it to a teddy bear or something."

"Why can't we keep your chest hair on your chest?"

"I'll get tartar sauce all over her."

"She's gotten worse on me." Corrected, in charity, "Us."

After they ate, she pulled over one of the boxes he'd brought in. He hadn't brought the head of Fred the Carriageless Horse, and she decided not to say anything about it because if Michael Moore was still angry on cable news, then they hadn't been forgotten. They'd go home. There'd be a home to go back to.

On the bed, she sat cross-legged with the box. Beside her, Gus scrolled through his phone. Paper and photographs shifted loose in the box, save the bundle of letters from G. She unfolded them. Thin as onionskin, like pages from a Bible. She had to lean into the bedside lamp to read some of them, the pencil lead faded to ghosts.

They moved me to nights. Wish I had those old blackout curtains from the war so I could get some damn sleep.

Monae read one aloud: *When you come back we can go down to the river, get a good breeze on us, watch the freighters.* Gus dropped his phone to his sternum.

"I don't remember my dad ever talking about anyone he ran around with in Detroit." She read the letter again. "And there's no *I love you* or *I miss you*. Who's G?"

"Some guy who sucks at writing and likes looking at ships." His eyes flicked up to hers. "Maybe G is for Gus. I could be a time traveler."

"So that's where you're going all the time." She hadn't meant to be mean. His eyes rolled away from her and up to the ceiling. But he was thinking.

"They remind me a little of talking on the phone with my mom when I was in rehab. She'd call and ask me what I'd eaten and ask me if I was reading anything and tell me dumb stuff her cat did. I think she didn't want to think about where I was, she just wanted to know I was still there."

Monae didn't press for details. She dropped the letters back into the box and pushed the box to the wall.

When she came back in from feeding the baby, August

was asleep in his clothes, the light still on beside him. She rolled his holey sock off and dropped it in the wastebasket. He blinked at her.

She tucked herself into the space her daughter liked. His heart beat under her ear. She felt his breath deepen. An arm folded her in.

She counted his ribs with her fingers. Ranged the knots of his shoulders. The line of his jaw. There was a little less of him than there used to be.

He mistook her touch for another kind of tenderness. He rolled into her, pressed her onto her back. She tried to remember precisely what this had felt like in bed, at home, where he was never so fleeting, so slippery; where there was too much of him sometimes, singing rock songs around the house and out in the yard, shaking his fist at the raccoons, those cucumber-thieving sons of bitches. She used to feel guilty for wanting to be alone sometimes.

He stopped kissing her. She was crying.

"Hormones," she said. At the bottom of the bed his one socked foot and one bare one. She threaded hers between them and hung onto him. "Maybe we could do something tomorrow. Get out of here for a while."

CHAPTER 18

August and Monae stood in the bright light of the Detroit Institute of Art's central courtyard, surrounded by Diego Rivera's murals of Ford's River Rouge assembly line. On the two main panels, workers in overalls and boots strained themselves diagonally against the machines. The assembly line was a twisting snake scaled in conveyor belts and chains. Behind the line, the foundry flamed and the men who fed it were black silhouettes, faceless.

August had Bea wrapped against him, the hood up on her fuzzy coat with the bear ears. A docent led a tour they weren't on, explaining Rivera's research at the plant and his relationship with Edsel Ford. In the mural, Monae's eyes met those of a white man in a suit glowering behind his workers.

August leaned into her ear. "Let's have a son and name him Edsel."

When she woke that morning, he was already up with the baby on his lap, coffee made, music low on his phone. "The Who are basically the Beatles for people with authority problems who don't want to admit they like classic rock. Your mother's more of a *Pet Sounds* on vinyl kind of guy," he said when she came in, digging the sleep out of her eyes. "She's got weird taste and she's touchy about it, so don't ask her."

She was too tired for quips, but for the sake of his rare good mood she did her best. "You seahorse out the next one, you can name it whatever you want."

Already his attention had drifted. He was looking up at the top panels of the east wall. In them, naked brown-skinned women held an abundance of apples and grain in their laps. Their breasts round and perfect fruits. Their glances sidelong and sad.

Between the two women, on the central panel, a giant baby was curled in the earth like a tuber. Its legs were crossed and curled, its head tucked and eyes closed, hugging itself. From the bulb that entombed it, or encased it, roots spread. On the panel across the room, men in gas masks and welding helmets built fighter planes and bombs. Below them what looked to be a cluster of diseased cells.

Monae had left her coat in the car and taken August's overcoat, heavy and blankety. She pulled her hands up into its sleeves. Behind her a docent said Frida Kahlo had lost their baby at Henry Ford Hospital, and August was whispering into Bea's bear ears. Monae stared up at the baby in the earth till she couldn't anymore. She walked ahead, out of the courtyard, trusting he'd follow.

The next gallery was made of cool stone and stained glass windows, a simulation of a cathedral. She was surrounded by white madonnas draped in luxurious red and blue holding their fat, glowing babies. Joseph seldom there, guiding a mule, watching from the far side of the nativity.

She felt August step beside her, heard his boots on the stone floor. He was telling Bea about the Gospels while she blinked and tasted her fingers. *"When they found out the Messiah was from Nazareth they asked, 'Can anything good come out of Nazareth?'* It was basically the Flint of the Roman Empire, Beebs. Which is a wild thing to think about."

Monae held the little snow boot Bea should've outgrown by now, for the winter that should've been over by now. August was saying something she couldn't quite hear, in her mind still the buried baby. Bea's foot kicked away from her, and Monae's hand moved to August's back, gathering a fistful of his sweater. She needed something to hold on to. She couldn't remember the last time she'd left the Holiday Inn, how long it'd been since August last drove them around Detroit (*Here's Motown, here's where I ate falafel sandwiches and wished I knew someone like your mother, Bumblebee*), and she wanted to sit down.

"Saint Jerome," August said, gesturing to a man in red with a book in front of him and a lion at his feet. She ignored him.

"Maybe I'll go wait for you in the café." When he offered to come with her, she told him to look at art with Bea instead. She was fine, she said; she was more tired than she realized. They'd meet her in the café in an hour.

Under the vaulted skylight, among strangers on leather sofas, Monae indulged in a glass of wine and a scone. It was calming, the sudden sense of space and anonymity, the buzz of sugar and alcohol, her husband and her baby walking above her. She pulled Gus's coat around her like a robe. Rich-looking women in big jewelry and bright cat-eye glasses drank tea at the next table. She pulled up all the text messages she hadn't responded to. She sent pictures of Bea to friends, her sister- and mother-in-law. In one selfie, she and Bea were lying on the white hotel comforter, Monae's lips pressed to Bea's cheek. Bea looked delighted, her dark curls getting thicker, her cheeks rounder. She scrolled to the last text from her mother, after Monae sent her a picture of the letter from G and asked if she knew who G was. *You should ask Harold.* She knew from the news that Harold was busy speaking to protestors and talking to reporters on the lawn of City Hall; she'd ask him sometime.

Zeniyah sent back a string of heart-eye emojis and OMGs.

It didn't surprise or particularly annoy Monae when August was fifteen minutes late. After twenty minutes, her call went to voicemail.

After half an hour, she went through the rooms of African masks and Buddhist statues and Islamic tiles. She tried his phone, each time looping back to the message that gave no greeting nor assurance he'd do anything with the missed call: "It's Gus." She returned to the café, asked the barista if a white guy with a BabyBjörn had been there, then climbed the stairs.

On the second floor she seemed to keep walking into the same galleries, the same flowers and dead rabbits and white girls in fluffy Victorian dresses. Stone passed to wood passed to marble beneath her boots. She tried to make sense of the map's "You Are Here" star, but she didn't know the street names that were meant to orient her, wasn't sure that the library across the street meant she was looking out at Woodward or John R. It felt like dreaming, like each hallway turned into the same hallway again, tunneled into an eternal maze. There she was again in the faux church with its fat and holy babies. Again in the River Rouge plant, the bulb of a baby above her. It was impossible to tell if the baby was gestating in its native soil or if it had been buried there; if the squiggles and cells in the dirt the roots tunneled through were nutrients or worms.

She checked the time again. It hadn't been that long. She called and called. *It's Gus, It's Gus, It's Gus.*

She asked a guard where the information desk was, and probably because she was crying he led her to the elevator and rode with her back to the basement. She thought how young he looked, in his loose uniform, and then she realized he was her age. He looked past her to the gold elevator buttons. "They're here somewhere, we've just never been here before," she said, as if he was the one who needed assuring.

He walked her to the desk. Her husband and her daughter, she explained to a white woman behind stacks of museum guides, were supposed to find her over an hour ago. Couldn't they page them? Wasn't there a PA? Wouldn't it be quicker? It was just that the baby was probably getting hungry. It wasn't that they were lost, but they needed to go home.

Then August walked out of the gift shop worrying a postcard. He'd turned the baby, asleep now against his chest, her head down, her hands in little fists.

Monae resented the concern in his face, as if it wasn't him that was doing this to her. She started to cry.

"I said meet me in the coffee shop an hour ago. I called you a thousand times."

"My phone's in the pocket," he said, gesturing to his coat, which she was wearing. She slid her hand in and there it was, the screen black anyway, the battery dead.

"I don't want to be here anymore," she said, wresting the baby from him. "Just get the car. I just want to go."

He did what she said without argument. She watched him leave. She was crying, stupid, embarrassed, and the people at the desk and the security guards were watching her. She lodged herself between the two sets of double doors to conceal herself from them.

"What's wrong?" August drove them back downtown, the buildings growing taller. Monae told him to just drop it, but he couldn't, and at a stoplight outside the baseball stadium, giant snow-dusted stone tigers lifting their paws, she asked, "Does everything have to be such an ordeal with you?"

His jaw twitched. His tongue moved inside his cheek with something he didn't say.

"Why do I never know where you are? Why do you have to make everything so much worse? Isn't this bad enough?" She swept a hand at the windshield, at all of Michigan outside his car. "You brought us here. You did this."

He drove the last few blocks in silence and dropped them at the front door. She fed the baby and gave her a bath, and the hours ticked by with the white noise.

When he came in, she stood, one of his sweaters over her pajamas, hugging herself. She watched him set a bunch of bananas, yellow and unspeckled, to replace the ones she wouldn't throw away. He jammed the freezer drawer with steam-in-the-bag vegetables. A bag of almonds dropped to the counter. A mesh sack of tangerines. A little bag of radishes. Formula and diapers, though they had plenty.

He glanced over at her. "Forgot your tea. Had to go back."

She thought it was fine, that that was it. When he went out to smoke, he came back immediately. Neither of them spoke, but in bed she put her head against his shoulder blades, her arm around him, and when his fingers grew fidgety, rubbing raw the same inch of her skin, she put her hand over his to still him, holding his touch against her. He exhaled too loudly. He'd been holding his breath.

When she woke, he was on the chair beside the bed, lacing up his boots. The alarm told her it was three in the morning. The heavy drapes permitted no moonlight, no streetlamps. A particular dark that reminded her she wasn't home each time she woke to it.

"Where are you going?"

"I figured I'd go to Flint early. Freezing rain. Roads are gonna be bad."

Monae never stopped watching the news: she knew this was not in the forecast.

"I'll see you in a couple days." He leaned in to kiss her, and his coat, unbuttoned, fell toward her. She caught his lapel and held his face close to her. "Where are you going?"

He reached around her to straighten the blankets, reordering what he'd disturbed. "I gotta head back," he said. She watched him leave them, listened to the door click shut. His phone, charging, vibrated on top of the dresser.

CHAPTER 19

1967

Around the Holiday Inn pool the after-party strutted and preened. They grazed from the table of booze and marzipan fruits, of all things, lighting each other's cigarettes and repeating to each other, *Brilliant show, yeah man.* Lights burned in the upstairs room, and people leaned onto the balcony, ashing into the swimming pool. Music came from somewhere in the smoke-thick hubbub, but the deejay had given up his post; "Respect" had been repeating for half an hour. Peals of laughter and British voices—*You must come see us in Soho, love!*—broke through the din. HAPPY BIRTHDAY, KEITH, the Holiday Inn marquee glowed over Bristol Road. Whoever the hell Keith was.

Goldie had long lost Sam, the owner of Engine Running Records who paid her peanuts to sing backup, and was standing alone by the marzipan. It was late August, and the air carried the coming fall in it. Goldie's dress had been pasted to her by the stage lights, and now it separated from her like dead skin. She was slick and new beneath it.

Goldie sang backup for a soul band from Flint, Peter J & the Metros. Homely white boys from Flint with funeral suits and a set of horns they'd learned to play in their high school marching bands. They'd been the least of the acts that night at Atwood Stadium: Herman's Hermits, the Who, Question Mark & the Mysterians. But the Metros were about to be hot shit, according to Sam. He'd gotten their song "Our Turn" onto a soul station in Detroit. After the show tonight, the record would be in every shop in the Lower Peninsula, or so he'd explained again to her and Loretta on the drive to the show. Motown who. Holland-Dozier-Holland my ass.

Goldie saw the horn player from the Metros with a chubby blonde sulking at his side. She was the closest woman to Goldie's age in this sea of false eyelashes and thighs. But that woman looked old, with her sour face and frumpy clothes, and Goldie only felt old; from a distance, with her hair swirled into a beehive and her delicate legs falling out of her minidress, you couldn't tell. She swung her hips in a shimmery dress with chiffon sleeves and floated her hands in the air, kept her nails long and done, which was no small feat when you worked the swing shift at Dodge and had no one at home to help you with the dishes. Up onstage she didn't look any older than Loretta, twenty-one with the hips and ass of a fertility goddess. On the drive to Flint she'd sat up front under Sam's arm, singing along with whatever came on the radio. Sam pronounced, "Heavenly," less a compliment to Loretta than to his own business acumen.

A girl swooped in for the cake box that sat among the marzipans and whisked it up the stairs, a flurry of girls behind her. Goldie kicked off one shoe and felt the rough cool of the cement underfoot. She could face it: she didn't have doe eyes and a big church voice like Tammi Terrell. She didn't have the range to belt like Aretha, or even to *sock it to me, sock it to me* behind Aretha, or sha-la-la with the girls with their big flipped-up hair at Motown. But it was kids' music, this stuff. Fuck Aretha Franklin, frankly, and fuck the rest of them, too. Singing just kept the noise out of her head.

A redheaded boy with eyes dreamy and glazed lurched toward her with an empty cup. His eyes slanted toward the empty beer cases. "Can I get a Jack and Coke?" he asked her. He shoved a marzipan in his mouth.

"I bet you can," she said. "I bet the world's your oyster."

Above them, a girl howled. A glass shattered. After the hell she'd been through this summer, the tanks rolling under her window, she still jumped at every bang. The redhead was too drunk to notice.

She pointed at the stairs. "Might be a supply you can tap into up there." But the man was staring toward the parking lot, his mouth moving but no sounds coming out.

Goldie hadn't been to Flint in thirteen years. A couple of miles from here, on the north side of town, Cora had her house and her husband and her boys, and maybe even that hateful little bird still. But it was Jerome she kept thinking about, though she wished she wasn't. Years of pictures Cora sent flickered through her head like film reel. She had envelopes full of photographs Cora sent with reports, like her son was the stock market. Jerome was up three inches this year. His grades were down.

She wanted to get stoned and let the rest of this evening glide away. She was going to ask the redhead, but there was a hot hand on her arm. On reflex, she swung back. "Goldie," the hand's owner said. Fingers wrapped around her arm as if to remind her of its smallness.

She turned to Sam; full moons of sweat rose under his arms, and his big tortoiseshell glasses were bugging his eyes. "I'm gonna take the boys to England. What'd I say? Didn't I say I had a hit on my hands?"

"We're going to England?"

His eyes were shining glass, ready to break. "Didn't I say God sent those white kids from Flint to me?"

"Sam, what are you talking about England?"

"Herman's Hermits' manager said they dig their sound. They're looking for a group to open up their shows back home. Said that northern soul sound is big over there and the Metros are the real deal." He laughed. "Northern soul. *Shit*."

"We're going to England?" Goldie said. "When?"

"Oh, Goldie, not *you*." His mouth in a sloppy smile. "*You* ain't in the band."

"I'm on that record, aren't I?"

"You're a session singer, Goldie. You know how expensive it is to tour? And England, goddamn! I mean, airfare, passports . . ."

Hadn't that been her, up on the stage, sweating under the lights, sashaying in front of Flint, Michigan, with the tits she barely had hanging out and the hairdo that cost more than she hadn't yet been paid for this show?

"I'm going to need more help around the office. We talked about this. You got any, uh, secretarial skills?"

If he thought she was going to stay in Detroit and suck his dick in the office, he might as well extend that offer to Loretta. She pushed into the crowd.

Goldie noticed in the parking lot, where the redhead had fixed his stare, people who weren't invited upstairs made their own private parties in the backseats of their Chevys and Fords. It didn't take long for her to sidle into a man still wearing sunglasses and a black suit coat, his hair an upturned bowl. She found herself in a Buick with its windows rolled up, her new friend reaching past her to the glove compartment for his rolling papers. In the back was a woman with hair frizzing over the shoulders of her paisley blouse and tiny eyes behind wire glasses. A thick bag open on the seat beside her with a notebook spilling out.

"You're the Question Mark?" Goldie asked the man rolling a joint on a map balanced on his thigh.

"I'm a Mysterian." He ran his tongue along the paper.

"I'm Dionne Warwick," she said. She gestured to the woman in the back. "Who's she?"

"I'm a writer from *Michigan Chronicle*. Are you here with a band?"

"Turns out I'm not," Goldie said. The writer wanted to know what that meant, but the Mysterian was saying to no one in particular, "What a fucking summer, man." She pulled the smoke down into her lungs. The journalist pitched forward.

"How do you think tonight's been affected by the mood, after the riots?"

"I think we're on the verge of utopia," the Mysterian said. "I think we're gonna drive through hell and take the first exit into paradise. We've released the pressure." The writer hummed like he'd quoted scripture.

The smoke massaged the ache out of Goldie's feet and her neck, sore from holding up her big hair. While it bloated her tongue fat and slow in her mouth, so that she didn't have much to say to the Mysterian, it didn't stop her thinking of all the boys shot and rounded up in jail that summer. It didn't stop her thinking of Jerome.

She thought they'd laced the shit with something harder when she heard the siren. A bad trip, sending her back to July. But then the lights swung through the car and the siren was blaring into her ears. "Oh, fuck me, man," the Mysterian said.

Goldie opened the door to throw the joint, and a body was there, silver buttons on a navy suit.

"Step out of the vehicle," he said, and then he had her cheek to the car, her arms wrenched behind her. Arms bound, braceleted in metal. The world tilted sideways, and she could see between the cars to the scene at the pool. Women clipping away in their big shoes. Men gesturing, shaking their heads, pulling out their wallets and handing over their IDs.

The Mysterian and the girl from the newspaper were pushed into one car, Goldie another. The officer who'd arrested her went into the crowd, looking for more people to arrest. Goldie closed her eyes. The backseat smelled like old puke.

A few cars away from her, a Cadillac rolled forward. She thought someone was making a cautious getaway, but then the car lurched up onto the grass and rolled into a crowd that screamed and parted.

From the back of the squad car, Goldie watched as it tipped headlights-first into the shallow end of the pool, metal on cement, a whoosh of water. Then the crowd re-formed, closing in between her and the Cadillac in the pool. She could only hear the screaming and the clamor.

Around her, people took advantage of the diversion. They slipped discreetly to their cars and backed out of the lot.

People in the hotel rooms twitched back their curtains, stepped out, and leaned over the balcony.

It seemed like years before a skinny boy in his underwear appeared in front of her, cops on either side of him holding him upright. The door opened, and he was pushed in beside her. He had blood from chin to chest, streaks of it smeared onto his cheeks. What appeared to be cake was clotted in his dark hair.

He rolled his head around, mumbling to himself. Through the blood it was hard to tell what his mouth looked like, if he was smiling or sad, not that Goldie cared to stare too closely. They'd wrapped him in a blanket, but he was seeping all over the backseat and she could feel a puddle of him lapping against her thigh.

He hummed, and it took her a second to recognize he was struggling out that Martha and the Vandellas song the Who had played that night. "Heat Wave." A spit of blood hit the partition.

"Knock that shit off," the officer said. They were pulling out of the Holiday Inn lot, leaving the other squad cars and the paddy wagon.

The boy turned his head to Goldie as if he'd just realized she was there. He had big black eyebrows made blacker still by the unearthly pallor of his skin, and round, dark eyes with baby-doll lashes. If you didn't look at him from the nose down, he looked like a sad little boy.

Heading downtown, the boy kept on humming, and she saw all the For Sale signs staked in front yards—the painted ladies that had been boardinghouses back when she moved up here. Flint wasn't so different after all. They were getting the hell out of here, too. "You been to Flint before?" she asked.

He'd seemed to realize he was bleeding. He pressed his

hand to his mouth, pulled it away and stared at the bright blood on his fingers, then repeated the process.

She turned her head to watch the city pass.

"You know I heard Berry Gordy and Smokey Robinson used to come up to Flint to get records pressed?" she said. "That's why they started Motown, so they didn't have to keep driving up to Flint. Can't say I blame them."

"Who are you, then?" he asked. There was blood everywhere now—streaked over his thighs, on the dark upholstery of the car, tangled in his chest hair, and dripped to his belly. A few bright splatters on her thigh.

"You don't care, and you won't remember."

Beneath the thick fringe of his hair, his eyes flicked up to the cops in the front seat. The fun seemed to be seeping out of him. "S'my birthday," he told her.

"Keith," she said. "Well, sorry your party went to shit."

By the time they rolled into the police station downtown, he'd puked. A little of it ended up on her dress and stunk up the car. She was escorted in; Mr. Moon—she overheard the sergeant and the man holding a change of clothes who'd come out to meet them—was being rerouted to a dentist.

There was only one Flint phone number Goldie had memorized. She dialed it, heard a young man's voice come onto the line. Not Jerome, she could just tell.

"Harold," she said. The receiver trembled in her hand. She nearly dropped it. "Is your mama home?"

* * *

Cora arrived in the morning with bail money. Goldie's heart plummeted at the sight of her, like she wasn't her blood, her little sister whom she'd known from the moment she was born, but an old flame. Someone she'd loved and disappointed. Someone whose heart she'd broken. She tried to swallow it down. She couldn't form a clear thought, and her body hurt from holding herself up all night, goddamned if she was going to lie on the floor like these girls with their miniskirts hitched up to their panties, handbags shoved under their heads for pillows. Goldie said she'd take a cab to the bus station and a bus to Detroit, but Cora said she'd drive her.

Cora looked good, though. A little heavy, but she'd always been big-boned, and she wore it naturally. Her floral blouse pulled a little at the chest, buttons gaping. She'd gotten all the good their mother had to offer, including her bosom.

She should've asked Cora to bring her a change of clothes, but there she was stuck in the sequined shift, her clothes in Sam's car. She'd spit-cleaned most of her eyeliner and mascara off and smoothed out her hair.

There were two boys in the backseat. One with her high forehead and sharp cheekbones, wearing sunglasses and a striped T-shirt.

"No," Goldie said.

Cora didn't hear her. She got in. Goldie considered turning, walking till she found a pay phone, but her brain had given up, underslept and hungover, and her body submitted to her sister's commands. Her body was impulse and reflex, its animal self.

This was her punishment. This was her sister shoving her face in it, like a dog who'd messed on the floor. Did Jerome know who she was? She could feel two sets of little-boy eyes on her mussed hair. The car was moving. She could've kicked the dashboard, pummeled it with her fists.

Goldie's voice came out hoarse. "I just need to get home.

I told you I could take a bus. Drop me off at the Grey-hound."

She watched Flint pass her window and tried to remember what it used to look like. The downtown streets used to be busier. There weren't so many houses for sale. She tried to remember all the places where she worked, all the bars where she sang, but in the panicked blank of her mind she couldn't. She'd tried to live like Flint didn't exist, and now her brain wouldn't let her go back there.

The radio wasn't on, and no one was speaking, so Goldie repeated the songs of last night in her mind to drive out the wildness of her thoughts. *Ain't nothing but love, girl.*

* * *

After Jerome was born, Goldie had the awful sense she was going to do something bad. She was already a burden, her sister and her husband paying her way. Raw-nerved in their tiny apartment with Jerome there beside her, all the time, fussing for reasons she couldn't figure out, pushing her tit out of his little mouth. She couldn't stop crying with him. Even when she tried going back to work, making beds at the Durant Hotel, she'd lock doors behind her and weep onto sheets a stranger had rumpled. Like a siren was going off in her head. And there was her sister, joyful and heavy-breasted with her own pregnancy, with her church friends crammed into the living room of that little yellow house. Women with wedding rings who wrote their mothers dutifully and spoke of babies as blessings so that you knew they never thought about leaving them.

Goldie had always been honest. Cora could say what she wanted, condemn her as silently as she pleased, but she'd never lied about it, and you couldn't help, could you, what God had made you in the first place. It had been Cora who said that she should've been grateful, and if she couldn't see that, how her life had been given a focus, someone to do better for, then there was something unnatural in her. She was depriving her son of the life he could have.

Once they got to her apartment, Goldie unlocked her door and left them to seat themselves. Alone in her bedroom, she peeled away her dress, crunchy and sour with sweat. She washed off what was left of last night's makeup. If her sister wanted to use her to scare the boy straight, wanted him to know the bad blood he had lurking in his veins, show him why he needed to be good, keep his nose clean, all the things his mother couldn't do, or chose not to do, well, then let her.

Instead, she walked back into the room, where her son stood to give her his seat on the sofa, the only place to sit. Harold hugged his knees on the floor.

She took it. "Get yourself a chair from the kitchen," she instructed, and after he left, she turned to her sister. "I guess you win," she said.

Cora shook her head. She was looking behind her, out the window at the charred remainder of a house.

Jerome returned dragging a chair behind him, a modest bicep flexing.

It didn't surprise her at all when Jerome glared at her and refused to talk. A heat spread through her chest. It was love or terror—you couldn't often tell.

"You think you've been wronged," she said.

He said nothing.

"Jerome," Cora said gently. "Harold and I could go for a walk, if you want a minute."

"You wanted for anything? You been hungry a day in your life? I couldn't be your mother like that, so I got you a different one. She said she'd take you. Said you didn't need to know me. You want to go hating somebody, take it up with her."

But Jerome just turned his eyes to the floor, nostrils flaring.

"Well?" Goldie said, as if he were any other person she'd loved and let down, anyone she'd had to give the what for when they had the audacity to ask anything of her, to cast judgment on her. Only it was her own pained face turned toward the ugly carpet. He looked so much like her. She'd seen it in pictures, but it was startling, in front of her like a mirror.

* * *

The concert made the paper the next day. Goldie saw it in the *Free Press* left in the ladies' break room, deep into the state news section. It wasn't the heralding of the next big thing, but a picture of that boy who drove into the pool, the collar of his coat turned up, standing in front of the marquee wishing him a happy birthday. "Musicians Banned from Holiday Inn," the headline said. And underneath the photo, "Chaos follows concert in Flint."

Goldie caught "Our Turn" once on the radio. She was heading into the grocery store. Sam had paid her for the gig, at least, and since it was going to be her last, she thought she'd spend it on something nice for herself. Cake and a bottle of champagne, like she was throwing her own birthday party, or marrying herself. She sat there and listened, watching women push their buggies out of Farmer Jack. She was on the east side, near the river, where the signal fuzzed with interference from the Canadian stations. The static buried her. She turned it up louder, strained, but it was hard to tell when the song gave its last cymbal crash and the next song followed. She couldn't make it out: either Marvin Gaye or someone trying their best to be him. She turned off the radio and sat, not much feeling like getting out of the car anymore.

It was almost funny. She'd gotten what she wanted, or some version of it, and there it went. She hadn't even gotten a copy of the goddamn record.

Her eyes followed a woman in gingham loading her milk gallon and grocery sacks. A little boy stood behind her, banging a toy truck meant to occupy him against the bumper of the car. One car crash after another while his mother put the laundry detergent and cat litter in, oblivious.

Goldie sang the song to herself—not the backing vocal but the lead—in the privacy of her coupe. *We've waited so long, girl.* If she'd known it was the last time she'd hear the song, she wouldn't have particularly cared.

She turned the key in the ignition. To hell with the cake, she didn't want it anymore. She'd go home and get ready for work. Some girls complained, but work for her was nothing, if you didn't give a damn what it was, and if it was mindless enough you could sing through the shift in your mind, train yourself not to think about everything you didn't want to think about. You didn't have to remember anyone you didn't want to remember. You could let your voice get so big in your head you sounded like you were singing in a cathedral.

CHAPTER 20

In the yellow house across the street from the park, curled in his coat and boots on Monae's old twin-size bed, her poster of Billie Holiday still blocking out the window, August woke. The heat and the electric were long turned off, and the old dog hair and mold smells had frozen out. He boarded the windows last summer after Monae cleared out the last of what she wanted. She was given the keys to the padlocks like a souvenir, and she hung them in the kitchen. There was a For Sale sign in the front yard with a number no one ever called.

The stagnant water in the basement had turned to ice. A currentless river under the house.

He was here because he couldn't sleep in his own house. He turned and woke over and over without his wife's head on his shoulder anchoring him to their bed, or on the couch beneath the verse from Isaiah she painted for him: *Your people will rebuild the ancient ruins and will raise up the age-old foundations; you will be called Repairer of Broken Walls, Restorer of Streets with Dwellings.* "See, there's proof God saw Flint coming," he'd said to Monae when he read her the passage the first time, a fool. He'd mistaken his dumb luck for blessings: the love of someone radically different from him, fiercely capable, and money he had no skills to earn. He'd thought they were doing something holy. She never seemed to believe it but seemed to like that he did.

Three days had passed listening to the raccoons and squirrels scuttle across the attic above. He had thought being in Monae's old house, its vacancy and monastic silence, would help him decide. It was their house on the river, the farm, that was the problem. The house was what kept them here. They needed to get rid of the house. They needed money and somewhere to start over.

He waited for clarity, for the certainty of what he should do, but instead his head was just radio static. Songs looped back to him: the syrupy doo-wop from his mamaw's records, covers his band thrashed through, the CDs that scattered abandoned in the backseat of Monae's fucked-up car. He tried to push it out, to focus on Monae's voice saying his name like she used to. His daughter's warm, tiny body against his while they stood at the Holiday Inn window, looking down to the statue of Casimir Pulaski below.

August moved his body, stiff with cold and exhaustion, through her old house, feeling his way along the picture-stripped walls, the floorboards protesting his weight. He went out the back door, locking it behind him. The house next door was unoccupied, its siding-stripped back spilling tufts of insulation, but the Red Cross had heaped cases of water bottles by the front door. A little relief no one was there to receive.

* * *

In their house by the river, August poured a few bottles of water into the coffee maker, listened to it gurgle and spit. Cases of water made a wall behind him. Months' worth of empty bottles scattered across the dirty, snow-tracked linoleum, labels picked off. Bottles for the baby's bathwater upended into stockpots. Bottles for brushing their teeth. Bottles for boiling grains, washing vegetables, rinsing out baby bottles. The recycling bins overflowing with plastic faster than could be collected so August started bailing them into garbage bags he tossed into the basement. When he went down to do the laundry, the washing machine corroding from the toxic water, the bags of bottles heaped like unburied bodies. Already, the house looked like a crime scene. The note his sister had left on the door—*looking for you. Mo says you don't have your phone. Come over tonight?*—might as well have been notice from the city that it was condemned.

Once in this house, when Monae still swore she didn't live with him but her laundry mingled with his on the bedroom floor and her textbooks were stacked beside the couch, she'd told him he was the most optimistic person she knew. He'd laughed, but it wasn't funny at all, she'd insisted: she carried so much grief, and so many questions. She didn't want things in the pure, unquestioning way he did. At the time it felt like a revelation, like she'd seen something no one else ever had, or had spotted an entirely new part of him breaking through, a new growth. Now it seemed that he'd sold both of them a delusion.

The coffee was done but the sugar was empty and the mugs were all dirty. He didn't really want it anyway.

He circled the house. First the baby's room, the bathroom

where he'd left the window open to air out the cigarette smoke, ice crusting the sill. Cracked plaster he hadn't fixed. Floors that groaned beneath carpet he hadn't ripped up. An abandoned house he'd been stupid to think he could fill. He ended up back down in the living room, in front of the windows that looked onto the river, gray through the still-bare trees.

He picked up St. Lazarus from a line of devotional candles bought on a whim at the grocery store and flung it at the closed door. Heavy, it left a dent. The glass splintered but didn't break, and the candle rolled toward a pair of Monae's shoes beside the door. A lamp broke easier, made a bigger sound, and the empty goldfish bowl on the bookcase crashed louder still, the man in the diving bell laid out on the substrate. He used to worry he'd grow into his father's disappointed violence, like he'd grown into his shoulders and dead-end jobs. It never felt good, though. Nothing ever released. Always he ended up destroying things on accident instead, ashamed and unable to clean up the mess.

He went through the house again, gathering what they'd want and need: baby pictures, clothes and books and things from the old house, Bea's birth certificate and sonogram images and printouts from the pediatrician, licenses, insurance policies, soil certification. He'd moved here with nothing and Monae, too, had little; everything cobbled together from thrift stores, family cast-offs. The house already seemed to belong to Bea, her soft, bright, animal-shaped things everywhere, and she was the one who needed the most to get out.

There was a gas can on the kitchen table and a box of matches. They had no neighbors to see him. He was in Detroit, at the hotel, one of those sad families with a poisoned baby, living on charity. The insurance policy was generous, and the fire department underpaid. He'd take everything to her father's house. He could do it in two trips. Then he'd drive down to Detroit, and maybe he'd sleep with her spooned into him. When the sun came up he'd give the baby her bottle so Monae could sleep, and there would be a quiet moment before he would accept whatever fate she'd give him. He wanted only to undo what he'd done, to give her back something in penance.

* * *

At one in the morning, the streets were empty and shiny-slick. August had the first carload heading to Monae's old house after he stopped at the one gas station he knew had a functioning pay phone, where he'd call her and say he was sorry, sorry, he was okay, he'd be back in a couple of hours. He turned the radio on to hear something besides the beat of his blood. On the college station he ran halfway into Question Mark & the Mysterians' "96 Tears," then Herman's Hermits' "Wonderful World."

The disc jockey came on, young and nasal and bubbling with the opportunity to talk into the FM void about his obscure enthusiasm. "So if you can believe it, the Who opened for Herman's Hermits in Flint back in the summer of 1967. The story goes that Keith Moon drove a Cadillac into the Holiday Inn swimming pool and knocked out a tooth. Got the Who banned for life from the Holiday Inn. Back then, the Holiday Inn was on Van Slyke by the truck and bus plant. I think it's a party store now. If you know, give me a call. Anyway, here's the Who's cover of '(Love Is Like a) Heat Wave.'"

Without the Vandellas assuring in the background *It's all right, girl / Ain't nothing but love, girl*, the song was just so much helpless thrashing. August turned it off.

At the first light August unbuckled his seat belt, lifted his ass, and dug his lighter from his back pocket. He cracked the window. In the backseat the head of Fred the Carriageless Horse.

He climbed Third Avenue, past the houses with sagging eaves lining the rim of Chevy in the Hole. Below him there were no factories, no people. A dark valley, a river chunked with ice. A clear lunar landscape, empty, stretching all the way downtown.

The last time August remembered coming through Chevy in the Hole this way, he was with his father. He was nine. His father had been out of work and on the couch for weeks. Beside the back door, grocery bags of beer bottles shifted and clinked. He'd been used to his father living another life on third shift, and so he didn't know how much his father hated him. Didn't like that he drew all over his homework, that he tied up the phone line calling for the time. When he saw Gus let Annie and her friend paint his toenails, he'd yanked him into the bathroom, told him to take that shit off, and Gus cried because he had no idea how. Soap didn't do anything, and he couldn't pick it off with his bitten and scraggly fingernails. Instead of just putting his socks back on his wet feet, covering it up, he'd had to knock blubbering on his sister's door and apologize and ask for her help.

But for a moment his father must have felt guilty. He took Gus for a bike ride. He remembered the sun on his father's bald spot on the descent, his shirt filling up with air; he was the fastest thing on earth. But then on the climb back out of Chevy in the Hole August fell farther and farther behind, alone in the ruin of the factory where his father used to work. At the bottom of the hole, where August was steering now, he stood there in the concrete and twisted rebar and wept. He didn't know how to get home. There was no one to ask. And when his dad circled back, looking for him, he was pissed off at August for falling behind, for being so small, and then angry at him for crying. They were alone. No one saw when his father hit him the first time, a smack across his wet face, or the second and third time, or when August lost count, when the shock of it was gone and all his father's pent-up energy came out of him too fast to stop. He was punching August in his chest and his belly, the way grown men hit each other on TV. Pushing him back down till the pebbles raked through his T-shirt and skimmed the skin from his back. The wind knocked out of him, and a film of tears spread between him and the sky.

That night Annie, who hadn't been there to help him, teased him till he threw his pizza at her. Sent the plate spinning. Knobs of sausage in her hair. His father yanked him up by the arm, so fast he couldn't see anything, only feel the force of it, sense the air around him and the burn in his socket and how his door was coming closer, and then his father was leaning over him, pinning him to the Teenage Mutant Ninja Turtles sheets, but he couldn't make out the words because his head was spinny and hot and he was bawling, which made it all worse. *What is wrong with you? Huh? The fuck is wrong with you now?*

And when his mother appeared, caught some purpling bit of skin, she pulled up his shirt to reveal the full evidence he was carrying. His father hated them, hated their life, their city, and he'd finally spelled it out on August's body.

August was too big to hold, so his mother gripped him to her, and that hurt, too, his skin tender and aflame. She called for Annie to get her shoes on. She dropped August's pillows from their cases and stuffed them with his clothes, pulled him by his hand to his sister's room to do the same thing. "I'm so sorry," she kept repeating on the drive to his mamaw's, crying so hard it scared him. He wanted to press himself through the upholstery. Run out into the night at the stoplight. He kept doing the wrong things, and it all kept getting worse, and everything was fragmenting, everyone hurt, the city blurring outside the car windows, just busted houses and empty factories.

August steered left, into the quiet and emptiness of Chevy in the Hole. Across the sweep of it the red eye of the weather ball, a promise of warmer weather August didn't believe. Why he had ever thought he could redeem himself here, and with love, of all things.

His feet tingled in the cold. He turned the radio back on to drive out his doubts and his craving for obliteration, turning it up louder.

Then, near the bottom of the Hole, past the Sit-Down Strike historical marker, past the ghost of his younger self struggling uphill on a bike after a father who didn't, or couldn't, love him, something crossed in front of August's headlights. He saw it out of the corner of his eye: a streak across the snow with a long tail behind it. He had just a second to make sense of it: some kind of animal, maybe a turkey or a pheasant, darting from the saplings of Chevy Commons.

August cranked the steering wheel. A reflexive mercy. The bird disappeared into the safety of Chevy in the Hole's reclaimed acres, but the tires hit black ice. The car fishtailed into a helpless circle, front tires jumping the curb, heading for the guard rail and the river below.

August slung forward, no seat belt on, the window still cracked open for cigarette smoke to curl through.

CHAPTER 21

1967

Myrna was watching television when Lester pulled up in his new Lincoln, his arm folded on the door and some girl group sha-la-laing on the radio. Royal blue with blue leather interior. He swung out with his trumpet case and headed for the neighbor's back door for band practice. They'd lost their younger son in Vietnam, and maybe in grief they figured to hell with everyone else on the street, let the thump of the drums rattle all the storm windows, let the trumpet blast like an alarm on this of all summers, when constantly the neighborhood was tensed for the worst.

The windows were open, and Myrna could hear Peter J & the Metros practice while she got herself ready. *Oh we've waited so long for our turn, honey*, Peter sang. She unlocked the back door and put the signal on the step—a pink flowerpot turned upside down—though she'd told Lester that Eamon and Rose would be in Florida, visiting his mother.

When she couldn't hear the trumpet anymore, she slicked on lipstick, fluffed her curls, and put on a dress. She was back in her size twelves from Obetrol and waiting tables. Since Eamon was going to drink through his promotion, she'd gone back to making her own money, same as when she met him. She resented everything but the taut line of her calves.

By the time Myrna stepped out of the bedroom, Lester had come in the back door, his trumpet case on the welcome mat and a box of records in crisp paper sleeves under his arm. When she saw him for the first time, she was hanging clothes on the line and he came out of the back door with his trumpet, his face glowing with sweat. He was twenty-three and looked a little like Frankie Avalon. He opened the spit valve into the grass and asked her favorite song. No one ever asked Myrna anything except what the soup and specials were. "Tears on My Pillow" was the answer. Little Anthony & the Imperials.

Lester's arms were around her, kissing her through a grin. "See those beauties?" A box of 45s sat on her kitchen table. Peter J & the Metros recorded their single at a little studio in Detroit, and, now they had it, Lester was convinced Berry Gordy was going to walk into Embers any night with fistfuls of cash. In the meantime, a couple of big-shot bands from England were playing that night at Atwood Stadium, and the Metros were opening for them. Myrna thought it was pathetic, but he'd just been promoted to foreman at the plant in Pontiac, and maybe being in a band was no different than being on a bowling league or building ships in bottles.

Lester didn't need to be congratulated anyway; his hands moved between kneading her sore breasts and stroking the curl out of her hair, and he was lifting her up onto the kitchen counter.

She waited until after, when he was looking at her in that syrupy way, to tell him.

"Oh, honey," Lester said, just like on the record. His eyes were so big and earnest, like a high school boy offering his letterman jacket. "Oh, honey, honey."

Myrna did up her dress. The box of records she didn't want sat ugly on the table. Engine Running Records. Detroit, Mich. Peter J & the Metros, "Our Turn."

"We'll get married," he said.

"I am married." She pushed her dress down to hide the stretch marks quivering on her thighs.

"But you're not *happy*," he said.

"I'm too old to be worried about *happy*." She righted the salt and pepper shakers and the napkins they'd upset. She straightened the rug with her foot.

Lester was behind her, pants still puddled at his ankles. He pressed his face into her hair and spanned her stomach with his hands. Eamon had a string of women on the line; she'd found the receipts for flowers she never received, the phone numbers, once even a creased picture of a woman draped over an old sofa with her bare behind smiling up at the ceiling. At first, she had thought, if he could have this, so could she. Then this pregnancy had fouled everything, forced her into choices she hadn't wanted to make. She listened to his murmured promises, let him draw the shape of the life she might have in the air of her kitchen.

"Come to the show tonight," he said. "Bring your things."

* * *

That night after she got off work, Myrna drove down Bristol Road, past the Chevy truck plant, to the Holiday Inn. The traffic seemed to move so slowly, all those people driving between the bars, pulling out of expensive restaurants, laughing and carrying on in their new cars. Earlier that summer people thought Flint was going to burn to the ground with Detroit, but for the time being everyone had gone back to having more money than they deserved, and for once Myrna didn't begrudge them. The city was doomed—let them stuff their faces and put their dimes in the jukeboxes.

It was the hormones, maybe, but all day she'd felt her confidence wobble. On break, she'd tried to compose the note to Eamon in her mind. *I have a chance to start over and I'd be a fool to let you keep ruining my life with your drinking and running around.* Still, each time she started to write, her eyes clouded with tears.

The lot at the Holiday Inn was full, and the sign out front said *Happy Birthday, Keith.*

Young people spilled out of rooms and milled around the pool, drinking on the lounge chairs and ashing their cigarettes into the potted ferns. Someone had upset a tray of pretty marzipan fruits, glistening with sugar, and they littered the tiles around the pool. It smelled like chlorine and marijuana, and all the women wore bright miniskirts and swinging earrings and wild swaths of eye shadow. Under the parking lot lamps they looked like exotic birds. And there Myrna was, nearing thirty in a shirt smelling of onions with her name stitched over the heart.

"I'm looking for Lester," she said to a man in a suit whose

eyes she'd caught sweeping over her, his mouth drawn into a tight line. "From the Metros. The trumpet player."

The man shrugged. "No idea, lady." He turned to a red-head with her breasts spilling out of a fringed top. Myrna pushed through the British accents and checked suits until she saw the neighbor's boy, his tie askew.

"Where's Lester?"

"Mrs. Molloy?" he said, but she could tell from his red eyes rolling loose in his skull that he wouldn't remember this later.

"Lester," she repeated. "Your horn player."

He pointed up the stairs, where more people were draped over the railing, beer bottles hanging from their hands like crystals from a chandelier. "Two-eleven," he said.

The door to 211 was open, and Lester and the Metros' unfortunate-looking drummer stood in their shirtsleeves, wearing those awful ties. Lester, bathed in sweat, looked like he'd just had a vision.

"I told my husband I'm leaving him," she said. It wasn't true, but it got the drummer to leave.

Lester gathered her up in his arms, crushing her into his cheap, sweat-soaked shirt, and though she didn't feel much like crying, she thought he'd like it if she made a show of letting him comfort her. She clutched the end of his hideous paisley tie. "We'll figure it out. Everything's going to be fine, honey." He pulled her down to the bed and kissed her, his mouth hot and beer-sour.

He fell back against the pillows. "You should've seen the show. Pete's been practicing these slides he saw the Temptations do on Ed Sullivan. The crowd just ate it up." Lester stood up. He looked absurd, jumping onto one foot and dragging the other across the carpet, and she told him so.

He gave her a wounded look. He looked like a pouting little boy.

"My nerves are just god-awful," she said.

"Ah, come on. We'll relax. Have a good time. We'll figure things out in the morning."

So she emptied her purse onto the cover, and Lester watched her sort through the tubes and lipstick bullets. She caught his face behind hers reflected in her compact. He kept turning to the door, and a pained impatience ticked in his jaw. She wasn't a woman in love in a hotel room with a husband in a jealous, passionate rage at home. Neither was she the girl who'd married a marine with his stories of Casablanca and Paris who bought her dresses and sweets from the best stores downtown. Not at all. She was just someone's knocked-up mistress with her Revlon.

Someone drummed on the door as they passed. "Hurry up, honey, I'll be down at the pool," Lester said, and closed the door behind him.

* * *

"This is Myrna," Lester said to men with woolly sideburns. "Lovely to meet you, darling," they said. "Brilliant party." Lester kept nudging her like she was supposed to be knocked out by these honest-to-God Europeans with their ridiculous band names.

Once in a while a mousy-looking thing in a pencil skirt came out from reception, swiveling her head at the scene, chewing her lipstick, before turning back in.

"Have you seen Keith?" everyone kept asking. Some of them laughed and some of them shook their heads, as though this Keith was a kid they'd wearied of disciplining.

"You only turn twenty-one once," someone said, gesturing toward the room on the second floor where the party seemed to be humming its loudest, and Lester laughed, "Hell of a guy," like this Keith worked at Chevy and played euchre with him on Fridays.

For a while she lost Lester to the crowd, and she hung back, ignoring the churn of her stomach with mouthfuls of marzipan. She considered leaving. Then he reemerged, throwing a heavy arm around her shoulder and guiding her to the parking lot. She pretended not to notice a couple necking in the backseat of a cherry-red Bel Air.

"I have a good feeling about this, Myrna," he said, letting someone's Buick support his weight. His eyes were pink, the whole of him drowning in liquor. "They're really impressed with us. Peter said he talked to the Who's manager about touring in England. He said our sound is really big over there. Northern soul, he called it. Isn't that funny? They don't even call it Motown over there. We could go to England."

"Well, that's nice for you," she said, and her heart fell into her stomach. She was only trying to get to Pontiac. "You just go to England and have yourself a hell of a time."

"I said *we*, Myrna. You could go with me. Take your little girl with us. Start over." He reached for her stomach—some gesture he probably saw on television—and she retreated.

She turned back to the party, Lester at her heels. She beelined back to the refreshment table and bypassed the marzipans, pouring herself a foul mix of rum and Vernors ginger ale. *Here's to you and England,* she thought, knocking it back. Lester looked sore and opened his mouth to begin again with all that talk of babies and running away, leaning into her, shouting into her ear to be heard over the party, and she started to wonder if maybe she could go to England. Just pack up with Rose and never see Eamon or the smokestacks of General Motors again. She let the thought expand. She could reduce some more and buy dresses at chic London department stores. She'd make friends with the other wives, raise this baby to say *biscuit* instead of *cookie* like Princess Margaret did on a television special she saw once.

But there was no time for any of this; above Lester and Myrna came a terrible gasp. She looked up to see Peter J stagger down to the pool, his eyes wide with shock. His undershirt was wet and smeared with frosting. Not fondant, but real fat-shiny buttercream. The crowd parted to fold him in.

"Keith Moon threw his birthday cake at us," he stammered.

Behind Peter, other bewildered victims followed. Girls with cake in their cleavage and clotted in their hair. A man with a shrimp tail emerging from his mop of hair like a question mark. Then came the sounds of breaking glass and women shrieking. Myrna couldn't tell if these girls were in distress or if they were just plain stupid.

"What's going on?" The mousy night clerk came out with a man behind her, stiff-haired and scowling. The poor clerk's eyes were wide behind her schoolmarm glasses. The man, probably her manager, kept repeating "Excuse me? Excuse me?" until, his question unanswered, he turned and left with the clerk close behind.

When the first wave of police sirens came shrieking toward the Holiday Inn, skinny girls clopped forward on their high heels, men with dope in their pockets disappeared around the building or into their cars. A boy emerged from the room upstairs, pushing through the crowd on the balcony and bolting down the stairs in nothing but his underwear. It was the first time Myrna had seen him, and she wouldn't have known him from Adam, but Lester said, "Jesus Christ, that's Keith—the drummer."

The drummer streaked past, scrawny and pale, blue and pink frosting from his big black eyebrows to his behind. Blue and red police lights swung over him. He skirted the pool, awful fast and determined for how drunk he must have been, and hurtled into the parking lot, darting through the cars.

Passports and licenses were extending when a Cadillac rolled out of the parking lot and into the crowd, heading toward the pool. Lester and Myrna pressed to the side of the hotel. Screaming women shuffled forward in their heels, though the car was only going a few miles an hour. Keith was behind the wheel, bare-chested and laughing. "Stop him!" someone shouted, but the Cadillac crept forward and then, just as slowly, tilted into the pool. There was a splash, and then the clunk of the fender hitting the bottom of the pool. The water was shallow enough that the party could see Keith Moon just sitting there behind the wheel, whatever he was exclaiming to himself muffled by the rolled-up window.

The crowd, police and all, stood there in gasping silence. Even Lester beside her was stunned and expressionless as they all watched Keith fumble with the door and push it open. He fell forward into the water, and three men waded in in their suits to make sure the poor fool didn't drown himself.

Before they got to him, though, he bobbed to the surface. His hair was slick, and the cake had washed away from his white and concave chest. He gripped the edge of the pool, his elbows pale angles. Through his soaked underwear Myrna saw the black crack of his ass. He squirmed onto his side until he could pull his legs out after him.

The whole crowd of them, all those women in their miniskirts, all those men, stood silent, watching. Even the police officers stood back, dumbfounded. A man offered a hand, but the boy yelled some gibberish, still creeping forward on his belly. Finally he staggered up to his feet and began to lurch forward, like some swamp creature out of a horror movie.

"Mr. Moon," one of the police officers said, stern and fatherly. Unlatched handcuffs swung from his hand.

Keith was advancing toward the marzipan fruits that had been strewn from hell to breakfast, and just like that he slipped on one. Fell face-first onto the tiles. Myrna heard his skull connecting with the ground. A few women screamed. She felt Lester shudder beside her, still clutching his driver's license. They watched the drummer lie there, still as death.

"Oh God," a girl howled behind her. "Oh God. Oh God."

But he pushed himself up, laughing, onto his elbows, his mouth gushing blood. "Whose fucking sweets are these?" he yelled. One of the men who'd tried to save him in the pool bent to lift him up by the arms, but he just flopped back to the tiles. He stayed down there, picking through the oranges, apples, and lemons on the tiles, and then he pushed one into his bloody mouth. "Gorgeous, this is," he said, and laughed through a mouthful of blood and sugar. One of his front teeth had been knocked out, and blood and drool dribbled down to his chin. He was still laughing when the police cuffed him and led him to the car, swaddled in a blanket like a newborn. What Myrna couldn't get over was how young he looked, and how he was probably the same age as Lester. How phenomenally stupid the whole thing was. Here she was, a whole woman, a mother, a wife, surrounded by flailing children.

A few girls knelt on the tiles and searched through the marzipans for his tooth. Lester ran up the stairs for his horn. She didn't follow him.

None of the cops stopped Myrna to ask who she was. Maybe because, in the dark, with her thick waist and her uniform, she looked like housekeeping. She sat on the stairs and watched the squad cars depart, then watched the tow truck slide the Cadillac out of the pool, water streaming from the grille, headlights cracked, fender hanging. Lester never came back, but she wasn't waiting for him anyway. When her sadness felt so big she couldn't stand it anymore, she walked down to the car Eamon bought with his employee discount. One of the girls at work would know whom to call, and she could pay for it herself. She'd take a couple of days, then she'd go see about a job for herself on the line.

*　*　*

Lester's box of records still sat on the kitchen table. There was no note there because Myrna never finished one. The house was dark, and Eamon's and Rose's suitcases had been left by the door. She could hear Eamon in the living room, on the phone. She stood in the door a moment, thinking about calling to him. Not his name, but what she wanted and didn't know how to ask for, or demand. *Divorce.* But she was so tired.

Through Rose's open door, some trick of light and shadow distorted the familiar angles of her daughter. Myrna went in and found her shorn: facedown on the pillow, her pale neck reaching out of her dirty clothes. The hair she'd given her daughter, buttery-blond and fine, chopped off. She felt around the pillow as if it had fallen off. She couldn't hear herself howling until Eamon came up the stairs and turned on the light.

"Oh, for Christ's sake, Myrna," he said. "It's just hair."

But Myrna was drowning. She couldn't pull any air into her lungs, and her eyes burned. She pushed past Eamon, shut herself in the bedroom. She slid to the floor, holding the door shut with her collapsed weight.

Through her sobs she could hear Eamon lying to Rose that it was nothing, that everything would be fine in the morning, that she looked beautiful. Myrna remembered when Rose was a baby, he'd get up with her, and Myrna would listen through the wall as he chattered to her like they were having a beer together. In the fragmented sleep of new motherhood, Myrna saw him as he was when they met, in his dress blues he'd worn to his father's funeral. In a closet somewhere was his sea bag with the names of cities inked on the side: Paris, Madrid, Seville, Casablanca, Tangier. When he told her stories, all the details of those far-flung places were superimposed over Flint in her imagination. Enough sand to cover Saginaw Street and fill in Chevy in the Hole, plugging up the Flint River and spilling out of the windows of the factories. A caravan of camels loping slowly up Chevrolet Avenue where cars were supposed to be.

CHAPTER 22

Monae dreamed of running through the Holiday Inn. She flung open doors into empty rooms, the hallways tunneling longer and twisting to mazes. When she found the lobby and was on the street, it wasn't Detroit she stepped into but Flint. She recognized the city, but she couldn't remember where they lived, and everyone was gone, all the houses empty. All the evacuated people had pushed their cars out into the river. Headlights and grilles and bumpers jutted out of the water like terrible fish. All morning, Monae kept seeing those cars in her mind as Bea watched the octopus-shaped rattle jiggling above her and sleet smeared the windows.

August had been gone three days. On the first, he dropped off a pallet of water at his mother's house and used her phone to call Monae, asked how the baby was, said no, he wasn't coming back to Detroit that night, he had a few things to do at home, and when she asked what, he said he had to go. And then he disappeared. Annie texted that she'd go by the house again when she got out of work. She'd called his work and was curtly informed that he hadn't shown up all week.

She rubbed Bea's belly through her onesie, tickled her so she gurgled and grunted. The white noise was off and music on, bright and brassy, to cover up Monae's devastation. She'd gone through every message and voicemail on his phone, including one from his mother, unopened and nearly two years old, that knocked the breath out of her. On his browser he'd left open one tab, an article about how Johnny Cash played his last full concert in Flint after he and June got stuck in the elevator of a downtown hotel now closed, and on another tab the YouTube video of the Peter J & the Metros song. She listened to it like it might have a message coded in it and cried while Bea napped. When she opened the door for housekeeping, she caught the sad look of Hiba, who didn't ask, because Monae already had plenty to cry about. That was the reason they'd been here nearly a month.

Monae put the rattle down. "Will you sit with me while I eat something? You ready, coney island baby?"

Monae pulled on one of her husband's sweaters. She'd packed up the rest of the room, left just what they needed for the night. Their bags were piled by the door. She'd tossed all the bananas into the trash basket and sat it out in the hall. Little in the room was August's, as if he hadn't left anything he might want to come back for. That was the best-case scenario: he just didn't want to be married to her anymore. The worst, she'd get a phone call from his mother, or the police, or a hospital, and then someone would come get her and Bea.

Monae slipped Bea's arms into her furry coat. Kissed her forehead and pulled her up onto her shoulder.

When the elevator opened on the first floor, she didn't feel like going outside anymore. It was cold, sunless, a high of twenty-nine. Her mother told her to eat and rest, but she had no appetite. August was gone, Monae had told her yesterday, matter-of-fact, rehearsed in the bathroom while the baby slept so she could wring the tears out of it. She waited for her mother to say, you should've known you were setting yourself up for a hard life, marrying a man with problems like that. Waited for her to ask, but didn't you see this coming? Didn't you know all the signs?

But she listened to Monae cry. "I'm calling Jim and we're coming down to get you now."

"Give me one more day," Monae said. One more day for him to return or for her to confront whatever she'd find at their house.

Instead of heading toward the front door, she walked to the empty pool and sat on a chaise lounge, pulling off Bea's mittens and unzipping her coat. She listened to the water lick against the tiles, the drain's gurgle.

A bachelorette party came in, a procession moving toward the hot tub, the bride spray-tanned and a novelty tiara balanced on her blowout.

They had water bottles with bright pink straws poking from them—poorly concealed cocktails they'd mixed in their suite. They bubbled and shrieked with laughter. They were in their midtwenties, maybe just a little older than Monae, and still she couldn't remember ever spilling herself into the space around her with so much bright, empty noise. She watched them take selfies, cheek to cheek, phones tilted over their heads.

Laughter sloshed out of the hot tub. One woman caught Monae looking and called, "She's *so* cute!"

Monae's phone buzzed with a Flint number she didn't recognize. She cleared her throat. Shifted Bea on her lap and fumbled with the screen.

As usual, not even a hello—Harold didn't have the time for that sort of thing, especially not in his office. "I spoke with your mother. I've been making some phone calls. I thought you might want to meet someone before I take you home."

"Uncle Harold, right now I can't—"

"Those letters you found," he said. Bea started to wriggle, and Monae pulled the rattle from her jacket pocket, pinning the phone to her ear with her shoulder.

The bridal party lifted from the hot tub, caped in towels, pedicures in flip-flops. As one paraded past she fluttered a hand to her heart and mouthed *adorable* at Bea.

Even after Harold explained, it felt like an elaborate hoax, or like further proof that Monae was in a bizarre dream from which she could not wake, with all those empty houses and submerged cars. She carried Bea back up to their room, pulled up the text Harold sent after he hung up. She dialed the number and asked for Goldie Byrdlong. She listened to the gravelly voice on the other end of the line pronounce, "You're Jay's girl." Monae's heartbeat slowed, and she suddenly felt the emptiness of her stomach and the ache of her face, swollen from weeping.

G for grandmother, August would laugh, this whole time, if only she could find him.

* * *

Harold had been to see Bea before they left Flint. "First baby I've held since you," he'd said, sitting in her living room while her husband, whom he clearly disapproved of, kept finding reasons to leave the room, fixing Harold a second cup of coffee he'd already declined.

Now Harold drove them across Detroit, Bea in a car seat he'd bought. He'd asked her twice if she was hungry. "Your mother was worried you weren't eating," he said. "She said you weren't sleeping much, either." Harold himself looked not so much thinner but deflated, like all the self-righteous pride and determination that puffed him up had leaked out. In the closeness of his car, the smell of his aftershave was comforting. He didn't bring up August, and she was grateful.

After they went to the nursing home, she was going back to Flint. He'd take her to her mother's, or to his house, if she wanted. He had plenty of space, he said.

"I have a home," she reminded him. But August hadn't gone to work again today, and Annie and his mother reported no sign of him.

"You're ready for this?" he asked. He'd pulled into the lot of Eastwood Convalescent Home on Grand Boulevard, a few blocks from the Detroit River, on a block of mansions repurposed for group living.

Monae was too tired for all this to register. Everything had spun out of focus. The government had poisoned her, and later she'd call the police and all the hospitals in Genesee County looking for her husband, and she had a secret grandmother in Detroit. Everyone had lied to her. But she got out of the car, bundled Bea in her arms, and followed her uncle inside.

A woman took them down a bright hallway to Goldie Byrdlong, who was, she chuckled, as if this was a joke they were in on, "something else." The hallways thrummed with white noise, a sound collage of oxygen machines and daytime television.

Goldie sat in a floral armchair, a skinny, ancient woman dressed for company in purple polyester slacks and a sweater with a brooch in the shape of a parrot with pearl eyes pinned to her breast. Her hair was a thin white dandelion frizz, and she'd drawn her eyebrows in waxy black. Her feet floated in loose leopard-print slippers. The only picture on the wall was of Barack Obama, hanging beside a calendar with illustrations of white women in full-skirted, red-lipped 1950s splendor with caustic captions. *Amazingly enough*, March said, *I don't give a fuck*. Unopened pudding cups, envelopes, and medication blister packs sat on the table beside her. The radio was tuned to an AM station playing Ella and Louis. "They Can't Take That Away from Me."

When she cleared her throat, it sounded wet and loose, like water sloshing in a glass.

Her uncle extended a hand. "Been a very long time," he said. Monae should have done the same, but instead she just stood there till Goldie told her to sit in the opposite chair. Monae handed Bea to her uncle. She watched his hand cradle the back of her head. Bea's fingers curled at the neck of his sweater.

There was some empty talk of the weather and the water. Harold talked about the protest while Monae and Goldie tried to make eye contact. Each of them settled on Bea.

"She's about the spitting image of your father. That face." Goldie squinted. "She look like her daddy at all?"

"Sometimes. Some faces she makes."

"He worth a damn?"

"I'm not sure anymore."

Goldie hummed with this information. She took a sip of her coffee, slurping it. She left a little of her lipstick behind.

"I bet it seems like you're the only person on earth who feels that way, but that's just what they do to girls. You don't look like you need him." She looked to Harold. "You agree?"

"They say no one's good enough for your daughter, and I suppose no one's good enough for your niece either."

It was the closest Monae'd had to a compliment from him. Whenever he indicated he approved of her, it was to someone whom it was advantageous for her to know. Someone who could help her need him less.

"It'd be nice for Monae if we could talk about Jerome." Harold cleared his throat.

"You and me met once at Cora's funeral. You couldn't have been four. I remember thinking you had my legs, just skinny little sticks, but it's hard to say with children, isn't it, can't tell till they're big, like you said." Her eyes flicked down Monae's legs crossed in front of her. "I'd say you got them."

"When's the last time you saw Jerome?" Harold asked.

"When he came home from the service. He used to come down and sit with me and listen to music. I think he couldn't stand much else." She folded her hands in her lap, all knuckle. "We didn't become friends, did we, when Cora brought him here. You were both still boys. He decided he hated me, and I couldn't say I blamed him. Then he started writing to me from the army. *In case I die over here, I guess I forgive you.* He didn't die, so we kept on writing. And when he got back, when he was drinking too much and not doing right by anybody, he started coming down here. Sometimes he didn't say anything. Just sat there, and I'd fix him something to eat." She looked at Monae.

Monae's eyes watered. The letters from G in the box at the Holiday Inn, waiting beside her suitcase and Bea's things.

"I hadn't heard from him in years. He had his own life, didn't he, and didn't I. Heart attack, was it?"

"Car accident," Harold said now, clearing his throat. Monae leaned forward to free a fistful of Harold's sweater from Bea's mouth, shiny with spit.

Goldie nodded. Maybe when someone was dead so long in your mind you couldn't get sad all over again about it. Maybe it didn't matter what had happened to her son, or maybe it was relief. She might've imagined something slower, crueler, a long suffering.

Bea gurgled and blinked at her great-grandmother's room, its colors, its particular light. In the quiet, Monae studied her grandmother's face and saw, beneath her father, herself. She would look like this someday. She had felt brittle and hollow, and she saw now a sturdiness. What she could endure.

"I think you should know your father forgave me. He knew I just wasn't suited to all this, and Cora did better by him than I could have. We understood each other, you could say. He was no grudge-holder. I loved him." She swallowed, reached for a glass of water.

Monae felt her uncle watching her. She was meant to respond, but it all felt so far away, like she was back on the hotel bed watching TV.

Goldie curled her skinny fingers around a few fat manila envelopes, wrinkled, the letter *J* scrawled across each of them. "Cora used to send me pictures of him, back when he was little. I figured you might want them." She looked at Harold. "Some of you in them, too."

Monae's fingers trembled. Inside, she found her father in a grainy late-fifties baby photo, then a toddler moving from black-and-white rooms into colored ones, Christmas trees, pastel Easter suits, an army uniform.

"Those letters from the army are in there, too. He wasn't really a writer and neither was I, frankly. They're in there, anyway."

"Why did everyone know this but me?" Monae asked. The envelope fluttered in her hand. With the other she reached a hand to Bea, gripping her foot.

Harold started to say something, but Goldie had an answer ready. "I think I hurt your father bad, and he didn't want me hurting you. He already gave you a grandmother, and Cora deserved to have you."

Harold murmured something to the baby. Monae's throat thickened.

"You didn't need me," Goldie said. "I don't blame you if you're mad. When Harold called me and told me where you were, I figured you were ready to hear bad news. I bet this doesn't mean that much to you right now."

Monae was too stunned, too tired, to cry or be angry. By the time they stood to go, and Goldie said, "If you think up questions for me, I'm no stranger to you," she was just sleepwalking to the car, her uncle opening the door, the baby secured.

Monae sat in the back beside her, one hand steadied on the car seat. It took a few blocks of silence, the drizzle on the windows of Harold's very clean car, before she seemed to float back into her own skin. Beside Bea, she pulled the pictures out of the envelope one by one. "Your grandpa Jerome," she explained to her. "That's your Jae, Beatrice Jae." Squeezed her soft-booted foot, fingers reaching inside her leggings to feel the reassuring softness of her skin. "You'll look like him because you're going to look like me."

Her heart was beating like a bird's. "Where are you going?" she asked her uncle.

"Back to the hotel. We'll finish packing you up."

"Let's go somewhere. Take us somewhere. We haven't seen anything." She didn't want to be back in that room. She didn't want to go back to Flint and what she'd find there. There was too much to process, too much moving too quickly, and she wanted to keep moving with it.

* * *

Harold drove them over the bridge to Belle Isle. Early afternoon, late March, the sky was a washed-out rag over the Detroit River, and the trees were bare. A freighter slowly crossed. "Used to come here on dates when I went to Wayne State," Harold said, pulling into the aquarium lot. He pointed to a domed glass building, like an ornate birdcage. "I had my heart broken by a library science major in the conservatory. Thought I was going to marry her."

"Then I guess we have that in common now," Monae said, lifting the baby from her seat. "We're both failures who got dumped in Detroit."

"You haven't failed anything," Harold said with a rare softness. She walked ahead.

The aquarium was one long, arched room of algae-green tile and hanging globes of light. On one wall a map of Michigan and the Great Lakes explained that the state took its name from the Ojibwe word *mishigami*, meaning "great water." On the opposite side of the room was an exhibit stuffed with plastic water bottles and trash, warning of the damage being done.

Monae read the signs to Bea, pointed out the fish as they

moved along the silver rail, stopping at each display. Her uncle trailed them, a few fishes behind, bent to his phone. Monae made one of her hands a pretend piranha mouth and chomped at her daughter's belly. "Look at the white bass. He looks like a moldy potato with eyes." She kissed her daughter's head through her bear hat. "That lungfish is a homely old snake."

"Miss," the woman at the front desk called to her. "Are you wearing nail polish?" When Monae stared, she repeated the question. Monae shook her head.

"That's a shame. He loves it. The lungfish. If you put your fingers on the glass and you're wearing a pretty color, he'll come right up to you."

The idea was absurd. Nail polish. She couldn't imagine caring about anything so stupid and small. She tried to remember the last time she'd painted her nails, and it couldn't have been the night before her wedding, but maybe it was. She'd bought blue nail polish from CVS in a last moment of superstition, and her mother painted them at the kitchen table of her new apartment in the suburbs. "I used to do this when you were tiny," she said. "Your dad just threw a fit about it. Let her be little, he said. Same thing when I got your ears pierced at the mall." It was spring, the farm's first season was underway, and already her fingers were calloused, the cuticles shredded. Her mother's hands trembled a little from the medicine, and the polish drifted. Monae forgot to clean it up before she went to bed, and when the ring went on, she saw that first, the imperfect streak of cornflower blue on her skin, before she saw the hand that was sliding it on, what had seemed so important and then was so quickly forgotten.

Monae stopped in front of the Texas cichlid. The males,

the placard informed them, could be identified by their pronounced foreheads. *The forehead bulge swells up on male cichlid fish around mating time.*

She started to say something to her daughter—"There's the Gus Molloy of fish"; "Beware a man with a lot on his mind"—and then she noticed the fish's blue lips.

Way down in Gus's voicemails, she'd found an unlistened-to message from his mother, the first of May, 2014. There was a staticky pause, then Rose said, "Your sister called me, sweetheart." It started to falter. "Gus, why are you doing this again? Why?" Then it broke apart. A full minute of sobbing until his mother gave up trying to form words, and the message ran out.

Monae couldn't support the weight of her body anymore. The bench was too far away. She lowered herself to her knees, Bea gripped to her shoulder. She didn't want to think about the fish, so she tried to imagine her father, young, in his dog tags and his natural, walking up his mother's front stairs. She hadn't asked where in Detroit Goldie had lived then. If she had another family. What she did. She tried to imagine the pulse of music on the other side of a closed door. Her father arriving at a kind of home.

"Miss?" Monae heard the lungfish lady call. She shook her head. She was fine. Bea was fine. They just couldn't stand. She was tired, and Bea was too small to support herself. They just needed a minute here, on the tile.

"Deep breath," her uncle said, then with his arm around her, he was guiding her out of the aquarium, back to his car. He was fastening her baby, crying now, into the new, plastic-smelling seat, and Monae was standing there in this winter that wouldn't let go, her skin quivering off her bones. Inside the open car door was her baby, her sick baby, their baby, who smiled like him when he was saying something he thought was funny, something he was getting away with, but who'd look more like her, who looked like her dad, who looked like her grandmother.

Harold pulled Monae into a hug like he was learning how, his arms stiff, his hand too tight on her shoulder. "Breathe," Harold was saying again, and she felt his chest rise against hers, his soft belly puff out, demonstrating how that elemental task was done. "I'm taking you to your mother's," he said, and she shook her head against his shoulder, his nice scarf scratching her face. His arms felt so solid. Over his shoulder she could see her daughter, safe and secure, marveling at her own tiny hands.

CHAPTER 23

"Who's there?" Annie shouted through the locked door to her apartment in a voice braced for bad news. According to the Methodist church, it was two o'clock in the morning.

"It's me, goddammit, come on."

The locks clicked open, and Annie stood there in her pajamas, staring stunned at her brother, back again from the dead. Rita appeared behind her, tying the belt of Annie's robe. He pushed past them to the bathroom and bent over the sink. He soaked a washcloth and held it to his throbbing face, too relieved to notice if the water smelled, if it was yellow or brown. From his nostrils to his chest was a wash of blood. The car had crumpled into the guardrail, and his face slammed into the steering wheel. There'd been a rush of stars, then a burn. A crack ran down one lens of his glasses.

He hadn't seen Rita in over two years, and when she came into the bathroom at first, he saw the mint-green robe on an unfamiliar shape and thought of scrubs. He remembered the questions nurses asked in emergency rooms. He was twenty-eight. It was the end of March, or maybe it was April now. Rick Snyder was still some-fucking-how the governor. He didn't want to die; he'd just bought the wrong house for a woman and a baby who deserved someone and somewhere so much better and he didn't know what else he could do to undo the damage, to give them something to start over again, without him if it was best, if it was what she wanted.

Annie was behind Rita, and then her hand was on his back. "Hey," she said, her voice low and gentle, as if waking him from a bad dream. "Who do we need to call, Gus?"

"A tow truck," he said.

* * *

At the bottom of Chevy in the Hole, they pulled everything from August's car into Annie's. Shards of headlight and plastic studded the ice. There was no sign of whichever animal he'd spared.

"What is all this stuff?" Annie's coat was unbuttoned over her pajamas, hair falling in her face. There was Fred the Carriageless Horse in Bea's car seat. August had swaddled it in a blanket, but it had shifted in the crash. Its big eyes stared out.

"Some stuff Mo asked me to take down to Detroit."

"Tonight? She needs a box of CDs and her creepy donkey head?"

"It's a horse." His frustration was amplified by the emptiness of Chevy in the Hole sprawling around them. He was shouting at her. "It's got sentimental fucking value and you don't fucking know, all right?"

Annie stopped, standing beside her open trunk. He watched

her pull open the box she'd just set down. A bilingual Speak & Spell chirped, "El Pájaro!"

The lights of the tow truck flashed at the top of Chevy in the Hole and lowered toward them. His sister tried to figure him out.

"Let's just take this to your place." He was pleading now. "Come on. Let's just fucking take this there."

"But Gus, why would we do that?"

Were he less exhausted, if he were in less pain, he might have thought of something. There was no way for her not to see it: the house kicked apart, the upturned drawers and emptied shelves. The rest of what was worth salvaging heaped by the door.

But he gave in to it. From Annie's passenger seat he watched the tow truck pull his car out. They drove to his house. He went upstairs with the first box, and when he came back down, he found her in his kitchen, her face slack and staring, a water bottle she'd picked up off the floor in her hand, broken glass under her boots. There were no excuses for the gas cans on the table, or at least he had no energy to search for them. When his sister said, "You're coming with me or I'm calling an ambulance," he submitted.

* * *

They passed Annie's apartment, kept heading west, and August thought for sure that the grand finale of this shitstorm would be a pajama-clad intervention at his mother's house. They could take him to the hospital. They could drug test him right now. He had never clawed this hard at sobriety, had never craved so badly to disappear from himself. But Annie passed the turn onto his mother's street, and they were driving in silence along the big-box store neon on the edge of town. A coney island sign assured WE SERVE DETROIT WATER where the specials should've been.

"Where are we going?"

She didn't say anything. He asked again. "Annie," he said. "Anneliese. Annie."

"I can't be alone with you," she said. "Just please shut up."

They passed the I-75 ramp and pulled into IHOP, the only restaurant open. Inside, a fake fireplace burned and "Billie Jean" followed "Working for the Weekend" on the speakers. It was four in the morning, and they were the only customers. August tried to ignore the waitress in her red button-down and name tag, staring at his bloody face as he lowered himself into the booth.

"Are you in trouble?" Annie asked after she'd ordered coffee for both of them.

"In trouble?" he repeated. "Am I eight years old?"

"Are you using?" And when he shook his throbbing head, staring bitterly away from her at the row of empty identical booths stacked with identical specials cards and syrups, "How long?"

"I'm not."

"There's no use lying. This can't get any worse."

"I said I'm fucking not."

"When's the last time you talked to Monae?"

"I don't know. Earlier."

"Earlier today or earlier in the marriage you're destroying?"

The waitress arrived with their coffees and asked if they were ready to order. Belgian waffles, please, Annie said, and after August said just the shitty coffee was fine, his head turned away from the waitress to obscure his face he hadn't cleaned, Annie said, "Oh no, my little brother's going to prison for insurance fraud and arson, bring him something special. This thing with the sprinkles." She clacked the plastic-coated menus back against the wall.

"The cupcake pancakes?" the waitress asked.

"Please," Annie said. Then to her brother, "Monae wanted to report you missing. Her uncle's down in Detroit with her. Honestly, I was the one who said there was probably no point, that you were probably fucked up somewhere. They don't put out an APB every time some asshole abandons his family. I don't remember a manhunt for Dad."

"You have no fucking idea what this is like."

"So you always say. But somehow I'm always the one that ends up with you."

"Because I was near your house. I knew you'd pull this—"

"You came to me because this is what you always do, because you know you can guilt me into keeping your secrets and figuring your shit out for you." Her voice rose over Morris Day and the Time. The napkin dispenser crossed the table to him; his nose was bleeding again. A fresh slickness on the dried blood and snot already crusted into his unshaven face. The change in the temperature, maybe. He held a fistful of napkins under his nose. At the front of the restaurant the waitress looked away, pretended to be on her phone.

"I used to feel sorry for you. Then when Mo came along I was happy for you—you never gave enough of a shit about yourself, or Mom, or me, but I thought maybe she gave you a reason to quit feeling sorry for yourself. And then Bea. But." There was a catch in her throat and she turned her head from him, her face scrunching as if in deep contemplation of the row of flavored syrups. "What do you want, Gus? You want to go wake up Mom so she can apologize to you for the thousandth time? You want to drum up an angry mob and burn Lansing to the ground? Do you—"

August watched his sister's mouth and her nose and her eyes all distort, her face wrecked. Watched her shake her head as she wept. If he felt guilty for this, he would have said, "I'm sorry, I'm sorry, stop, I'm sorry," but this was about someone else.

The waitress circled with coffee refills, asking Annie and Annie only, "Are you okay?" Annie forced a smile behind the napkin she was blowing her nose with and said, "Long night. Long state of emergency. Probably for you, too." After a few steadying sips, August watched her pull out her phone from the coat she was still wearing over her pajamas. The only name he could make out upside down was his wife's. Or he couldn't, really, but knew it was her because he could see a photo of his daughter on the Holiday Inn bed, a few messages back.

At Annie's apartment, she'd thrust her phone at him and told him to call, and he said no, there was no point waking her up. "No one who knows you," his sister snapped, flinging the phone at him, "is getting a great night's sleep right now." The phone missed him and bounced to the carpet.

The waitress returned, setting their plates down. She leveled a wary glance at August and left them.

August stared down at a pile of sprinkles. His nose dripped a dollop of blood onto the whipped cream.

"Just take me home," he said. "I'll fix this. I won't do anything." But she was tapping a message onto her phone, and when she looked up at him again, it seemed she was waiting for him to explain. The sentences that started to form—*Don't you worry that because of Dad I—I bought her this house and I buried them in it*—all dissolved. It was possible Annie was always the one he turned to, the one whose number he offered, because she was the only one who'd borne witness to all of him. When their mother was working three jobs, when she got calls from school offices—Gus didn't show up again, Gus nodded out in class—it was always a crisis, an emergency, an occasion for her to cry and go through all the ways she'd failed him. Annie was the only one who all-the-way knew him and still mostly liked him, or at least liked to tell him what to do, which he both resented and desperately wanted.

He dropped his head into his hands. All of him was slick, every orifice seeping. He added another napkin to the wadded pile rising like strange coral from the booth.

The waitress approached to check on them, and he stood up, gesturing for his sister to give him her phone. He took it to the bathroom.

There was blood on his T-shirt and the lapels of his coat. His eyes were red from sleeplessness and a jewel of blood bubbled in his nostril. His breaths echoed down the tile.

He scrolled through her phone for the pictures and videos he'd sent to her from Detroit. He had a group thread with his mother and sister; for a while, fatherhood had made him a better correspondent. There was Monae walking through the Eastern Market stalls with the baby on her back, thick stalks of Brussels sprouts and flowers rising around them. Bea and Monae in the blue shallows of the Holiday Inn pool, Bea padded in orange floaties and puffy with diaper.

He scrolled back to their first week in the hotel, where he

found the video he wanted. Monae would've been embarrassed if she'd known he sent it, but at the time it had seemed important to share. Like it proved something.

In it, Monae was cross-legged and barefoot on the bed, Bea propped on her knee. At the end of the bed August had the eye of his smartphone steadied on them. They were going to send this to Aretha somehow, a tribute, a thank-you.

Monae sang "I Say a Little Prayer." She swayed, fingers curled around Bea, who didn't squeal but didn't resist. Her eyes were her mother's, round and bright, watching him.

Together forever, that's how it must be
To live without you would only mean heartbreak for me.

Then Monae's eyes flicked up to the camera, and the song dissolved in laughter. A look on her face like she'd been suddenly caught in her own happiness, remembered an old self-consciousness. "Keep going," August said behind the camera. "It's glorious." She bent to kiss their daughter. "Tell Daddy uh-uh," she said. The video ended. Just a few seconds. In the IHOP bathroom, he held a wad of soaked paper towel to his burning face and played it again.

August paused the video a moment. He expanded the image with his fingers. Monae looked clearly, unquestionably delighted. She looked like she trusted him. August kept replaying the video, pausing and enlarging the image of his family with his fingers, till their faces filled the frame. You could only see how happy they were. How blessedly ordinary it looked, like they could be in a Holiday Inn commercial, or one of those Pure Michigan tourism ads, Monae and Bea between shots of rolling sand dunes and lighthouses. You couldn't see the question mark hanging over their daughter. You couldn't see what they'd been through, couldn't feel the knot of love and guilt and terror in the man holding the camera. You didn't question their joy, or all the good that was ahead of them.

When he lowered himself back into the booth, Annie didn't say anything. The cook had come out and was sitting with the waitress at a booth, watching them. There was a bright spatter of blood on August's untouched pancakes, a trail across the table. His chest felt tight, and he tipped his head back in an attempt to pull the pressure from his nose.

He could pull his hat down over his eyes and curl up in the booth. He could crawl under the table and sleep for just a minute or two on the industrial carpet. He pushed his fingers under his cracked glasses and pressed on his eyelids till watery streaks of white and gray stitched across his vision. He sensed Annie get up and settle beside him. She fished ice cubes out of his water with a fork and wrapped them in a handful of napkins. One hand held his head still. The other pressed the ice against his nose.

"I guess I'll take you home," she said. He waited for the ultimatums, the appointments he needed to make, the self-reflection the situation called for, the sweeping changes. When they didn't come, when a ride home was just that, he said, "Thank you."

"Whenever I worry about Bea I remember she's got two parents who love her, and that's twice what we had."

The ice was melting against the heat of his face, water seeping through the napkin and down into his mouth. "One of them's me."

"Then work on your shit so you can be better at loving her."

"I thought I'd worked out my shit. I thought shit was old news."

"Nobody's shit's ever really done with them, Gus. Every-one's figuring out new strategies for confronting their shit. All the time."

"Can I get you some boxes?" he heard the waitress ask.

"You know what, yeah," Annie said, putting down the ice. "We'll take this biohazard with us."

August cracked his eyes open. The colors and shapes of this anywhere restaurant had resettled. He'd go home and sleep, and he'd stitch the house back together. Somehow he'd get back to Detroit.

Annie's phone on the table lit with an incoming call from Rita. She flipped the screen to the table.

"Rita bring you some water from Chicago or is she finally back to pick up her record player?"

"You of all people should appreciate a secret romance." She wiped her wet hand on his coat sleeve.

* * *

In the unlit room, beneath the quote from Isaiah, there was his wife on the sofa, still wearing her coat with his *Qua-drophenia* T-shirt underneath it. She was the still point in a tumbling mess. She'd picked up a cracked devotional candle, St. Lazarus, and it sat on the coffee table beside the head of Fred the Carriageless Horse, freed from its swaddling blanket. He wanted to curl fetal with his heavy head in her lap and weep. Instead he stood in his own doorway, holding her gaze through cracked glasses, bloodied and open in the chaos he'd made.

"I took Bea to my Mom's. I didn't know if it was safe here. Annie said you wrecked the car on Chevrolet. Where were you going?"

He started where it made the most sense. "I've been trying to figure out how to get you out of here. I was going to store some things."

"And you stranded us so you could make that decision. So you could take my home and my work from me."

"I'm trying to fix this for you and Bea."

"Did you ever ask me what I want? Wouldn't that have been easier?" Then, "August?"

He tried to remember if he had. He couldn't untangle now what he thought and what she told him; what had happened to them and what had been distorted by fear and rage and confusion. She kept repeating his name, and her voice was low, even tender, as if Bea were asleep on the other side of the wall, and he couldn't tell if this was forgiveness or pity. If she was sitting there in her coat because she was going to get up and leave.

"I don't know," he said. His voice broke apart like a plate flung at a wall. Nearly two years and he hadn't cried in front of her. Even when she was pregnant and she kept reading things about stillbirths and defects. He'd leave the room. Long walks up the river trail, through Chevy, his headphones on. Not the Bible but dumb pop songs to drive out the noise, cover it over with pleasant gibberish.

"I'm sorry," he said.

"Sorry for what?"

He couldn't talk. His throat felt full, like his lungs were filling with water. He gestured at everything around them. The glass and the Bible verse and the sun just sparking on the Flint River on the other side of the window.

"What are you sorry for?"

"I'm the worst thing that's ever happened to you. You'd

have gotten out of town with your mom. You're all I wanted, and I fucked up everything for you. The insurance money would give you something. You could go where you wanted."

"Where do you think we would go, without you?"

He'd been trying to get away from himself for most of his not-quite-thirty years, and yet he couldn't say.

"You told me that me and Bea were proof God wanted you to be happy. You don't believe that anymore."

"It's really hard to believe I've got a father somewhere who loves me unconditionally. That's the bottom-line thing you have to believe in, you know. Some guy just watches you fuck up over and over and knows your heart and loves you for it, and everything makes sense in the end."

"You know what I believe?" Monae said, and he wasn't sure he did. "I think you decide on someone and somewhere and that devotion is the sense it all makes. You choose someone and you try your best for them. I'll take it if there's more, but that's enough for me. That's the way I love you. That's the way I love this place."

There was a surge of relief like a hit, his muscles releasing. He wanted to lie down in it. He wanted to sink to the floor with his head in her lap. But she stood. "Come on," she said, and he followed her up the stairs.

* * *

Monae ran the bath, tipping in the lavender salts her mother had given her at her baby shower in a little pampering basket. There were filters on all the faucets, and if you believed the state, then the water was fine for everything but drinking. If you believed the news, it would take five years to replace all the pipes in Flint, and that was if you believed they'd be replaced at all. Monae got in first, submerging the lightning bolts of stretch marks across her hips and breasts and belly. She watched him pull his bloody shirt over his head. He folded his glasses on the sink. A little lavender-scented water sloshed over the sides when he got in. There was more of her than there'd ever been, and he'd worn himself so thin.

She held him by the chin and inspected him, pulling clots of dried blood from his sideburns, his beard. Flicked it away with her wet fingers.

There was a bottle of water beside the sink, and she angled for it. She upended it over his head. Water beaded in his eyelashes and the purpling skin beneath. A droplet quivering on his cupid's bow she pressed away with her thumb, and he winced as her hand moved down his face. A pain he tried to ignore. Imperceptible, maybe, if she wasn't so close.

She pushed the wet hair from his forehead. He kissed her. A brush of a kiss from a swollen face. A kiss that wanted a deeper, reassuring kiss back that it was too embarrassed to ask for. Instead, she resettled with her back against his chest. His arms circled her, then ranged the differences in her body, the new shape they made together. Her shoulder blades sank back into his chest. Below the water, his arms crossed over her belly. The sun was up, slanting over the tile. They stayed that way till the water grew cold. She opened the drain with her toes.

They went to bed, dripping bathwater all over. The water from his hair mixed with the damp on her face, puddled between her breasts, made their fingers slippery when they laced so that they gripped tighter. On the mirror above the dresser a verse from Song of Solomon: *Flowers appear on the earth; the season of singing has come.*

"Does this hurt?" he whispered when she gasped into his neck.

It did, but only in the way she'd prepared for. Only in the way she knew would pass.

EPILOGUE

2022

August and Bea sat on their knees on the sofa, elbows propped on its back, looking out the window as diggers in their yellow vests and hard hats uprooted the old pipes. A giant yellow claw dipped into the earth. The machines rattled the windowpane at the end of Bea's nose.

August kept checking his phone and repeating, "We're running late, bumblebee," and not moving. "Your mom's gonna be here any minute." They were going to church.

Monae had gone to the other house, and she was coming back to pick them up. With a grant, they'd knocked down the yellow house across from the park where Monae had grown up, and soon they'd have another place that wasn't a farm but a community garden. There were plans on the refrigerator: permits, sketches of the lot, potential names. Our Turn Community Garden was circled and starred and question marked.

Finally, August stood. He gestured with his coffee cup toward the men on the other side of the window. "So we're running a few minutes behind. These guys were supposed to be here five years ago." He upended the plates into the sink and handed her a dinosaur-shaped vitamin and rattled a few pills out of orange bottles for himself. They stuck their tongues out at each other. He followed her out the back door, the air buzzing with the diggers.

Carriageless Horse Farms had expanded into the adjoining lots. The rows multiplied, and maple and apple saplings reached up behind the greenhouse. Chickens, illegal, strutted over ground waiting for new seeds. August called them the anarchists, enemies of the state of Michigan. In the summers when Aunt Annie and Aunt Rita came up from Chicago, they called them the Myrnas, named after one of her other grandmothers, like Goldie, who had gone to heaven and whose ashes they'd scattered on Belle Isle while the freighters cut through the water and music played from their car, the windows down. Her mother had explained what death meant, and though she said it was a nice thing—you went to a place where you had everything and everyone you needed—on the riverside she'd pressed her face into August's chest for a moment and then bent to scoop Bea into her arms, stroking her curls.

After church they were going to the beach. It was finally warm enough to swim. And so they went to the back shed, where they kept the boat they'd built.

It had started with the barrels overflowing with water bottles. After school in the fall and winter, when the farm slowed to root vegetables and Monae took her grad school classes, Bea went into the shed with him, warm from the electric heater and spilling music. Some of the bottles were crumpled, the adhesive long dried up, rims caked with dust. Some of them had bugs and cigarette butts and dirt inside, like terrariums, and August held them up for her to see—cicadas and Japanese beetles—before tipping the bottle outside.

The blueprints and the instructions were tacked to the wall. The bottles bundled together, secured with zip ties and garden mesh, a plywood platform fastened on top. He steadied her while she stood on her knees on the stool, so that she could see it, too. "You use Archimedes's principle to figure out how many water bottles you need. 'A body immersed in a fluid is buoyed up by a force equal to the weight of the displaced fluid.' Big-time, right? It'll be the greatest engineering marvel since the carriageless horse."

While August knit together the bottles with zip ties and mesh, he spun stories of all the places they'd go. The river would take them through Chevy Commons and they'd dock there. Grandma Rose would pick them up and take them to the Korean grocery store for lychee gummies and banana milk, and then they'd get back on their raft and keep going, all the way to Saginaw, then Bay City, and it would be the Fourth of July so fireworks shimmered overhead. Sometimes they docked on the shores of Lake Huron, caught fish and grilled them, and split a can of beans, two forks in the same can, and called her mother so she didn't worry.

Someday he could add the water bottle raft to the farm's online offerings and give tours from the river, pointing out all the places white men got rich in Flint a hundred years ago and all the ways people like her mother and the people from the growers co-op and the farmers market had tried to repurpose the space they left behind. Her mother once gave tours at the history museum, and she could be the tour guide.

Monae had found the project less exciting. "You told me you took those bottles to the recycling center," she said. It was just a raft, he insisted. "A raft of our suffering you think you're going to launch on that horrible river, from in front of my house."

So there wasn't a fleet yet. Only the one boat, ready on its side.

But the truck tires crunched up the drive and Monae stepped out, her belly round with a new baby, and she smiled when Bea held up her shirt to show the swimsuit beneath her T-shirt. They packed a cooler of snacks while August strapped the boat onto the roof.

They turned onto the main road, the diggers and the old pipes and the new pipes behind them. He turned the radio on and put *Bebe* where baby was supposed to go in the words. Her mother watched the rearview mirror for a cascade of water bottles. At a stoplight, she pressed a laugh behind her hand when she caught the people in the next car gawking, and August said, "Jealous."

* * *

On Bluebell Beach, her dad stood with his hands on his hips, his white fish belly gleaming in the sun, and gave his daughter a geography lesson while her mother rotated her, her fingers working the sunscreen down the backs of her arms.

Mott Lake, her dad explained, where they stood, connected to the Flint River, which rolled on to Saginaw Bay and Lake Huron, which was a Great Lake, as she of course knew, and lapped the shores of Canada. His thumb out and fingers pressed together to form the lower peninsula's mitten, he traced the river over his right hand, up to the crook between forefinger and thumb. With his left hand he gestured inexactly to the mass of Canada floating right of his hand. If their vessel proved seaworthy—riverworthy, Great Lake–worthy—they could end up in Ontario.

"If you two end up in Canada," her mother said as she rubbed lotion into the crease of skin beneath Bea's butt, "you just start a new life for yourself over there and pray I don't find you. There'll be no saving you, August Molloy."

She patted her daughter's behind. "Stay inside the state line, please." She held up her own map of Michigan. Clarified, "Lower Peninsula."

Bea's father tossed his glasses onto their blanket. He threw her onto his shoulder, and she scrabbled for a grip on his sunscreen-greased neck. "Come on," he goaded Monae, who said, "I'm having no part of that thing." He took off toward the water.

At first Bea couldn't see the water but she heard it, splashing under her father's feet, then as it whooshed up his body, swallowing his hairy legs, his knees. She couldn't make out her mother's face anymore, only the black orbs of her sunglasses beneath the brim of her hat.

Then Bea felt his shoulders give way beneath her, and water engulfed her, cold and surprising. Her head was the last part of her submerged, and the whole world—Flint, her mother and father, the empty beach, the gulls pecking through the trash cans along the path—was gone. Only the water and its utter silence. When it came back, it was all brighter, louder. She blinked and sputtered. Her father said something, but she had to shake the water out of her ears, and then he picked her up and tossed her back in.

After she'd practiced headstands and rode her father's back

till he wheezed, "All right, Beebs, that's all I got in me," they went back to the car for the water bottle raft. He waded the raft out, dropping an anchor he'd made with a rope and a milk jug filled with sand, then held it still while Bea climbed on. She felt the water pushing up beneath her, buoying her. Her father walked the raft out, the rope of the anchor uncoiling, and then he heaved himself on. The boat rocked with his weight, and Bea gripped the sides of the plywood. The sun moved over the crinkled plastic.

"Well, dammit, Bebe, we're boatwrights," he panted. "Plenty of room out here," he called back to the beach, then hissed to his daughter, "Help me out."

Bea yelled for her, too, feeling down for the air at the bottom of her lungs like she'd learned in mindfulness class. Her mother stared back behind her sunglasses, unmoving. Her father waved wildly. *Mommy, Mom, Mom, Come out with us, Mom*, Bea howled, until finally, her mother stood, Ziploc bags of chopped vegetables and fruit slices in one hand, the sunscreen bottle in the other. She tossed the bags onto the deck first, then offered her arms to be pulled up. "This is ludicrous," she said, but she laughed when the raft drifted from her and she splashed back into the water. "Just let me do it myself," she said. "You're messing me up."

Monae lay on her back with her knees up. "Now neither of you say another word to me. Give me peace," she said, but her father was laughing, and her mother lifted a hand and smacked his wet, fleshy belly.

Her mother took off her sunglasses and handed them to Bea. She resettled her head on her husband's lap. Bea slipped the sunglasses onto her face: the seagulls pecking through the trash cans now a more shadowed and sinister bird, tumors of rust on the playground equipment, the pavilion empty.

"Swim, boatwright," her dad said. He pointed to the sunglasses and then to his own eyes. Bea slid them over his face, stabbing him with the arm before successfully tucking it behind his ears. Her mother watched, shading her eyes with her hand.

Bea took a big gulping breath and dove. This time she made herself look. She imagined dog skeletons and sunken cars, submerged bottles with messages folded inside them. This was where the river emptied out, ended, and the river was dirty, the river was full of all the bad things. Instead she saw only water, sand-spangled and bright with sun.

When Bea came up, they'd resettled on the raft, her mom's head nestled on her father's shoulder, one hand splayed over his heart. Without the sunglasses, Bea could see her mother's eyes, watching her. She waved, so they knew she was fine, then she plunged back down again, propelling herself forward.

ACKNOWLEDGMENTS

I was blessed to have people who believed in this book: Jonathan Freedman saw my rage and reminded me of what I could do with it; David Wanczyk sharpened my sentences and showed me how to write about shitty cars; Betsy Teter gifted me the time to write. My agent, Chris Bucci, had an unwavering faith in this book in all its Vernors and rock 'n' roll. My editor (and fellow Midwesterner), Caroline Zancan, lifted up the joy and the grief in this story and made me a better writer. Thank you to the team at Holt: Molly Bloom, Jane Elias, Kenn Russell, Vincent Stanley, Christopher Sergio, Meryl Levavi, Sarah Fitts, and Nicolette Seeback. Special thanks to April Mosolino for her generous insights and Lori Kusatzky for her patience.

I'm grateful for my community in Detroit, especially Adrienne Gołota, Kristy Sue Bishop, Omni Odum, Poppet and the crew at MCSDA, Detroit Friends Meeting, everyone at InsideOut Literary Arts, and all my friends who remind me of the joy of writing: Lia Greenwell, Liana Imam, Monjoa

Likine, Rochelle Marrett, Evan Paddock, and Christin Lee, who gave me the space to work. I wrote all the best parts at Room Project.

Thank you to Mike Campbell, Julie Henson, and Natalie Lund, who read these pages at their raggediest; to Rebecca McKanna, my first and dearest reader, and to Connor Coyne, the truest Flintstone I know. Thank you to Brian Allnutt, who answered all my questions about urban agriculture, and to Anna Clark, Dr. Mona Hanna-Attisha, Andrew Highsmith, *East Village Magazine*, and all the Flint activists and journalists whose work informed these pages.

To Lindsey Alexander, P'arry Drew, Lisa Perry, Mom, Bunnie, Papa in heaven, the Lockes, and the Dohertys—I love you. To Dylan: thank you for helping me go back home. Tell Alva, Harry, and Lewis I love them, too.

And to Bryan. I started out writing a love letter to Flint and ended up writing a prayer for you.

ABOUT THE AUTHOR

Kelsey Ronan grew up in Flint, Michigan. Her work has appeared in *Literary Hub*, *Michigan Quarterly Review*, *Kenyon Review*, and elsewhere. She lives in Detroit and teaches for InsideOut Literary Arts. This is her first novel.